A Rookie reader®

PLEASE, WIND?

By Carol Greene

Illustrations by Gene Sharp

Children's Press®
A Division of Scholastic Inc.
New York • Toronto • London • Auckland • Sydney
Mexico City • New Delhi • Hong Kong
Danbury, Connecticut

MAY 12

Dear Parents/Educators,

Welcome to Rookie Ready to Learn. Each Rookie Reader in this series includes additional age-appropriate Let's Learn Together activity pages that help your young child to be better prepared when starting school. *Please, Wind?* offers opportunities for you and your child to talk about the important social/emotional skill of **development of self: becoming resilient**.

Here are early-learning skills you and your child will encounter in the *Please, Wind?* Let's Learn Together pages:

• Rhyming
• Patterns
• Concept: left and right

We hope you enjoy sharing this delightful, enhanced reading experience with your early learner.

Library of Congress Cataloging-in-Publication Data

Greene, Carol.
  Please, wind? / written by Carol Greene ; illustrated by Gene Sharp.
    p. cm. -- (Rookie ready to learn)
  Summary: A child begs the wind to blow hard enough to make a kite fly.
Includes suggested learning activities.
  ISBN 978-0-531-26502-4 – ISBN 978-0-531-26734-9 (pbk.)
  [1. Winds--Fiction.] I. Sharp, Gene, 1923- ill. II. Title. III. Series.
  PZ7.G82845Pl 2011
  [E]--dc22
                          2010049998

CHILDREN'S PRESS, and ROOKIE READY TO LEARN, and associated logos are trademarks and or registered trademarks of Scholastic Library Publishing. SCHOLASTIC and associated logos are trademarks or registered trademarks of Scholastic, Inc.

1 2 3 4 5 6 7 8 9 10 R 18 17 16 15 14 13 12 11

It is still.

It is so still.

There is no wind.

Wind? Wind?

Blow!

Please, wind?

Listen.

It is a whisper.

A wind whisper.

Whisper, wind.

Whisper and grow.

Grow, grow…

and blow!

Oh!

Oh!

Blow butterfly and bird.

Blow cat and dog.

Blow…

hat!

And, wind?

Please blow kite.

Blow.

Blow!

Go.

Go!

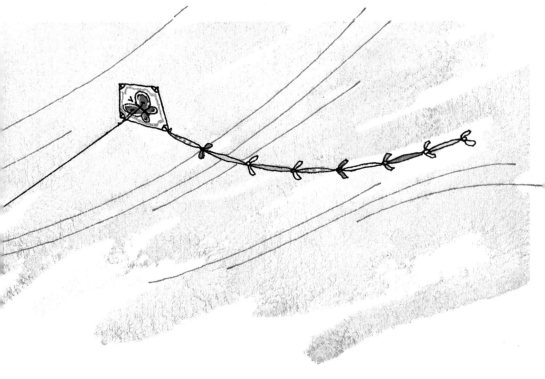

There!

31

Congratulations!

You just finished reading *Please, Wind?* and learned about air and wind.

About the Author
Carol Greene has written more than 20 books for children, plus stories, poems, songs, and filmstrips.

About the Illustrator
Gene Sharp has illustrated books, including schoolbooks, for a number of publishers.

Please, Wind?

Let's learn together!

I Fly My Kite

I fly my kite high in the sky.
(Use one hand to mimic a flying kite.)

It sails and swoops by and by.
(Sway your body side to side.)

Twisting and turning and dipping around.
(Twist and dip your body.)

My kite goes up high and then it flutters down!
(Raise arms over head, stand on tiptoes, and then lower yourself down.)

PARENT TIP: When the wind didn't blow and the kite didn't fly, the little girl was patient and kept waiting. She kept trying and trying. This is a great opportunity to discuss patience and resilience. Perhaps you can share with your child a time when you were patient and resilient, and ask him if he has ever had that kind of experience.

What Blew in the Wind?

In the story, the wind blew many things. Read a rhyming story about what the wind blew.

The wind blew a
sock

It did not blow the
clock

The wind blew a
dog

It did not blow the
log

The wind blew a
hat

It did not blow the
bat

PARENT TIP: Explain that wind is moving air. It can move slowly, like a gentle breeze, or quickly and strong, like a hurricane. Look outside. Do you see any signs of wind? Talk with your child about how to tell if the wind is blowing, even if you are not outside to feel it.

Colorful Kites

The girl in this story waited for the wind so she could have fun flying her kite. Look at the kites in each row. Point to the kite that comes next in each pattern.

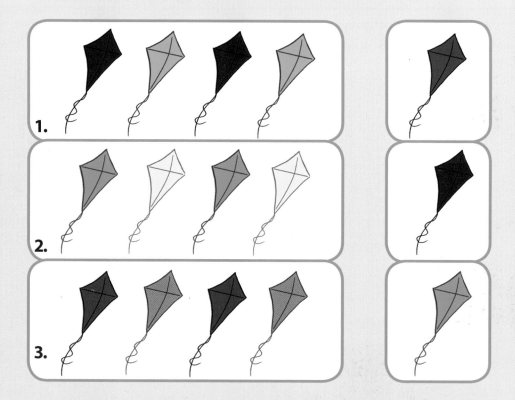

Right Side/ Left Side

Play this fun game to see which way the wind blows: left or right.

YOU WILL NEED: Masking tape **Paper**

Markers **Newspaper**

1
Place a piece of tape down the center of a table. Tape a piece of paper that says LEFT on the left side edge of the table. Place one that says RIGHT on the right side.

2
Roll a small piece of newspaper into a ball and place it on the edge of the table on the tape.

3
Blow the paper until it goes on the right or left of the tape. Do this several times, keeping track of when the paper goes "left" or "right."

PARENT TIP: Although it takes time for children to accurately and consistently associate the words *right* and *left* with the concept, rest assured that your child knows that one side is different from the other. Continue to model the use of the words and concepts in your everyday activities. For example, say, "Let's place the fork on the left side of the plate."

My Kite

The little girl flew a huge kite. How long is it? Use a six-inch length of yarn or string to find out. • Using a ruler, mark one-inch spaces on your string. • Measure the kite with the string. • Count how many spaces long each side of the kite in this picture is.

PARENT TIP: Use the string to compare two items, such as a pencil and a paper clip, to reinforce the concept of longer and shorter. Which one is longer than the other?

38

Will It Move?

The little girl in the story wanted the wind to blow. Wind can move many things. What can it move? What can it not move? Try this experiment.

YOU WILL NEED: Small or large pieces of paper

Stones **Leaves** **Crayons** **Marbles**

1 Put one of the objects on a table in front of you. Do you think that wind can move it?

2 Be the wind! Blow on the object as hard as you can. What happens?

3 Repeat with each object.

PARENT TIP: Whether or not something moves in wind has to do with its size, shape, and weight. It also has to do with how strong the wind is. This simple experiment, which lets children pretend to be the wind themselves, encourages early scientific thinking and observation.

Please, Wind? Word List (22 Words)

a	grow	please
and	hat	so
bird	is	still
blow	it	there
butterfly	kite	whisper
cat	listen	wind
dog	no	
go	oh	

Prospect Heights Public Library
12 N. Elm Street
Prospect Heights, IL 60070
www.phpl.info

PARENT TIP: One of the words on this list is *whisper*. Play a listening game with your child. You point to each word and say it out loud. Invite your child to repeat each word in a whisper.

Twayne's United States Authors Series

Sylvia E. Bowman, *Editor*

INDIANA UNIVERSITY

Edward Taylor

EDWARD TAYLOR

by NORMAN S. GRABO

 8

Twayne Publishers, Inc. :: New York

MANUFACTURED IN THE UNITED STATES OF AMERICA BY
UNITED PRINTING SERVICES, INC.
NEW HAVEN, CONN.

To Effie

Preface

Thy crumb of dust breathes two words from its breast,
 That thou wilt guide its pen to write aright
To prove thou art, and that thou art the best,
 And shew thy properties to shine most bright.

EDWARD TAYLOR'S poetry, his prose, indeed, his entire
life were informed by one central purpose, hammered
on one anvil, aimed at one end—a blissful eternity in the
heavenly city, basking in the radiant vision of Christ, singing
His praises and glory. The frontier community near the Connecticut River, pleasant though it must have been at times,
was a far cry from the City whose visions dazzled the poet.
Yet Taylor saw no impossibility living in the "Suburbs of
Glory" even there. His attempt to achieve the glorious life
of spirit while still in time accounts for his poetry which is,
however, only a part of that attempt. Anticipating the life
to come, Taylor could echo Donne's

 Since I am comming to that Holy roome,
  Where, with thy Quire of Saints for evermore,
 I shall be made thy Musique; As I come
  I tune the Instrument here at the dore,
  And what I must doe then, thinke here before.

This was Taylor's regular tune, the petition he made constantly: that he, like a musical instrument be attuned to the
heavenly harmony; that his spirit, like the string of a lute
or a harp, be screwed to the highest pitch, be stretched till
it quavered with the angelic choirs. The tension of the image
of a soul yoked to a carnal body, yet yearning to fly free of
all carnality emblemizes the vital energy behind Taylor's
poetry. Unlike Donne, he does not tune his own instrument;
he prays Christ to stretch it to heaven.

 He might, of course, have relieved the tension by mini-

mizing his worldly attachments, by retiring from the world
to a life of pure contemplation. Certainly there is precedent
sufficient for this in Christian tradition. But he did not. The
social implications of Congregationalism, of the Covenant
theology, and of the analogy between New Englanders and
the Jewish nation provided little room for a recluse. Consequently, Taylor's religious life forced him into the activities
of his own community. And these activities of which we
have some record stand, like the poems, as parts of Taylor's
religious devotion. His marriage and his children; his leader-
ship in the church and his controversies; his preaching and
his poetry are all, in a sense, equal acts of devotion. Believing
with John Cotton that "not only my spiritual life but even
my civil life in this world, all the life I live, is by the faith
of the Son of God," Taylor could never, in good conscience,
have withdrawn from his worldly involvement any more than
he could have expelled his soul prematurely to its heavenly
rewards by suicide.

This is not to say that every living act of the man was a
conscious act of devotion or that his affection for the world
was so weaned as to make his activity in it impersonal.
Taylor was, on the contrary, deeply involved in the world.
But the simple action of setting pen to paper makes a man
conscious of his choices and his values, and Taylor was a
ready and voluminous writer. Those activities which moved
him to write—college assignments; the thrill of a trip across
the Atlantic; his love for his wife and his grief at her death;
his letters of state and of controversy; and, most eminently,
his sermons and poems—were activities engaged in with
full consciousness. It is this life Taylor sometimes describes
and sometimes, in a sense, betrays, a life almost uniquely
unified in its godliness. And this is the only life of Taylor
we really have—that reflected in his own writings.

Perhaps by thus spreading out his devotion, by giving it a
wider base in his entire life, by denying as strenuously as
he could in his whole behavior the duality of body and
spirit, and by making himself personally and socially, in his
family, church, and community, the whole creature of God,
he somewhat relieved the tension that nearly undid John
Donne. Lacking Donne's egocentricity and Herbert's am-

bition, Taylor was incapable of their dramatic excellence. But, more positively, the interrelationship of all the aspects of Taylor's life puts his other activities in peculiar relationship to his poetry. In a way that is true of few other poets, all that Taylor is known to have done comments upon, explains, glosses, accounts for, and provides the motives and the occasions for his poetry. Conversely, to learn what Taylor's poetry is about requires knowing what Taylor was actively about. For his poetry was not merely an ornament to be hung among Taylor's social graces but, like his marriage and his ministry, a duty owed to God.

None of the critical views of Taylor published thus far has been long enough to permit a comprehensive appraisal of his work. The primary difficulty, of course, has been its inaccessibility. Only a few lines of verse were published in Taylor's lifetime, and those probably without Taylor's knowledge. At his death he prohibited his heirs from publishing any of his writings. They have, as a result, remained in manuscript. Chance apparently selected the manuscripts still extant, of which time has yielded the majority of the poetry only recently. Few critics have, therefore, had the not always pleasant opportunity of reading all that Taylor left behind. His handwriting is difficult and nearly three hundred years have not been kind to the manuscripts themselves. Their fragility and uniqueness require that they be handled with the utmost care. Indeed, some are even too fragile to microfilm.

The purpose of this critical study, then, is—as the first extensive study—not only to define the character of Taylor's poetry analytically but to place that poetry in the context of the life that produced it. To view Taylor in the light of his own values, it becomes necessary to explore the quality of his unifying mysticism, the structure of his thought, and the poetic and critical theory he evolved over years. Such study reveals Taylor to be not simply an historical oddity but a gifted and complex poet who offers increasing enjoyment as more is known about him.

All quotations from Taylor—modernized in spelling, capitalization, and punctuation—have been edited from Taylor's own manuscripts. He numbered his *Preparatory Meditations* in two series; references to these poems appear as follows:

Meditation 33, First Series, is reduced to 1.33; Meditation 33, Second Series, becomes 2.33.

I wish most earnestly to thank Sam S. Baskett, Meredith Baskett, Russel B. Nye, Clyde Henson, D. Gordan Rohman, and my wife Carrol for their critical reading of the manuscript. An All-University Research Grant from Michigan State University enabled me to prepare materials for this study. I am also indebted to Mr. Zoltán Haraszti of the Boston Public Library, to Mr. Stephen T. Riley of the Massachusetts Historical Society, and to Mr. David R. Watkins of the Yale University Library, for their kind permission to quote from their manuscript collections of Taylor material.

Permission to quote extensively from copyrighted material has generously been granted by the following: American Antiquarian Society for Harold S. Jantz, *The First Century of New England Verse;* Duke University Press for Donald E. Stanford, "The Earliest Poems of Edward Taylor"; E. P. Dutton & Co., Inc., for Evelyn Underhill, *Mysticism;* Oxford *University Press* for L. C. Martin, ed., *The Works of Henry Vaughan,* Helen Gardner's *John Donne: The Divine Poems,* Robert Bridges, ed., Gerard Manley Hopkins' *Poems,* and H. M. Margoliouth, ed., *Thomas Traherne: Centuries, Poems, and Thanksgivings;* and the Yale University Press for Louis L. Martz, *The Poetry of Meditation* and Donald E. Stanford, ed., *The Poems of Edward Taylor.*

NORMAN S. GRABO

Michigan State University

Contents

Chronology

1642 Born, probably in Sketchley, Leicestershire, England, at beginning of Puritan dominance; strict Christian upbringing.

1662 Restoration of Charles II; turn of Puritan fortunes; Taylor refuses to subscribe to Act of Uniformity and loses his teaching position at Bagworth, Leicestershire; Half-Way Covenant proposed in New England; Taylor may have attended Cambridge University around this time; writing satirical and occasional poems.

1668 Sails to America; begins diary; his vocation is definitely the ministry by this time; enters Harvard with advanced standing on July 23; enjoys friendship of Hull, Mather, Sewall, Chauncy, the leading men of the time; writes several elegies and begins to develop a theory of poetry.

1669 Frontier town of Westfield, Massachusetts, is incorporated.

1671 Taylor commences B.A. from Harvard; decides reluctantly to serve as Westfield's minister; at first unwilling to remain there.

1673 Westfield urges Taylor to organize the church formally.

1674 Courts in verse and marries Elizabeth Fitch of Norwich, November 5.

1676 King Philip's War spares Westfield, but the plans to organize the church are again postponed.

1679 Westfield congregation finally enters into a church covenant on August 27; Taylor is elected pastor and launches his first attack against Solomon Stoddard's "liberal" practices in "A Particular Church Is God's House."

1682 At the age of forty Taylor begins his major poetic and devotional activity, the *Preparatory Meditations,* to be composed at monthly intervals for the next forty-four years.

1689   Wife Elizabeth dies on July 7; Taylor vents his grief in "A Funeral Poem."

1692   Taylor marries Ruth Wyllys, daughter of a prominent Hartford family; his concern with Stoddard's "apostasy" increases.

1694   Attacks Stoddard in eight sermons about the Lord's Supper.

1701   Outlines his Christology to his increasing congregation in fourteen "Christographia" sacrament-day sermons.

1712   Faction threatens to wreck Westfield; Taylor withholds sacraments to maintain pastoral authority and defends his action in two sermons on church discipline the following year.

1720   Taylor's fruitful ministry brings him a new and larger meetinghouse; he receives M.A. from Harvard.

1723   Aged and ill, Taylor requires temporary assistance of Isaac Stiles.

1725   Taylor writes his last *Preparatory Meditation,* October 8; unable to perform his duties, Taylor accepts the help of Nehemiah Bull and assists in his ordination the following year.

1726-
1729   Taylor bedridden most of the time after his last sermon from Zechariah 1:5, "Your fathers, where are they? and the prophets, do they live forever?" Westfield adopts Stoddardeanism.

1729   Edward Taylor dies, June 24; buried in Westfield.

Edward Taylor

CHAPTER 1

The Active Life

W ITH SOMETHING of the pride of a spiritual descend-
ant, John Hoyt Lockwood, twentieth-century minister
of the church at Westfield, Massachusetts, wrote of Edward
Taylor: "It is not an extravagant claim to assert that had he
settled in Boston, instead of spending his life on the frontier,
he would have been famous in the annals of colonial times."[1]
But Taylor did spend his life on the frontier; and, while he
remained in high esteem among prominent men of his time,
he has been largely ignored by the annalists. In fact, more
than two centuries elapsed after Taylor's death before Professor Thomas H. Johnson examined the manuscript book
of poetry in the Yale University Library that is now bringing
Taylor his deserved praise. By publishing some of these poems
in 1937, Johnson made the American literary world aware of
a long-forgotten, distinguished son.

Professor Johnson was not the first literary scholar to
appreciate Taylor's poetic skill—both Thomas Goddard Wright
and Josephine Piercy called attention to it earlier—but he
was the first to bring specimens of Taylor's work to light.
Taylor's poems established him almost at once and without
quibble as not only America's finest colonial poet but as one
of the most striking writers in the whole range of American
literature; he had an exceptional quality of mind and spirit
for an American Puritan. For in Taylor's poems man is no
creature chained by the flesh to a position midway between
angels and beasts. Far from being lower than the angels,
man comes as close to Godhood as a created nature can; and
Taylor boasts that his own nature has been seated in the

Trinity. He exults proudly; and he commands even the angels, as a lower order of creation, to "give place" and show him obeisance. "Oh! Admirable," he gloats, "Give place ye holy angels of light, ye sparkling stars of the morning. The brightest glory, the highest seat in the kingdom of glory, the fairest colors in the scutcheon of celestial honor, belong to my nature and not to yours." Even more defiant in verse, he declares without the slightest humility:

> I'll claim my right: give place ye angels bright.
> Ye further from the Godhead stand than I.
> My nature is your Lord, and doth unite
> Better than yours unto the Deity.

For the highest honor imaginable has fallen to mankind—God has married man—and this is reason for exultation. Were this notion man's own invention, it would be the grossest blasphemy; but God, not man, makes the claim; and, though the orbs of human reason are dazzled by it, man's only recourse is to accept the God-stated fact.

Like other marriages, this one requires mutual duties; and Taylor does not hesitate to admit that God is dependent upon man as much as he is upon Him. In fact, God needs man. Divine Wisdom has worked out a plan for salvation that permits the loss of no saint whatsoever—a great and enduring source of comfort to those who find signs of God's favor in their own lives. Moreover, the Divine Husband shares His strength with His human bride, communicating to her His Truth, grace, life, and wisdom. Hereby man shares God's inmost secrets, knows and participates in the Blessed Life. Again, like earthly marriage, divine wedlock requires consummation; and Taylor sings ecstatic and rapturous songs of love to the Lover of Lovers.

This picture of Taylor, a *rara avis* singing solitary in the New England wilderness, hardly squares with the common picture of stern Calvinists preaching the depravity of man in a world where moral gloom has overpowered all systematic gaiety. In Taylor there is no stench of sulphur and fiery burning brimstone, no bleak fatalism. Instead there is honor, pride, sensual and erotic delight, and almost arrogant confidence. Taylor undoubtedly was a rare bird; and, consequently, he has confused critical readers who find him drastically at odds with most evaluations of seventeeth-century Puritanism. Taylor furthered the confusion himself by prohibiting his heirs to publish any of his writings. A sense of mystery has grown about this injunction—a suggestion that Taylor set pen to paper only "secretly,"[2] and that, therefore, he must have had something to hide. Either Taylor entertained beliefs or attitudes that orthodox New Englanders could neither have sanctioned nor permitted, or the writing of poetry itself was offensive: theologically or temperamentally, he leaned too much toward the rituals and trappings of Roman Catholicism.

But the significant fact is that all historical evidence shows Taylor to have been a very conventional and perfectly orthodox—indeed, conservative to the point of reactionary—Calvinist of the New England school. No full biography of Taylor has yet been written. But the known facts—meager as they seem at first glance—bear out the conventionality of the three major activities of his life: his education, his ministry, and his defense of the New England Way.

I *Education*

Taylor was born in England in 1642, the year in which decades of religious and constitutional agitation finally boiled over into civil war. Parliament had in effect declared itself supreme executive of England; and King Charles I readied for battle in Nottingham, not many miles north of Taylor's home in Sketchley, Leicestershire. Puritans generally joined the parliamentary cause, some even returning from New England where as many as 20,000 religious and political exiles had been erecting a Bible commonwealth for the preceding twelve years. In 1645 the King's forces were defeated decisively at Naseby; and, though Taylor would not have been aware of that event, he was certainly to enjoy its benefits. At least socially and politically there was no stigma to being a Puritan in Taylor's youth.

He retained two especially clear memories of his earliest childhood—the strictness of his parents and his conversion. He seems only to have thought of his parents in terms of

[19]

discipline. Several times he refers to them together, remembering that their Puritan rigor in no way compromised their Christian love. His childhood habit of lying called forth such sharp reprimands from his mother that in his thirties he could still remember the vividness with which she pictured fire and brimstone; he never mentions his father specifically. But the single event that impressed him mostly deeply was his own spiritual birth. This occurred early enough in his life for him still to be regularly awakened and catechized by an older sister (there were at least four children in the family). Two mornings in a row his sister recounted stories of the creation and of the life of Christ, and they so impressed him that he dated his real conversion and dedication to Christ from those mornings.[3] From then on he saw his spiritual life as a constant conflict between love, faith, fear, anger, sorrow, joy and hope—a tumult to be controlled only by a well-informed and well-trained reason.

A way to such training and knowledge was open to young Puritans in Taylor's time, but to what extent he took advantage of it is not clear. Certainly instruction in reading and in Bible history were his at home. And probably he began to study Latin, Greek, and logic quite early. A certain proficiency in languages was required for entrance to the universities, and a long tradition holds that Taylor spent some years at Cambridge. If he really went to Cambridge, his Latin and Greek would have been necessary for exploring the recesses of scholastic learning. For the universities in England, as on the Continent—and for that matter Harvard —still taught the traditional curriculum of the medieval schools.

Cambridge undergraduates studied three main "arts": logic, which taught correct patterns of thinking; rhetoric, which taught expression according to ancient principles; and ethics, which taught the principles of moral behavior discoverable in the natural world.[4] At Cambridge Taylor may have first absorbed the logical "method" of the educational reformer Peter Ramus—the method later to reveal itself in the construction of Taylor's sermons and in the intellectual structure of much of his poetry.[5] Then, too, the Cambridge system of oral examinations, disputations, and declamations also appear

in his American sermons. Taylor might very well, then, have
accomplished some of his famous learning in England, but
this is not certain. At Harvard the curriculum was so close to
Cambridge's that the symptoms of scholastic training in Taylor
might have been rooted in either school.[6]

By 1658 Oliver Cromwell was dead, and two years later
the fear Taylor must have shared with many another Puritan
became a lamentable fact—Charles II was restored to the
throne. The years that followed saw one Puritan disappointment after another as Charles reduced the freedoms and
privileges of dissenters from the Anglican faith. Taylor felt
the pinch of religious intolerance and sovereign displeasure
as he never had earlier. Through Charles's Act of Uniformity
in 1662, he even lost a position—whether at Cambridge or at
Bagworth, Leicestershire, where he reputedly taught for a
time, is not clear.

There is no record of Taylor's activities for the next six
years. But early in 1668 he made arrangements to try his
fortunes in America, and on April 26 he set sail. His little
convoy took nearly five weeks to skirt the lower part of
England from Gravesend to Land's End. Taylor's impressions
of the trip—recorded in a diary—show him about equally conscious of three things: the uncertain state of his stomach; unfamiliar birds, fish, and meals; and the necessity of preparing
sermons. On May 24 he reports: "I then, being put to exercise, spake from John 3:3."[7] The word "exercise" indicates
that Taylor was not a licensed preacher; but the reference
establishes the earliest date we have for Taylor's commitment to the ministry. The exercise was not extemporaneous;
he indicates in another place in the diary that he worked
on his Sunday sermons from at least Thursday.

Appropriately, Taylor first spied New England and the
approach to Boston on the fourth of July. Boston, the heart
of New England's dream and the center of her commerce,
numbered between five and six thousand inhabitants when
Edward Taylor walked ashore; and it was the largest city in
all the English colonies. Settled in 1630 as the beginning of a
Puritan Utopia, Boston in 1668 had not enjoyed the warmth
of God's smile for some time. Of course there was the college
designed to "advance learning and perpetuate it to posterity";

and, though it had recently fallen on hard times, it showed no signs of surrendering its hopes of training a learned clergy. But the early dream had been compromised. The year of Taylor's birth, 1642, had seen a great and troublesome outbreak of sin, and the English Civil War had made New Englanders feel like deserters rather than the van of the Puritan movement. The restoration of Charles II had been a certain sign of God's disapproval, and the compromise of 1662 that threw the doors of church membership halfway open to souls of questionable purity proved again that God's face wore a frown. New England was worried—at least Boston, the conscience of New England, was worried—and its ministers were searching their stores of knowledge, imagination, and ingenuity to find means of weaning New Englanders from their worldliness, sinfulness, and neglect.

This was the Boston in which the twenty-six-year-old Taylor, armed with several letters of introduction, presented himself to Increase Mather, only three years his senior but already a leading light in Boston's intellectual life. Mather must have welcomed him warmly, for Taylor spent the next two nights at Mather's home. Another letter—to John Hull, Massachusetts Bay's mintmaster and one of New England's wealthiest residents—brought more generous hospitality and flattering attention.

After a week, Taylor went to Cambridge to talk to Charles Chauncy, president of Harvard College. From the seventy-eight-year-old President Chauncy he received both encouragement and an invitation to return in a week. Taylor later spent the night of July 22 in Chauncy's home, and the next morning was admitted to Harvard. Whether making Taylor the college butler and permitting him to take his degree in only three and a quarter years instead of the usual four were acknowledgments of his advanced age and prior education or whether these were inducements to attract another student to a college badly in need of students is not clear. Johnson has attributed Taylor's warm reception to his congeniality,[8] but it may in large part have been due to everybody's recognition that in Taylor stood a potential prop to New England's slipping dream.

Taylor records three experiences from his college days;

only one concerns his studies. The first involved Thomas Graves, the senior fellow who tutored Taylor:

> Mr. Graves, not having his name for nought, lost the love of the undergraduates by his too much austerity, whereupon they used to strike a nail above the hall door catch while we were reciting to him, and so nail him in the hall, at which disorder I was troubled. Whereupon, being desired by him to go into the buttery privily and watch who did it, one morning I did so; but being spied by the scholars I was fain to haste out and make haste to Boston before I spake to Mr. Graves, the better to cloak over the business that so the scholars might conclude it was accidental and not *ex propositio* (for I was fearful of incensing them against me). . . .⁹

But Taylor's attempt to cover his duplicity with flight did him little good, for Graves "checked" him when he returned to school. Shortly after this episode Taylor joined his classmates in refusing to study a reputedly inadequate text; the issue forced Graves's withdrawal from the college.

The third incident occurred in the spring of 1670 when Taylor went to pay for his winter's wood. The woodman's wife, Elizabeth Steadman, accused Taylor of aloofness because he had not visited them more often. Recognizing that "she was a woman of a troubled spirit," Taylor visited her frequently, bringing her "comfort and support." She in turn acted as his nurse when he "was in any kind of affliction," but gossips made him so uncomfortable that by spring of 1671 he talked to Chauncy about quitting school. The president, still fighting to keep his classes together, persuaded Taylor "by his incessant request and desires" to graduate with his class. In fact, Taylor even planned to return to Harvard that fall as Scholar of the House.

Although Taylor wrote a couple of elegies in his last year at Harvard and delivered a verse declamation in May of that year, no one remarked about his poetic ability. Samuel Sewall, an indefatigable versifier himself, had been induced to go to Harvard by Taylor—they even shared the same bed for two years—and often refers to Taylor in his diary and letter book; but he never says a word about his poetry, which emphasizes Taylor's lack of reputation as a poet. But though his colleagues

did not know it—Taylor probably did not know it himself—
his Cambridge years were training him to be one.

An interest in medicine led him to compile a five-hundred
page description of herbs and other medicinals, and this material appeared in his poetry later. Perhaps it was through
his acquaintance with John Hull that Taylor first became
interested in metallurgy; the interest led him to copy the
greater part of John Webster's *Metallographia* (which also
found its way into his poetry). The friendship with Increase
Mather apparently warmed during Taylor's Harvard years,
for Taylor left college an avid follower of all Mather's ecclesiastical teachings. But the college itself was the crowning
experience of Taylor's education. It secured his control of
Latin, Greek, and Hebrew; it opened for his explorations the
tremendous continent of Patristic writings; it grounded him
thoroughly in biblical studies and church history; and it honed
his abilities against the grating necessity of regular disputations. In short, by the fall of 1671, though he had planned
to continue his studies, Taylor was ready for the opportunity
that came to him.

II *Ministry*

In 1636 Mr. William Pynchon, seeking to take advantage
of a growing trade in beaver furs, founded a settlement on
the Connecticut River about one hundred miles west of Boston. Trade was good, and the settlement—called Springfield—so
flourished that by 1667 there was room for another trading
post nine miles further west. John Holyoke, son of one of the
principal settlers, served as minister to the Westfield outpost
for a year and then quit. He was succeeded for three years
by Moses Hill, but 1671 found the trading post turning into
a little farm community and in need of a permanent minister.
So in November, 1671, Westfield sent Thomas Dewey to
find one.

Dewey first went to Increase Mather in Boston, who sent
him with a letter to Taylor. Taylor immediately passed the
problem on to the President Chauncy and the Fellows of the
College. They in turn refused to advise Taylor positively,
declaring that they had to consider the good of the college
first; and this attitude suggests that they thought it to

Harvard's advantage to keep Taylor there but did not want to interfere with his job possibilities. Because Chauncy was dead set against the Westfield offer at first, Taylor asked for a week to consider the matter. Taylor's indecision was natural, of course, but in this case it represents a special problem that was to vex him for eight more years. On November 18, Increase Mather advised Taylor to take the job; and on November 27, 1671, finding that he had raised Goodman Dewey's expectations so high he could not back out and having secured Chauncy's blessing, Taylor began "the desperatest journey that ever Connecticut men undertook." Eight days later he arrived in Westfield.

Congregations customarily tested prospective ministers over an extended time. But in 1673 Westfield urged Taylor to continue among them, and his initial indecision returned. He found himself not sufficiently encouraged to organize the church formally; he sensed his intellectual isolation; and he felt he had no roots in the community. Still a student, Taylor purchased what books he could; others he borrowed, making manuscript copies of them for his own library, stitching, gluing, and binding more than a hundred such volumes with his own hands.[10] And when he met with an author's manuscript seeking publication, he willingly wrote to Boston to promote the project.[11] The 192 printed books he managed to collect are impressive for their quality and expense rather than for their number.[12]

But maintaining the intellectual life in the wilderness was not easy. On September 29, 1696, Taylor sent a letter to his college chum Samuel Sewall, now a judge of the Superior Court in Boston. In accepting Sewall's friendly challenge to a debate on the symbolic meaning of the word "Euphrates" in Rev. 9:14, Taylor begins apologetically, saying,

> it is so long since I have been engaged in such sort of combats that my weapons are rusty in their scabbards. Yet I have been casting mine eyes into my quiver to find a friendly shaft or two suitable to my poor, simple bowstring. And what I find I entreat you to accept, as heretofore when we were at our pros and cons. I am far off from the Muses' copses, and the foggy damps assaulting my lodgen in these remotest swamps from the Heliconian quarters, where little save

clonian rusticity is à la mode, will plead my apology: the mind's arrows are not feathered with silken rhetoric nor piled with academic eloquence.[13]

Perhaps because they recognized Taylor's problem, the townspeople "encouraged" him to stay among them by writing him a formal letter of commendation and by making several attempts to secure David Wilton from Northampton to bolster their struggling church. They hoped that Wilton would encourage their young minister "unto the comfortably carrying on that great work before us, which, when begun in a right way and managed after a right manner, ends in God's glory and our salvation. . . ."[14] Northampton was, however, unwilling to surrender Mr. Wilton; and representatives from Westfield wrote their brethren to the north rather resentfully that "Mr. Taylor is utterly averse to any coalition into a church state without further encouragement, and where to have it, if not from you, we know not."[15] This letter was dated August 21, 1673—the coalition did not come about until six full years later—but within a year Taylor found encouragement from an unexpected source.

How and where Edward Taylor met Elizabeth Fitch we do not know. The first record of their relationship dates from about a year after the rather discouraged letter to Northampton, and it comes in the shape of another letter, this time by Taylor himself and addressed to his "Tender and Only Love." The letter has two parts: the first is a complicated rhymed acrostic in which he promises his heart will be a "ring of love," "Truly confined within the Trinity"; the second is a prose love letter that carefully reaffirms the relationship of the heart to the Trinity. Human love must be subordinate to the mystical love of the soul and Christ, and Taylor begins the prose part of his *billet-doux* with the rather blunt "I send you not my heart, for that I hope is sent to heaven long since, and unless it has awfully deceived me, it hath not taken up its lodgings yet in anyone's bosom on this side of the royal city of the Great King. . . ." Yet he assures Elizabeth that she commands all the love he can devote to created beings. Perhaps mockingly, but yet with a sense of seriousness, he falls midway in the letter into a sermon form, arguing the doctrine that "conjugal love ought to exceed all other love"; and after three "proofs," he concludes that "though conjugal love must exceed all other, yet it must be kept within bounds too. For it must be subordinate to God's glory. The wish that mine may be so, it having got you into my heart, doth offer my heart with you in it as a more rich sacrifice unto God through Christ. . . ."[16] Thus did the minister of Westfield work upon another Puritan heart and tie it, as he was later to say, into a true-love's knot with his own.

Elizabeth, too, was afflicted with the Puritan "lust of versification"; for on October 27, 1674, Taylor wrote another love poem to her that seems to refer to poems received from her hand: "I had thought that my Muse should have added a quaver or two unto your music, but that stage being so thick a-crowded already, there is scarce any room for it. All therefore that she shall do shall be only to take the tune where you left it and answer, as it were an echo, back again unto your song in this following ditty."[17] The sixty-four line ditty begins with an apology for writing in coarse iambics rather than silken Sapphics, and it then proceeds to instruct the bride-to-be in the duties of marriage. In one of his favorite images Taylor develops the conceit of marriage as

> That long'd for web of new relation gay,
> That must be wove upon our wedden day,

a whole cloth decorated with honors, duties, pleasures, faithfulness, and "cares and crosses too." He warns Elizabeth that, if duty, faith, and love are not maintained, the threads of the cloth will snap and the whole web become as irritating and "black as haircloth." Then he concludes:

> It now remains: let's clothe ourselves, my dove,
> With this effulgeant web and our pickt love
> Wrapt up therein, and let's, by walking right,
> Love's brightest mantle make still shine more bright,
> For then its glory shall ascend on high
> The highest One alone to glorify,
> Which rising will let such a glory fall
> Upon our lives that glorify them shall.

Within two weeks they were married.

Thus Taylor sunk roots into the Westfield community, but there was yet another discouragement to keep him from organizing the church. Indian hostilities had threatened for months; and in the spring of 1675, Metacomet, chief of the Wampanoag Indians, united several tribes into a more or less organized series of attacks. Metacomet became known as "King Philip" to the English, and it is by this name that Taylor refers to him in describing the movement of the Indian wars into the Connecticut Valley in the summer of that year. "Summer coming opened a door unto that desolating war begun by Philip, Sachem of the Pakonoket Indians, by which this handful [at Westfield] was sorely pressed. . . ." By late autumn Westfield was still "sovereignly preserved"; but its preservation was "yet not so as that we should be wholly exempted from the fury of war, for our soil was moistened by the blood of three Springfield men."[18] Through the winter of 1675 and into the spring of 1676, Westfield, now somewhat fortified and garrisoned, suffered occasional raids from what Taylor calls "skulking rascalds," but remarkably escaped a full-scale assault. Agitation to desert the frontier completely had been staved off by Solomon Stoddard at Northampton, who rejected a plan to consolidate the forces of the frontier towns at Hadley and Springfield. Taylor likewise managed to keep Westfield intact, and the spring action really ended King Philip's War for Westfield. Philip's death that year completely concluded the struggle.

The end of the war allowed Taylor to return his attention to the problem of organizing the Westfield congregation into a formal church. Although four of the nine reliable communicants left Westfield with the war, Taylor felt sufficiently encouraged by 1679 to proceed with the ceremonies. Now, thirty-seven years old, with a growing family and eight years of close involvement with the town, he felt firmly rooted there. So in July he circulated letters to several neighboring ministers, requesting their presence. They arrived on August 26, and, in typical New England fashion, immediately objected to Taylor's plans for the following day.

Their most serious objection was with Taylor's failure to provide a written confession of faith for the congregation. He had intended merely "a professing the doctrine laid down

in the *Catechism* of the Assembly of Westminster, so far as
it goes, and where it is deficient, to acknowledge the platform
of church discipline put forth by the reverend elders and
messengers in a Synod held at Cambridge in . . . 1647."[19]
But the ministers simply would not accept so casual a confession. The significance of this episode is double: first,
Taylor's theology and church polity were so conventional he
deemed them covered exactly and completely by the Westminster Confession and the Cambridge Platform—more orthodox he could not be; secondly, the ministers, by forcing
Taylor to write out the "heads" or principal tenets of his
faith, compelled him to reveal the matters of faith he thought
most significant. Taylor dutifully entered these doctrines
in a manuscript book titled "The Public Records of the Church
at Westfield Together with a Brief Account of Our Proceeding in Order to Our Entrance into That State." Nothing
Taylor wrote in the following fifty years indicates the slightest modification of these doctrines.[20]

Taylor and six other Westfield men then made "relations"
of their qualifications for entering into the church covenant.
All seven had arrived at as full assurance as any mortal could
that they had been predestined to eternal salvation; that in
spite of their heritage of original sin from Adam, Christ had
died to redeem them as members of his elect church; that
they had experienced special signs of God's saving grace; and
that they were, therefore, ready to persevere in God's service.
They then signed a brief document called the "Church
Covenant," in which they agreed "to give up ourselves unto
the only God in Jesus Christ to walk in his ways with all our
hearts" and "to walk together according to the rules of the
Gospel in the communion of saints in a particular church
instituted state for the carrying on of all gospel ordinances,
the ministry of the word, sacrament, and discipline, and also
all those mutual duties of helpfulness and subjection in the
Lord one unto another. . . ."[21] They then elected Taylor
pastor, and were formally welcomed into the family of independent New England congregations.

Taylor's covenant agreements foreshadow his major activities over the next fifty years. Two more wars threatened the
frontier during his ministry—King William's War (1690-1697)

and Queen Anne's War (1701-1713)—but while the records note Taylor receiving several pounds of gunpowder or fortifying his house, Westfield never again came quite so close to falling under the brandished tomahawk as it had in 1676.

He preached regularly—usually twice a week—and occasionally displayed his eloquence at Boston.[22] His relationships with his Boston and Cambridge friends remained cordial, and Taylor found himself by inclination and by conviction contributing to Increase Mather's plan to entice people back into active church life by advertising God's illustrious works in New England. This plan, which originated in 1681, resulted in 1684 in Mather's *Essay for the Recording of Illustrious Providences*—a collection of weird occurrences, witchcraft, strange deaths, and even stranger recoveries. Its last chapter is largely the work of Taylor's father-in-law, and Taylor himself sent Mather descriptions of mighty hailstorms, supernatural interventions, and monstrous births.[23] In short, there is no reason to suppose that, had Taylor been closer to the witchcraft activities of 1692, he would have differed at all from the unhappy position of Increase and Cotton Mather.

Meanwhile his family cares increased. Elizabeth had presented him with eight children—five of whom died—before her death in 1689. Three years later Taylor married Ruth Wyllys, and by 1708 had six more children. Throughout this period he filled his commonplace book and his church records with legal opinions about divorce and rape, with admonitions to churches, with advice and inquiries about matters of church discipline, and with a constantly lengthening list of baptisms, marriages, and deaths. By 1703 the meetinghouse had to have galleries built to seat the increasing congregation, and by 1721 an entirely new structure was necessary.

But there was one aspect of Taylor's ministry that overshadows all others and has far-reaching implications for the poetry he began composing in earnest by 1682. The main task Taylor set himself and his congregation was to live a life in imitation of Christ. Christ's life, as Taylor constantly reminded the congregation, was a teaching life. Secondly, and somewhat more peculiarly, Christ's life was an artistic life—Christ was the paragon of poets—and in this, too, Taylor

sought to imitate him. Over years of study Taylor achieved an exceptional unity of thought in which both views of imitation coalesced; and the result was that his ministry and his poetry became inextricably bound. Taylor's poetry is what it is because of what he believed and taught as a Christian. For this reason it is important to review his central teaching.

III *Defending the New England Way*

When speaking of the sacrament of the Lord's Supper, Taylor once wrote: "this rich banquet makes me thus a poet."[24] Certainly the sacrament was the occasion for, as well as the subject of, most of his poetry. Also the central concern of his ministry, it naturally occupies a significant position in his preaching.

In part this prominence was a fact of the times that Taylor could hardly have avoided. He had arrived in America only six years after the Synod of 1662 adopted the famous Half-Way Covenant. The Synod urged individual congregations to baptize the infant children of church members, but not to admit them to full membership until they were at least fourteen years old, knew something about the faith they professed, and provided in a public confession or "relation" some evidence that God's saving grace had visited and converted them. The partaking of the Lord's Supper became a lure to struggling half-way members to discover their right to full membership and a public sign of the purest in the congregation. Promoted by prominent churchmen like the Mathers, the practice gained widespread—but by no means total—acceptance in New England. Taylor, whose association with Increase Mather was close, seems never to have deviated from this position. By 1679, the Half-Way Covenant was coming under severe attack, especially from Solomon Stoddard, Taylor's powerful neighbor from Northampton. Taylor was to find that the Christ-like life of teaching meant a life of controversy, and he threw himself into it willingly.

Though Stoddard (1643-1729) and Taylor were nearly the same age, Stoddard graduated from Harvard in 1662, six years before Taylor came to New England, and during Taylor's stay at Harvard was the librarian of the college. While Taylor was finishing his last year at school, Stoddard

was being tested by the congregation of Northampton, where he received a call and was ordained in 1672. By that time Taylor was down river in Westfield, looking to Northampton for encouragement to organize the church. So far as is known, both men put into practice the principles of the Half-Way Covenant.

But in 1677, Professor Miller writes, Stoddard began to baptize "every adult who consented to the articles of faith, and admitted him to the Supper,"[25] thereby giving full support to many who had been unable to accept the conclusions of the Synod of 1662. It is questionable that Stoddard had gone quite so far by this time, but there is no doubt that he publicized his desire to do so; for in 1677 Increase Mather, without naming Stoddard, preached to the General Court "A Discourse Concerning the Danger of Apostasy," attacking Stoddard's doctrines.

What Stoddard objected to was that, according to the Half-Way Covenant, no man was permitted to partake of the Lord's Supper until he had certain knowledge and full assurance of his salvation; without this knowledge, his attendance at the sacrament was damning. But Stoddard insisted that no man could know he was saved with absolute certainty. The only safe course, therefore, was to admit all well-behaved Christians to the sacrament in hopes that they might thereby secure saving grace, that they might, in other words, be converted by it. Since they presumably had not yet experienced conversion, they need make no "relation" of their religious experience prior to church membership. Stoddard also argued that the widspread concept of *particular* church covenants was neither scriptural nor necessary; because God covenanted with a whole people or nation "there is no necessity of any covenant between the Members of a particular Congregation among themselves."[26] He concludes that "the supream Ecclesiastical Authority doth not lye in particular Congregations; if there be no National Church, then every particular Congregation is absolute and independent, and not responsible to any higher Power: this is too Lordly a principle, it is too ambitious a thing for every small Congregation to arrogate such an uncontroulable Power, and to be accountable to none on earth. . . ."[27] Increase Mather

sniffed the dangers in this as early as 1677, and in 1679 his discourse was published.

Of course, 1679 was the year Taylor formally organized the Westfield church. When neighboring ministers arrived that August, Stoddard was among them; and he had just come from the first of his five "harvests" or revivals demonstrating the efficacy of his methods by the great number of young people brought to a concern for their salvation in Northampton. He assumed the role of leader at Westfield, as he was to do throughout the Connecticut Valley; and on the following afternoon he listened to Taylor preach "A Particular Church is God's House," in which he categorically dismissed each of Stoddard's arguments and strongly upheld the Half-Way Covenant.

Perhaps Taylor's final injunction to the gathering to avoid contentions, to knit themselves one to another in love and charity, and to walk in the ways of the Lord moved Stoddard to hold his peace. At any rate there is no record that he tried to defend himself at this time. Instead he arose and, after the new church members signed their covenant, extended his right hand to Taylor with these words: "I do in the name of the churches give you the right hand of fellowship." Taylor approved of neither the form of this speech nor its brevity, but Stoddard's restraint is a remarkable instance of self-control and good sense. Everybody connected with the ministry must have recognized that Taylor's sermon was largely an excuse to face Stoddard down, and may even have been amused by the splendid deviousness with which he wielded his long and complicated weapon.

Within two weeks Stoddard had a chance to make his side of the argument clear. At Boston to attend the Synod called to deplore the spiritual deadness of the times, he found himself challenged to a debate by Increase Mather. Urian Oakes, then president of Harvard, was to act as moderator. But seeing that wrangling at the Synod itself was not likely to go far to reform the times, Oakes managed to defer the debate until a later time. There is no evidence that Stoddard forced the issue before the meeting on September 10 which Mather reported in *The Necessity of Reformation* (Boston, 1679). In May of the following year Stoddard had another

opportunity when the second meeting of the Reforming Synod gathered to draw up a *Confession of Faith*. The only frontiersman on the committee whose task it was to draft the confession, he again avoided pressing his case.[28]

Meanwhile, Taylor carefully copied his sermon into the "Public Records of the Church" and then made another copy of it to send to Boston. The realization, as Perry Miller puts it, that "there already had been more controversy over the Covenant than the society could stand, and another split over anything fundamental would wreck it,"[29] may have kept it out of print. Or it may simply be that the printer recognized it as a sad piece of writing. In any case, there is no known reaction to Taylor's sermon, and he was content to preserve not only his friendship with Stoddard but peace and amity in the society. By the beginning of 1668, however, he again became alarmed over Stoddard's proselytizing, and he sent him a long letter pointing out that the controversy Stoddard had raised was contrary to the ideal for which New England had been working for over half a century; that his idea was impractical and disturbing to the peace of the church; and—rather prophetically—that future generations would "be ready to date the beginning of New England's apostasy in Mr. Stoddard's motions." Stoddard answered the letter cordially, but did not attempt to argue with Taylor.[30]

But early in 1694 Taylor, who had worriedly noted Stoddard's growing popularity over the years, preached a series of eight sermons directly against him. These sermons are his longest single treatment of the Lord's Supper; and, therefore, they are most important in respect to his poems. He suggests that sacramental controversies were really what brought the Puritans to America in the first place; for, unwilling to submit to the improper administration of the Supper, "the old and new Noncomformists . . . deserted episcopal governments and suffered persecution, loss of their public ministry, poverty, imprisonment . . . to avoid such mixt administrations of the Lord's Supper; and to enjoy an holy administrating of it to the visibly worthy was that that brought this people from all things near and dear to them in their native country to encounter with the sorrows and difficulties of the wilderness. . . ."[31] To throw over the

"thoroughly studied" practice of the founders of New England, as Stoddard was doing, was "grand presumption." Taylor also laments that the "Popish error" of considering the Lord's Supper as a converting ordinance "should bud and blossom among us in New England . . . and yet the same hath been publicly preached to and urged upon the church and people of God at Northampton by the Reverend Mr. Solomon Stoddard the Pastor of the church there" (*1694*, p. 53). Taylor warns that acceptance of Stoddard's tenets must lead to "downright Arminianism or Pelagianism" (*1694*, pp. 107-8).

Taylor insists that only the really pure, holy saint may come to the sacrament; for, without the wedding garment of true sanctity, the sacrament is fouled. If, as Stoddard contended, the unsanctified could attend the sacrament merely "to see Christ presented, under the signs, as crucified," this was —to Taylor—reducing the sacrament to a stage show: "as if a man was to go to see a tragedy or stage play; and it doth not answer the case in hand" (*1694*, p. 103). The sacrament requires the most devout preparation: baptism, hearing the Word, conversion, and "prayer, meditation, and self-examination," which Taylor says "are of special use [to] prepare the soul for this feast." To these he adds contemplation, and so fills out the preparatory requirements for the sacrament.

In describing the preparatory act, Taylor uses the terms "meditation" and "contemplation" interchangeably. Contemplation goes hand in hand with self-examination; they are so close, in fact, that "examination cannot be without contemplation." As a result, he exhorts his congregation to "meditate upon the feast—its causes, its nature, its griefs, its dainties, its reason and ends, and its benefits, etc.—for it carries in its nature and circumstances an umbrage or epitomized draught of the whole grace of the Gospel." Of course this is exactly what Taylor did in his own poetic meditations, which he called *Preparatory*. Such preparation, he adds, will "stir up all sacramental graces: repentance, faith, love, humility, a discerning eye, hunger and thirst after communion with God in Christ, thankfulness, and holy joy in the Lord" (*1694*, p. 168); and these are the very affections expressed in his poetry.

But contemplation is a reward as well as a preparation,

for the sacrament strengthens the soul's yearning for union with Christ and sharpens the spiritual eye for a clearer view of Christ:

> Thy contemplations will be raised upon the glory of the wedden, and these will affect thy soul to the glory of God. Think of this. For this will be great benefit. The wedden will set thy contemplations going upon the glory of the wedden, the glory of the king, the glory of the prince the bridesgroom. Oh, the king of glory! How doth it shine forth here? The beauty of the bride, the happiness of the bride, and her honorable preferment. The dowry laid down as his estate to redeem her, to pay her debt, to purchase her freedom, her furniture, her felicity. And that he came to her out of his father's bosom, from his father's palace, on his father's errand, and here in this dirty world was attached to her account, imprisoned, arraigned, condemned, executed, put to death, held a prisoner in the grave till the third day: then he broke the bands of death asunder, threw the prison door off of its hinges, came a valiant conqueror, ascended up into glory, sat at the father's right hand, set up ordinances, sent out suitors his spokesmen, sent down gifts to bestow on his bespoken for, contracts them to him and celebrates the contract now in this wedden feast. So that here you see at the Lord's Supper that contemplation is set awork about these, and that they tend to raise the affections thus, and to bring them to God (*1694*, p. 156).

And so he describes the Lord's Supper as the highest kind of human activity short of the everlasting life: to belong fully to the church and to partake of the sacrament are to live, he says, in the "suburbs of glory."

Six years after the completion of these sermons, the argument between Stoddard and other advocates of Taylor's position erupted into print. Increase Mather's *The Order of the Gospel*, Cotton Mather's "Defense of Evangelicall Churches," and Stoddard's *The Doctrine of Instituted Churches* were all issued in 1700. But at this time Stoddard and the Mathers have not faced off squarely. Each argues as if unaware of the other's position: Increase Mather defends the Half-Way Covenant as Taylor would have done, and Stoddard positively states his differences for the first time in print. Eight years later, however, with Stoddard's sermon *The Inexcusableness of Neglecting the Worship of God under a Pretence of Being in an unconverted Condition,* the polite fencing ended. Increase Mather attacked "Mr. S" in earnest in *A Dissertation, wherein The Strange Doctrine . . . is Examined and Refuted* (Boston, 1708). The refutation was unfortunately hurried, as Stoddard showed the following year in *An Appeal to the Learned . . . Against the Exceptions of Mr. Increase Mather.*

To come to this debate after reading Taylor's sermons is to court disappointment. For Taylor had exhausted the arguments. Mather lacked either the invention or the time to do a decent job, and Stoddard shames him often with his point-by-point rebuttal. Mather turned to vilifying insinuations; he made it appear that Stoddard was out to deform the church —not reform it—and that his arguments smacked of both treason and Papistry. Stoddard, of course, managed to insinuate the same about Mather and to return the injury in a way that reflects upon Taylor, too. Stoddard declaims: "It seems to me that many Persons do make an idol of the Lord's Supper; crying it up above all Ordinances both of the Old & New Testament, as if it were as peculiar to Saints as heavenly glory. . . . It may be this is some of the relicks of Popish Idolatry, in making the Bread and Wine to be the natural Body & Blood of Christ."[32] He found it easier in this manner to parry Mather than he would have to fend off Taylor, but Taylor's sermons never reached the printer. In 1709 an anonymous pamphlet titled *An Appeal, of Some of the Unlearned, both to the Learned and Unlearned* was published in Boston—a sarcastic retort to Stoddard. The concluding sentences of the pamphlet read: "We hear that Deacon Prince of Sandwich, is preparing an answer to him [Stoddard]. We wish him *good Success;* only we will *Wonder* if he shall convince the Appellant of his *Error,* when all the *Learned Men in the World* have not hitherto been able to do it."[33] Deacon Prince was probably Samuel Prince (1649-1728), or perhaps his son Thomas, who had just received his degree of B.A. from Harvard and was visiting his father in Sandwich in 1709.[34] At some time Taylor's "A Particular Church," the eight 1694 sermons, and a number of other notes in Taylor's hand on Stoddard's notions came into Thomas Prince's possession. Had Prince ever produced the proposed answer to Stoddard, Taylor's influence on American theology might have been considerable; but the book was never written, and Taylor's manuscripts became part of Prince's famous New England Library. These unpublished contributions to the most crucial ecclesiastical controversy of the times prove to be the earliest as well as the most comprehensive refutation of the position called Stoddardean.

Because Taylor based his sacrament-day poems upon his sermons, we know he must have been preaching on the Lord's Supper again from the middle of 1711 through the end of 1712; we have the eleven poems, but not the sermons. At this very time, however, Stoddard was enjoying another harvest at Northampton, and was to have yet one more in 1718. He seems to have made some inroads in Westfield by 1712, for Taylor was having difficulty with his own congregation.

Two sermons in 1713 show Taylor's use of the sacrament as an instrument of pastoral power. In these sermons Taylor defines the minister's authority very much as Winthrop had defined the magistrate's almost a century earlier. He tells the story of a faction that once threatened to wreck the Westfield church until he subdued it by withholding the sacrament not only from the malcontents who opposed him but from all eligible church members. "I knew my office well enough," says Taylor, "and I would not be imposed upon by any."[35] Surely this disciplinary use of the sacrament accounts in part for its eminence in his preaching and poetry.

Taylor's purpose in recalling this unrest to his congregation at the same time of Stoddard's successes in Northampton may well have been to remind them of his knowledge, his power, and his will to keep them to the New England Way. His fight with Stoddard was a long one, and these 1713 sermons may be the first clear sign that it was a losing one.

By 1726 Taylor was quite decrepit, though in that year he attended the ordination of his successor, Nehemiah Bull. The very next year Jonathan Edwards went to help his equally aged grandfather at Northampton. By that time Taylor "had become imbecile through extreme old age,"[36] and may not have been aware that in 1728 Bull put before the church at Westfield the following question: "Whether such persons as come into full communion may not be left at their liberty as to the giving the church an account of the work of saving conversion, i. e., whether relations shall not be looked upon as a matter of indifferency." A matter of indifferency! The church requested six weeks or so to think about the matter, and then "voted in the affirmative"; and it undid in that short span the work of Taylor's entire ministry. On June 24, 1729, Edward Taylor died, and by 1750 only four congregations in the Connecticut Valley still held out against Stoddardeanism; Westfield was not among them.

CHAPTER 2

The Contemplative Life

A REVIEW of Taylor's active life demonstrates beyond question his social and theological orthodoxy, his involvement in the intellectual life of his times, his commitment to all that colonial New England represents. Except for the accidents of place and event that distinguish any individual, Taylor's upbringing, education, and vocation were typical. He was a learned man in an age of many learned men, a frontiersman when the entire continent was yet a wilderness, and a man of God in a land swarming with ministers. He detested monarchy, but he played the despot in his own congregation. He denounced Quakers and hated Roman Catholics. He knew there were devils and witches. He believed God exerted His providence in all the minutiae of nature. He thought he was among God's chosen few and that by God's great design the mass of men skidded to everlasting and inescapable damnation. Viewed from the outside, from his "activities"—even his habit of versifying—Edward Taylor was a typical Puritan.

How then is Taylor's obvious unusualness—his peculiar quality of mind, his undeniable artistic accomplishment—to be explained? The kernel of the problem lies in the fact that in our concern for the uniqueness of the New England Way, our search for the native grounds of American ideas in Congregational church polity, and our fascination with the intellectual matrix that distinguished the Puritan from his Christian forebears, we have ignored a most crucial side of Puritanism. We have painted our picture in blacks and grays because we at first took the color and light of the Puritan faith for granted—and then forgot about it; and our picture no more squares with the colorful world than a black-and-white photograph does. For the Puritan faith had a gloriously bright side, too; but, in the dark and complicated folds of reform and controversy, we have lost the golden thread of private devotion. Prayer, meditation, and contemplation were as colorfully vivid to the Puritan as to the Catholic, as full of joy, delight, and ecstasy—devotions fundamentally indistinguishable in New England from their practice in medieval Europe and the primitive Christian church. Taylor's best service to his faith may, indeed, lie just in this correction of our view of Puritanism: he casts the color and light of devotional tradition over the historically gloomy face of early New England.

In a sense, Taylor does indeed reflect a Catholic tradition, but he does so with no jeopardy to his own orthodoxy. The boldness of his conceptions, the devotional practice reflected in his writings, the form of his poetry, and even his images and symbols derive unquestionably from the literature of mysticism. Evelyn Underhill indicates the dangers inherent in the term itself in her description of the mystical: "One of the most abused words in the English language, it has been used in different and often mutually exclusive senses by religion, poetry, and philosophy: has been claimed as an excuse for every kind of occultism, for dilute transcendentalism, vapid symbolism, religious or aesthetic sentimentality, and bad metaphysics. On the other hand, it has been freely employed as a term of contempt by those who have criticized these things. It is much to be hoped that it may be restored sooner or later to its old meaning, as the science or art of the spiritual life."[1] And in his recent translation of *The Poems of St. John of the Cross,* John Frederick Nims feels obliged to apologize for using the term "that to many suggests something suspicious or lurid. . . . We may connect it with parapsychology or ESP [extrasensory perception] or candles in a darkened room or hallucinative mushrooms or delusions of the endocrines."[2] The unfortunate dilemma is that the epithet *mystic* evokes these suggestions and is, at the same time, the only name which properly describes a distinct concept of reality and the process by which that conception is attained.

Mysticism begins with the belief or faith that the real nature of the universe is transcendental; reality lies, therefore, beyond the world of phenomena, of sense impressions, and of intellectual abstractions or ideas in the Platonic tradition. The mystic has faith that beyond these is Pure Being, an ultimate spirit or vital principle or energy from which all other forms of being are derived or under which they may be subsumed. Moreover, mysticism contends that men, perhaps especially gifted ones, may, through the discipline of their own spirits, attain a direct experience of this pure being—and not merely a rational conviction of its existence, but a direct and personal acquaintance so complete that it can only be described as a union with ultimate reality. Such a view of reality is ancient and universal, but Christianity has provided a particularly rich proving ground for its development. Its three-personed God, creator of all things, and maintainer of them by His unresting providence, is the Christian's Pure Being, the source of all life and truth, the original and ultimate reality. Omnipresent, and therefore immanent in His creation, He is to the Christian yet distinct from it; He is not pantheistically confused with the nature He has made. The Christian mystic often startles his brethren by claiming that he has attained an intensely close and personal relationship with his transcendent maker—has actually achieved union with God.

The mystic's attempts to describe this ineffable experience, to assure others that the mystical union is really possible, and to urge them to seek to attain it comprise the literature of mysticism. Its documents are strikingly parallel in the process they describe and in the symbols by which they attempt to apprehend the tremendous experience—so parallel, indeed, that they may be called conventions. The mystic process is usually described as an ascension; it begins with curiosity or study of the world and with a growing awareness that the natural world of sense impressions is too transient—too unenduring to answer man's questions about what and who he is. This recognition which often comes suddenly—like the experience of conversion in traditional Christianity—often results in contempt for the world. Turning from it, the soul rises to a transcendent realm, partly by its own mental efforts, but frequently without any control. This is conventionally described as the soul's being rapt or snatched to heaven, actually vacating the body for a very brief time. During this enraptured state, the body becomes senseless and the person lapses into a trance. The soul, at this time, usually experiences a sensation of Divine presence and has a vision perceived not by the eyes, really, but by the mind's eye, the divine spark, or "Funklein," of the soul. Frequently the soul does not attain union with its "vision" immediately; but, by persistently contemplating this source of all wisdom and object of all love, it is eventually beatified. The affinity of this experience with sexual ecstasy accounts oftentimes for the mystic's turning to terms of sex, love, and marriage to express it. Like Plato's philosopher of the cave, the mystic does not remain perpetually enraptured; he must descend to a world of shadows and images again. Having viewed ultimate reality, he desires to communicate his vision to others. His union with God informs every aspect of his active life.

I Awakening

The mystical process is the subject of Taylor's poetry. The first step in the process—"the awakening of the self," as Underhill calls it,[3] or conversion from the world of sense— Taylor called "conviction." We must remember that Taylor subscribed to a complicated and highly refined theology; and its vocabulary came, in a sense, with his faith and is, therefore, seldom original with Taylor. Rarely so dramatic as St. Paul's conversion on the Damascus road, conviction was yet absolutely necessary in Taylor's theology. Often very ordinary occurrences occasioned sudden enlightenment: a natural object, a familiar passage from scripture, or the example or exhortation of a well-known friend unaccountably triggered the significant experience. Taylor's own conversion occurred in his childhood; he described it to his congregation on the day of the formal organization of the first church at Westfield:

> As for the first time that ever any beam of this nature did break upon me was when I was but small, viz., upon a

morning a sister of mine while she was getting up or getting me up or both, fell on the giving an account of the creation of the world by God alone and of man especially and of the excellent state of man by creation as that he was created in the image of God and was holy and righteous and how Eve was made of Adam's rib and was the first woman, Adam's wife, how both were placed in Paradise and the garden of Eden, a most curious place and had liberty to eat of all the trees therein *except* the tree of knowledge of good and evil, and *this* God would not suffer them to eat of.

But the serpent did betray them and did draw them to eat of that fruit and thereby they did sin against God, and God was angry and cast them out of the Garden of Eden and set angels, cherubims, and a flaming sword turning every way to keep the "Tree of Life" and so man was made a sinner and God was angry with all men for sin.

But oh, this account came in upon me in such a strong way that I am not able to express it, but ever since, I have had a notion of sin and its naughtiness remain and the wrath of God on the account of the same.[4]

This awakening to the sense of the reality of sin, of its dreadfulness, and of his own participation in it betrays Taylor's full realization of an infinite and transcendent God whose will man had crossed. What accounts for his awakening through this rehearsal of a story undoubtedly well known to Taylor even as a child, Taylor calls the special "work of the spirit of God." He elsewhere considers it a miraculous effect of God's grace. Typically Puritan, Taylor awakens to a conviction of the reality of sin and his own sinfulness as grace affects his conscience. But grace also affects the understanding, according to Taylor, in which case it is called illumination.[5] The two faculties of the soul function together but in opposite directions: conscience struggles to push the soul free from the carnality and worldliness which have led it into sin; and the understanding pulls the soul to the source of light illuminating it, to the personification of Wisdom—Jesus Christ.

Taylor's man is above all a rational animal. He cannot legitimately be brought to God without reason. This is a point on which seventeenth-century Puritanism insisted: faith and reason were not utterly opposed; and faith without reason was most suspect. What distinguished man from the other creatures was his rational soul, the link between man and God; and, therefore, God had to be explicable to human reason. Taylor emphasizes this side of his faith even more than most of his colleagues, and they are startling for their rationality. The emphatic point of Taylor's conception of the rational soul is the intellectual faculty—the spark or eye of the soul. Not unique with Taylor, the conception is, however, uncommon among Puritans; it is not so rare among mystics from at least the time of the German Dominican Meister Eckhart (1260?-1327?).

Taylor's God, as we have suggested, is a thoroughly transcendent one; and the frequently reprinted "Preface" to *God's Determinations* makes this concept abundantly clear. In it God is maker of the world: turning it on a lathe, blowing the bellows of a mighty furnace, and holding the mold into which the molten Nothing is poured; finally setting it upon pillars, lacing it with rivers and seas, and locking it "Like a quilt ball within a silver box." God's "handiwork" is a very pretty trinket, whose works are under the constant surveillance and control of its Creator's providence. But it remains somehow frivolous: even the glorious sun is reduced to a brilliant bowling ball. Undoubtedly a mighty work, the world glorifies its Maker, but it always remains apart from him. Unlike Jonathan Edwards' God, Taylor's never becomes so intricately a part of his own creation; for, although Edwards sidesteps the error of pantheism, his expressions walk the very brink of that abyss. He describes the change in nature that follows an intense experience of God's presence: "The appearance of everything was altered; there seemed to be, as it were, a calm, sweet cast, or appearance of divine glory, in almost every thing. God's excellency, his wisdom, his purity and love, seemed to appear in every thing; in the sun, moon, and stars; in the clouds, and blue sky; in the grass, flowers, trees; in the water, and all nature; which used greatly to fix my mind."[6] Nature never in this way affected Taylor.

The mystic's problem was to find some way of bringing created man to his utterly transcendent God. Unlike the rest of creation, man was made in God's image; Eckhart suggested that this image had nothing to do with man's physiognomy but was a divine nucleus[7] in the soul, which was implanted there to act as a point of contact between man and his Maker. This divine spark seated at the apex of the soul is identified with the highest rational faculty[8] by Eckhart and the German school of mysticism that flowered in the fourteenth century. Taylor, whether aware of their concept or not, echoes the same idea and uses the same image in the last lines of the "Preface." God, having created his glorious trinket the universe,

> Gave all to nothing man indeed, whereby
> Through nothing man all might him glorify.
> In nothing then imbosst the brightest gem
> More precious than all preciousness in them.
> But nothing man did throw down all by sin:
> And darkened that lightsome gem in him.
> That now his brightest diamond is grown
> Darker by far than any coalpit stone.

Sometimes, as in this selection, the divine nucleus is a gem; at others, a seed, a candle, a coal, or a kernel; but most often it is the spark or eye of the rational soul.

God's grace, like light, shines upon the rational soul and awakens it to the source of all wisdom, Christ. Taylor's Christology emphasizes this aspect of the Savior, fusing him with the classical image of Sophia, or Sapientia, the goddess of Wisdom.[9] One entire sermon in Taylor's "Christographia" is devoted to making Christ intellectually and rationally appealing to his congregation. Arguing that since all men desire to attain wisdom and the honor it can bring, he tells them they must "apply themselves in Wisdom's treasury, and trade in Wisdom's markets," which is Christ, in whom wisdom shines "as a clear candle in a golden lanthorn."[10] Of course, St. Paul had warned against the pursuit of wisdom;[11] but, while Taylor is careful not to go contrary to the Apostle, he seems to have felt with the Englishman Thomas Traherne (1637?-1674) that "to be a Philosopher a Christian and a Divine, was to be one of the most Illustrious Creatures in the World," and that it was impossible to be truly one without being the others as well.[12] Traherne restates Paul's opinion: "We must distinguish therefore of Philosophy, and of Christians also. Some Philosophy, as St. Paul saith, is vain, but then it is vain Philosophy."[13] But Christ, in both Taylor and Traherne, is true wisdom, and not vain.

The beams of Christ's wisdom strike "the intellectual faculty, filling the eye of the soul with a clear sight into all things that are the proper objects thereof" (*C, 4*, p. 88). This intellectual faculty is the spiritual organ designed especially to receive the "divine light" which Taylor calls "the knowledge of the will of God." "The intellectual faculty is the special seat of this knowledge. This is the eye of the soul whereinto the light of the sun of righteousness is sent and seated. The whole heart is the house into which this sun shines; yet the very cabinet wherein this sparkling pearl which the prophetical office doth hand out is more especially treasured up. The beams of this sun do more especially flutter in this nest, and therein hatch the sanctifying eggs of grace. Oh! Consider this. The sanctifying beams of Christ's prophetical office do gild over the intellectual power with the holy light, whose influences graciously touch the will and affections. . . . The intellectual faculty is the golden candlestick in which the glorious candle of Christ's prophetical chandling is set" (*C, 12*, pp. 247-48). The highest intellectual organ or faculty is housed in the heart, and the knowledge it brings affects not only the understanding but also the will and affections. Ultimate wisdom and love are inextricably bound together. Taylor declares that there is in human nature a principle for choosing the best; when the intellectual faculty is enlightened, therefore, man must inevitably pursue with all his love and desire that which the intellect has learned to be most valuable.

But not all men are graced to see the wisdom that is Christ. Their souls' eyes are, like the "lightsome gem," covered over with sin. Their understandings may occasionally catch some glimpse of Divine Wisdom; but, for full illumination, they require divine and saving light. And this is not given to all: God splits all mankind, exercising what Taylor calls "Selecting Love."[14] The New Covenant or Covenant of Grace, by means of which saving light is distributed, is made only with "the elect of God" (*C, 12*, p. 248), and not with reprobates who can never attain salvation. Real conviction, when experienced by a man of Taylor's faith, signifies that

God is exercising saving grace upon his soul; and therefore proves that that man belongs among God's chosen. The experience of enlightenment or the awakening of the soul, of the illumination of the understanding, and of the conviction of sin—all that marked real conversion—brought assurance and hope of salvation; and such conversion was, indeed, the most reliable sign that God's love had selected him and also the strongest motive for seeking communion with God.

Taylor also was concerned with the soul's awakening at a most mundane level. When God made his "dichotomy" of all mankind, selecting each "name by name," he sent for his chosen

> A royal coach whose scarlet canopy
> O'er silver pillars, doth expanded lie:[15]

The royal coach is the church in which only the sanctified may enter. Some test of the sanctity of those desiring to ride to God's "sumptuous feast" in the royal coach had to be established.

On this question the churches of New England divided in Taylor's time. As to the admission of adults to church membership, liberal practice tended through the last quarter of the seventeenth century more and more strongly to favor admitting all persons of non-scandalous behavior who had a basic knowledge of the principles of Christianity. Many hoped that easy entrance would encourage more people to seek full church membership and thereby, perhaps, reduce the growing sinfulness of New England. But to Taylor and other more conservative ministers, such a course of action was an abandonment of the principles laid down by the founders of New England Congregationalism, and it could only lead the churches to ruin against the rocks of hyprocrisy.[16] Therefore, on the very day he and six other Westfield men gave their own accounts of God's spirit illuminating their understandings and convincing their consciences, Taylor preached a sermon setting out the principles by which the Westfield church was to be run. Long and complicated, the sermon clearly indicated the importance of testifying to the signs of God's special grace awakening the soul: "It is necessary," insisted Taylor, "that the person seeking church fellowship with any church of Christ, give an account of some of his experiences that he hath had of the workings of God's spirit upon his heart. . . ."[17]

Supporting this contention in over twenty pages of argument, Taylor constantly shifts the terms by which he identifies the "matter" or subject of these accounts. Sometimes he calls it a confession of faith, sometimes a confession of sin, a sign of repentance, or a proof of God's "saving work." But essentially it seems that Taylor meant it to be a "confession or relation of some experiences of God's gracious working upon the heart, by the means of grace, holding forth some grounds for Christian charity to judge the old man is put off and the new man put on" (*PC*, p. 14). In his insistence upon admitting only truly sanctified persons, as far as sanctity could be determined, Taylor frequently argued this question of the soul's twofold awakening: the positive illumination that brought faith in Christ, and the negative conviction of sin.

II *Purgation*

Conviction and illumination, working simultaneously, draw forth Taylor's descriptions of the second stage of the mystic way: repentance for sin, disgust at its sight, the attempt to keep the soul's precious eye clear from the foulness of sin, and the denial of carnality and worldliness—in short, the stage of purgation. According to Plotinus, the purpose of purgation is to learn "the meaning of *order* and *limitation* . . . which are qualities belonging to the Divine nature."[18] And Underhill says that "that which mystical writers mean . . . when they speak of the Way of Purgation, is . . . the slow and painful completion of Conversion. It is the drastic turning of the self from the unreal to the real life. . . . Its business is the getting rid, first of self-love; and secondly of all those foolish interests in which the surface consciousness is steeped."[19] On one hand, then, purgation involves self-denial and perhaps even self-punishment; on the other, it requires a positive self-discipline and self-formation; on both, it means self-struggle.

The first struggle upon awakening to the sign of God's

spirit at work upon the soul is described by Taylor in *God's Determinations* as the soul's exertion to accept the fact that it has been chosen—or as Taylor puts it, "The Elect's Combat in their Conversion."[20] In this poem he pictures the soul as at first bewildered, unbelieving, and resisting God's call in an allegory of war. The soul's resistance arises from its knowledge of its own sin; for, like Michael Wigglesworth's men surprised by the Day of Doom "in their Security," Taylor's elect have been

> Lull'd in the lap of sinful nature snug,
> Like pearls in puddles cover'd o'er with mud:[21]

Souls completely free from outward sin "are nigh as rare / As black swans that in milkwhite rivers are." Some few immediately give in to the sweet wooing of God's grace, but more commonly their awareness that they do not deserve God's favor sends them in headlong retreat. The second rank of souls surrender to God's Mercy: that is, they accept the argument that, as sinful as they may be, God's mercy is stronger and greater than their own sins; and they yield to God's ability to forgive. The third and last group gives in neither to the first sign of Grace nor to the unassisted power of Mercy, and it promptly divides into two ranks: the first gives in only when convinced of the justice of election according to God's all-wise plan; the second succumbs only to the combined strength of God's mercy and justice.

But this dramatic allegory of conviction is accomplished very near the beginning of the poem; its greater part is devoted to the accusations of Satan, who represents the convinced conscience, as S. Foster Damon hints rather worriedly. "Satan is the Accuser," Damon says, "and comes perilously near being identified with the conscience. . . ."[22] There is really no peril in this identification. In pointing to the complete unworthiness of the soul to be saved—inwardly and outwardly, even in its worship of God—the conscience functions quite properly; it is Satanic in that its accusations purpose to pull the already elected soul away from God, and so run counter to God's will. Taylor is saying that once the soul has evidence of its election, it need not fear the accusations of conscience. Indeed, the Wise and Happy Saint assures the bewildered soul that its doubts are "Satan's temptations," and that the soul must persevere in faith no matter how vicious its conscience claims it to be.

But Taylor does not mean that conscience is absolutely wrong in its condemnation. Like all Puritans, Taylor accepted what Jonathan Edwards was to call "The Great Christian Doctrine": the inheritance of all mankind, and indeed one of its defining characteristics, is the defect of sin—the doctrine of original sin. Calvin writes that man as a whole is in every way defective; he is, in a sense, the blotch and defect of nature itself: "man is of himself nothing else but concupiscence." Carefully defining the term as he finds it used by Paul and Augustine, Calvin asserts: "Original sin, therefore, appears to be an hereditary pravity and corruption of our nature, diffused through all the parts of the soul, rendering us obnoxious to the Divine wrath, and producing in us those works which the Scripture calls 'works of the flesh.' "[23] Not the work of nature but the proud disobedience of man himself in the person of Adam is responsible for our defect, he insists. Calvin isn't concerned with how this sin is transmitted; the important thing is to accept the fact that Adam's sin is inherited. "Nor," he says, "to enable us to understand this subject, have we any need to enter on that tedious dispute, with which the fathers were not a little perplexed, whether the soul of a son proceeds by derivation or transmission from the soul of the father, because the soul is the principal seat of the pollution."[24]

But the transmission of original sin—exactly the kind of question that fascinated a mind like Taylor's—received his attention as he preached about purification in 1701. What would have to be done, he asked, to permit a pure and undefiled human nature to come into being? Human nature, according to his considerations at that time, was composed of two essential parts: (1) the physical materials, and (2) the rational soul. No creature can be sinful unless it is rational; but the rational soul is, for each individual, "made immediately *ex nihilo*, of no preexisting matter, and therefore is in itself pure. As soon as it is infused into the physical materials, however, the combination becomes sinful. But neither are

the physical materials, before this infusion, sinful in themselves; they are merely what Taylor calls "fallen nature."
Though not properly sinful, this fallen nature requires purification because it is the part inherited from Adam. What
identifies it as fallen or defective is its "inclination to any
vice, or sensual motion disordinate. . . . There is in the sper-
matic principals, the original of all indisposition unto, and
opposition against, all sanctity and righteousness, as a con-
sequent of the loss of God's image in holiness, by sin . . .
which, when the rational soul is infused, making it perfect
human nature, then this original of these things is indeed
original sin inherent; and this is found in all conceptions made
in an ordinary way." Of course, since Adam, only one human
nature had come into existence purified prior to being infused
with a rational soul: the extraordinarily purified human nature
of Christ.[25]

All others faced the impossible task of purifying a nature
already thoroughly sinful. Taylor's personal offenses, confessed in his "relation" to the Westfield church, seem singularly unworthy of the great work they illustrated. And Taylor
himself admitted that "being under the rigid and watchful
eyes of my parents who would crop the budding forth of
original sin into any visible sins with wholesome reproofs,
or the rod, I was thereby preserved from a sinful life. But
yet the transgression of the Sabbath and some degree of
disobedience to my parents, and too often the evil of lying
and also inward evil were things that did more prevail, all
which have had their oppositions by one reproof or until
they have been a burden unto me."[26] The founders—"foundation men," or "pillars"—of the church were never chosen
easily in New England; for public confessions of "innocency
of life" were viewed by partial and impartial neighbors
alike with sharp and not always charitable criticism.[27] Yet
no one seems to have questioned the mildness of Taylor's
confession.

Moreover, Taylor provides two strong reasons for sup-
posing that had there been more to confess to, he would
have made it public. First, of course, the blacker the sin, the
more powerfully God's spirit could be seen to have worked
in the repentant sinner; and, therefore, the better and more

encouraging an example he would be for others in the gathering. And secondly, the strength of the church grew from the
mutual dependence of its members. One way to secure that
strength was to submit to the charitable love of others in the
church by throwing oneself upon their loving forgiveness.
Presumably the more self-degrading the spectacle was and
the more love required to forgive, the more intimate one's
reliance on fellow church members became, and the stronger
became the church itself (*PC*, pp. 50-51). But apparently
Taylor could muster no such visible sins.

Invisible sins, however, were another matter—if we may
judge from his *Preparatory Meditations*, the 217 poems
written at regular intervals from 1682 to 1725. The very first
confesses to a "streight'ned breast," a "lifeless spark," and a
cold love; and late in 1722 he still complains that his soul
is diseased, too barren a ground for him to expect Christ to
be implanted there. In fact, his poetry, in which he never
mitigates the foulness of his sins by euphemistic language,
creates a picture of his sinfulness in startling contrast to his
public confession. "Filth" recurs frequently throughout the
meditations, and Taylor is rich in figures of speech to vivify
the word: he calls himself a dirt ball, a muddy sewer, a tumbrel
of dung, a dung-hill, a dot of dung, a varnished pot of
putrid excrements, drops in a closestool pan, guts, garbage,
and rottenness. He wears a crown of filth, his cheeks are
covered with spiders' vomit, and he is candied over with
leprosy. He is also a pouch of passion, a lump of loathsome-
ness, a bag of botches, a lump of lewdness; and he gives off
a nauseous stink. He is wrapped in slime; pickled in gall; a
sink of nastiness; and a dirty, smelly dish cloth: he is, in
short, "all blot." The violence of his deprecation strikes
modern sensibilities more offensively than, no doubt, it
would have Taylor's contemporaries; they would probably
have admired the vividness of his self-vilification.

Much of Taylor's language is conventional, and certainly
his attitude is. But the images bark too energetically to be
discounted as mere shams or conventions; Taylor very really
felt himself to be sinful; in fact, to be utterly helpless against
his sins. He allegorizes in military terms the struggle in his
own soul in *God's Determinations*. The thousand griefs that a

man faces in life violate his integrity and make him surrender
to sin itself; as soldiers of sin, they

> march in rank and file, proceed to make
> A battery, and the fort of life to take.
> Which when the sentinels did spy, the heart
> Did beat alarum up in every part.
> The vital spirits apprehend thereby
> Expos'd to danger great the suburbs lie,
> The which they do desert, and speedily
> The fort of life, the heart, they fortify.
> The heart beats up still by her pulse to call
> Out of the outworks her train soldiers all,
> Which quickly come hence: now the looks grow pale,
> Limbs feeble too: the enemies prevail.
> Do scale the outworks where there's scarce a scout
> That can be spi'd sent from the castle out.[28]

We should notice that, while it is the heart that becomes the
last stronghold against sin, the heart is not the symbol of
emotions in our common use of the word: it is the proper
seat of knowledge, which houses the divine spark, the intellectual faculty. Sin penetrates most deeply in the form of
"peeping thought, sent scout of sin" (2.42), so the struggle
against sin becomes an intellectual combat in the heart. "For
the battle must be fought where the enemy is quarter'd,
and that is in the heart. You see, they are enemies in the
mind. So the carnal mind is enmity. . . . Now then the
enemies to be slain are the inhabitants of the heart. The
rebels are quarter'd there" (C, 2, p. 18).

The thoughts most injurious to the clear sight of the eye
of the soul are those of the "carnal mind," the attraction to
things of this world. "I'm but a flesh and blood bag," he
complains: "Passion, pride, lust, worldliness, and such like
bubs . . . bow my heart aside."

> They do inchant me from my Lord, I find,
> The thoughts whereof prove daggers in my mind.
> (1.43)

He finds his love hugging the brambles grown around his heart rather than his Lord. His heart is too small, "Tartariz'd with worldly dregs dri'd in't." Knowing his heart should be turned to God, he sees it nonetheless "run out to

> Poor bits of clay: or dirty gays embrace.
> Doth leave thy lovely self for loveless show:
> For lumps of lust, nay sorrow and disgrace.

Willing to prize his Lord, his worldliness interferes:

> I fain would prize thee, Lord, but find the price
> Of earthly things to rise so high in me
> That I no precious matter in my choice
> Can find within my heart to offer thee.
> The price of worldly toys is grown so dear,
> They pick my purse. Thy gain is little here.
> (2.42)

And thus his conscience interminably accuses him; Satan tells the convicted soul that its worldliness, like all its vices, are natural to it, "For sins keep sentinel within thy heart."[29] Humiliated to the edge of despair, Taylor cries out,

> Unclean, unclean: my Lord, undone, all vile
> Yea for all defil'd: What shall thy servant do?
> Unfit for thee: not fit for holy soul,
> Nor for communion of saints below.
> (2.26)

The work of ridding his heart of its worldliness cannot be carried on but by "the heart searcher, and this is God alone" (*C*, 2, p. 18). It is He who must "Scour these quarters," gibbet up "each peeping thought" of the world, and "quarter here each flourishing grace." Because Taylor finds the source of his sins not merely in his passions or will but in the very root of his being, he is incapable or removing them by his own exertions. Only Christ can purify him:

Christ's name
    Propitiation is for sins. Lord, take
It is so for mine. Thus quench thy burning flame
    In that clear stream that from his side forth brake.
    I can no comfort take while thus I see
    Hell's cursed imps thus jetting strut in me.

    Lord, take thy sword: these Anakims destroy:
        Then soak my soul in Zion's bucking tub
    With holy soap, and nitre, and rich lye.
        From all defilement me cleanse, wash and rub.
        Then wrince and wring me out till th'water fall
        As pure as in the well: not foul at all.

                                        (1.40)

In this poem the purification is in terms of cutting, washing, and wringing. But Taylor's ways of purgation are almost as many as the kinds of filth he finds in his heart.

Taylor insists so much upon ceremonial cleanness in talking about the church that one would expect him to emphasize the Old Testament rite of circumcision. But he concerns himself with it very little; in Meditation 70 (1706) he considers circumcision most directly: there is no question but that man must undergo the knife to cure his soul of sin and "proud naughtiness":

    The infant male must lose its foreskin first,
        Before God's Spirit works as pulse, therein
    To sanctify it from the sin in't nurst,
        And make't in grace's covenant to spring.

Must there be actual cutting then? Taylor says

    No, no. Baptism is a better mark.
    It's therefore circumcision's rightful heir
    Bearing what circumcision in't did bear.

Circumcision, therefore, a part of the Mosaic Law, is merely a symbol or "type" of the New Testament's baptism, which ceremonially purifies the new-born soul after conversion. Its symbol changes from a "keen and cutting sharp" one to one of washing. As important as this sacrament is, however, Taylor says very little about it directly in either poetry or prose. Circumstances, as well as his own interests, turned his attention from the initiatory seal of baptism to the confirming seal of communion.

But this turn of attention in no way limits the variety of purification images. Arrows and swords of God's righteousness play an active part, but purification comes much more frequently through washing or scouring. Christ is a spring or a well, a pool or a cleansing shower, a laver, or fountain of *aqua vitae,* whose blood scours the soul of all sin. Most often, however, the purification is by fire; and in repeated images, Christ is the sun whose hot rays melt the frozen lake of Taylor's affections, disperse the black clouds of sin, or enlighten the eye blinded by it. Sometimes He is a spark falling into Taylor's tinderbox of sin; at others, a flame dropped into the poet's hearth, burning up the trash of worldliness; or again, a furnace in which Taylor's heart is melted like ore. Purification is compared to the refining of gold from the dross of sin and worldliness. Taylor pleads repeatedly for a coal from God's altar to be placed on his tongue, or for himself to be made a sanctified altar upon which to offer his own heart as a sacrifice:

> I'll offer on't my heart to thee. (Oh! take me)
> And let thy fire calcine mine altar's wood,
> Then let thy spirit's breath, as bellows, blow
> That this new kindled life may flame and glow.
> (2.82)

Often his heart itself is a coal covered with ashes that must be blown clear before the fire of love can burn, or it is a candle that must burn sin's fat to remain lighted.

In another set of related figures, purgation is a grinding process, or his heart is hammered into a Godly frame on the anvil of Christ's authority. He begs to be made the valley in which the Lily Christ is planted; but he must consequently be prepared by tearing, plowing, and harrowing—thus the dung of sin is made the fertilizer for sweet graces (2.84). From the purified field come the sweet graces and herbs, medicinals in the hands of the Physician of physicians. Purgation is always left to Christ in Taylor's writing; for, although men can will to be pure, the doing remains with Christ. "Without a miracle there is no cure," writes Taylor, and so the Sun of Righteousness becomes a "surgeon's shop" where Taylor presents his sinful soul for cleansing.

In this negative aspect of purgation, Taylor often seems to approach traditional asceticism; but his self-punishment never reached the extremes of mortification reflected in Catholic hagiography. The "loathsome ordeals" described by Underhill in the lives of St. Francis of Assisi, St. Catherine of Genoa, Madame Guyon, St. Ignatius Loyola, and other mystics[30] appear neither in the writings nor in the life of Taylor. But because Taylor did not put stones in his shoes or wear chains next to his body or seek out ugly sores to kiss, he is not to be disqualified from the spiritual life. His ascetic training satisfied his spiritual needs; and, as we have seen, the extensive and intensive humiliation evidenced in the poems testifies to his spiritual determination. Perhaps to a man as highly sensitive to words as poets must be, the verbal whiplash provides as effective self-flagellation as a physical whip could.

Abundant as the evidence is for the darker side of the purgative way in Taylor, proof of a more positive self-discipline and self-formation also abounds. It comes not from Taylor's poems, however, but from his sermons, especially the "Christographia" sermons preached from 1701 to 1703. Actually a unified study of the nature, properties, and operations of the Redeemer, the fourteen sermons commonly sound one distinctive note: the necessity of imitating Christ. Taylor tells his congregation that it is one thing—and a very necessary thing—to worship and praise God with the mouth, "But this honor without the heart is but a vain shew"; and so he urges his congregation: "Strive to hold forth the glory of the person of Christ in your Christian life and conversation." In almost every exhortation he returns to this duty. It being God's plan to redeem fallen man through divine mediation, He, in the person of Christ, took on a human nature. For this gift, men ought "to live more to the honor of God, than the angels themselves in that our nature is more honored" (*C, 1,* p. 50). Our will and judgment being under the cloud of original sin, our surest way to a virtuous life is through the imitation of the most Godly of men.

In fact, man imitates by nature, instinctively: "We were made and formed with an imitating principle in our nature, which cannot be suffocated or stifled, but will act in imitating some example. God, to prevent us from taking wrong patterns to follow, hath presented us with a perfect pattern of right practice in our own nature in Christ, which is most exemplary, being a most exact copy, written by the son of God with the pen of the humanity on the milk white sheet of an holy life. Hence our imitation of him is his due and our duty, and to leave this pattern is to dishonour him, deform our lives, to deviate from our pattern, and to disgrace ourselves" (*C, 1,* p. 52). For this reason, Taylor's task in the "Christographia" is to write an extended character sketch of the perfect model and to encourage his congregation to follow it.

What Taylor pursues in the "Christographia" is not a dramatic characterization like *God's Determinations* but a profoundly analytic study of the character of Christ; it is rational rather than emotional, representing that traditional stage of mystic development that often accompanied "the Purification of the Self"—the process of recollection or meditation.[31] In Taylor's mind, meditation and faith go hand in hand, though he employs a rather more bovine image. Meditating on Canticles 6:6, "Thy teeth are like a flock of sheep that come up from washing whereof every one bears twins," Taylor writes:

> Hence methinks they the righter judge, that hold
>   These teeth import true faith in Christ alone
> And meditation on the gospel, should
>   Be signified thereby to every one.
>   Teeth are for the eating of the food made good
>   And meditation chawing is the cud.
>
>   (2.138)

He extends the image further a few lines below:

> This faith and meditation a pair appears
>> As two like to the two brave rows of teeth
> The upper and the nether, well set, clear,
>> Exactly meet to chew the food, belief.
>> Both eat by biting: meditation
>> By chewing spiritually the cud thereon.

"Christ's milk white righteousness and splendent grace"—the perfect pattern to imitate—become the particular food to be chewed by meditation.

From the beginning of the sixteenth century there appeared on the Continent and in England an increasing number of guides to the spiritual life—to prayer, contemplation, and devotion generally. Emphatically they urged the duty of prayer, both public and private; and they gradually identified private prayer with meditation, which they treated sometimes as self-examination, sometimes as secret prayer or that of the closet; but they made it a necessary action of the devout life. Progressively they came to define meditation, distinguishing it subtly from other very similar acts of devotion. Until the beginning of the seventeenth century, the most prominent of these works were written by Catholics and were brought to England largely through the proselyting of the Jesuits.

Quite naturally, then, Professor Martz, in his fine study of *The Poetry of Meditation* (New Haven, 1954), turns to Richard Gibbons of the Society of Jesus for a contemporary definition of meditation. Gibbons succinctly defines it as thought "deliberately directed toward the development of . . . 'love and exercise of vertue, and the hatred and avoiding of sinne.'" St. Francis de Sales modifies this definition somewhat by distinguishing the exact mode of thought: ". . . when we thinke of heavenly things, not to learne but to love them, that is called to meditate: and the exercise thereof Meditation."[32] Love, not knowledge alone, is the end of meditation; and the peculiar relation between love and knowledge is its distinctive feature. Underhill comments that "there is a sense in which it may be said, that the desire of knowledge is a part of the desire of perfect love: since one aspect of that all inclusive passion is clearly a longing to know, in the deepest, fullest sense, the thing adored. . . . But there is no sense in which it can be said that the desire of love is merely a part of the desire of perfect knowledge: for that strictly intellectual ambition includes no adoration, no self-spending, no reciprocity of feeling between Knower and Known. Mere knowledge, taken alone, is a matter of receiving, not of acting: of eyes, not wings: a dead alive business at the best."[33] Gaining knowledge, not for its own sake, but for the sake of love, "comes to be regarded," writes Martz about the first half of the seventeenth century, "as an exercise essential for the ordinary conduct of 'good life' and almost indispensable as preparation for the achievement of the highest mystical experience."[34]

While Taylor describes the act as a chewing of the cud, others also emphasized its nature as an exercise. The most exacting and detailed of these descriptions is probably Saint Ignatius Loyola's *Spiritual Exercises,* which details a series of ordered and predictable but not utterly inflexible stages. First the "exercitant"—as Loyola calls one who meditates—attempts to fix his attention on some "heavenly thing" such as some scriptural incident or venerated object in order to secure as lively an apprehension of it as he can by an effort of memory and imagination. Then he submits the object of his contemplation to a lengthy, rigorous, and thorough intellectual examination until his understanding of it is complete. The next step is to judge or evaluate the object, after which the exercitant submits his evaluation to his will and affections, which are moved according to the attractive excellence or repulsive sinfulness of the object. The final stage expresses these moved affections—usually joy, love, praise, gratitude, or sorrow—in a colloquy with the Lord. Loyola's directions, in one form or another, gained wide distribution in England; and they exerted, with De Sales' *Introduction to the Devout Life* and Lorenzo Scupoli's *The Spiritual Combat,* a considerable influence upon the devotional practice of English writers, notably upon Donne, Herbert, Crashaw, and Traherne; they also created a demand for similar books by non-Catholics.

In 1648 the popular *Shorter Catechism* of the Westminster Assembly—the statement of doctrine about which Puritans of

Old and New England agreed, and which Taylor in 1679 wanted to make the primary basis of the Westfield church's statement of faith[35]—made the practice of meditation a clear duty in approaching the sacrament of the Lord's Supper; and a year later Puritans had their own handbook of meditation in Richard Baxter's *The Saints Everlasting Rest.* The fourth part of this book, "one of the most popular Puritan books of the entire seventeenth century,"[36] expounds at greater length and in greater detail than any other English book what Baxter calls "this Art of Heavenly-Mindedness." He titles this section "a Directory for the getting and keeping of the heart in Heaven: by the diligent practice of that Excellent unknown Duty of Heavenly Meditation."

In defining meditation, Baxter echoes De Sales' emphasis on love. Too often Christians "have thought that Meditation is nothing but the bare thinking on Truths, and the rolling of them in the Understanding and Memory! when every School-Boy can do this, or persons that hate the things which they think on."[37] Baxter's strength lies not only in the vigor of his expression, but in the boldness with which he calls upon the rich Catholic tradition of mystical literature. His marginal gloss ranges widely, once citing Jean Gerson's *De Monte Contemplationes* with the surprising advice: "Read this you Libertines, and learn better the way of Devotion from a Papist!"[38]

His meditative method itself, like Loyola's, follows the exercise of the various faculties of the soul. First the understanding "must take in Truths" and store them in its "Magazine or Treasury"—the memory. Bringing these truths from the memory to the affections requires "Ratiocination, reasoning the case with your selves, Discourse of minde, Cogitation or Thinking, or, if you will, call it Consideration."[39] This is also Taylor's understanding of meditation; like Baxter, he sees this intellectual analysis preceding the act of love itself but tending always to produce it. "Impower my powers, sweet Lord," he petitions, "till up they raise / My 'fections that thy glory on them blaze." For Baxter makes the rational discipline the necessary bridge between the head and heart, over which the truths of the understanding must pass to be judged good or bad by the will, and then submitted to the affections, usually love and joy.

Taylor knew Baxter's work, as did most New Englanders of his day; consequently, it is not surprising to see one of Baxter's ideas affirmed in Taylor's practice. Baxter sees this positive aspect of purgation closely related to the negative one—as closely involved, in other words, with the struggle against sin. He urges meditation as a duty, even when the spirit is dry and unresponsive. "I know," he says, "so far as you are spiritual, you need not all this striving and violence; but that is but in part, and in part you are carnal; and as long as it is so there is no talk of ease."[40] The exercise must be performed, willingly or not, until the heart achieves the joyful rewards it seeks. Verbalized, this self-struggle takes the form of a soliloquy, which Baxter describes as "a Preaching to ones self."[41] Martz writes that "a curious and typical Puritan twist" then occurs when Baxter says that "Therefore the very same *Method* which a *Minister* should use in his preaching to others, should a Christian use in speaking to himself." Actually the twist is neither so curious nor so typically Puritan as Martz suggests since similar injunctions recur commonly in sixteenth-century devotional guides.[42] But the injunction was singularly appropriate to Puritans, whose "method" in preaching was quite distinctive; and to Taylor in particular, whose preaching conforms essentially to Baxter's meditative discourse of mind.

Echoes of Baxter's *Saints Everlasting Rest* resound through the pages of American devotional guides, especially those written by Increase and Cotton Mather and their colleague Samuel Willard, whose writings were undoubtedly known to Edward Taylor, and whose works appear in Taylor's library. Evidence indicates that Taylor's practice of meditation dates from at least the time of his emigration to America, but it is nonetheless appropriate that Increase Mather's *Practical Truths* should have declared the nature and aim of meditation as Taylor observed it the very year Taylor's *Preparatory Meditations* began.

Mather's eight sermons of *Practical Truths* comment on the duty of public and private prayer; and he identifies meditation with the latter in a consideration of the practice of Isaac (Genesis 18:23), of whom it is said: *"That he went out to meditate*; or (as the *Hebrew* word . . . may be read,) *to pray*. The word signifieth both to pray and to meditate, and it is not improbable but that *Isaac* did at that time nothing but what was his daily custom to do, even retire himself from all company, for secret prayer and meditation."[43] Mather describes the aim of such secret prayer, as he frequently refers to it, as a mystical "intimacy of Communion with God"; its method is primarily a careful "particular" examination of conscience, the logical divisions of which correspond to the number of sins in question; and its effect is to stir the affections to "a *godly sorrow* for sin." But with this conviction of sin there also comes a "hungering after Christ. The soul must stand affected towards Christ as a hungry man doth towards food." Of course the Lord's Supper is the only feast at which Mather imagines that this "hungering after Christ" can be satisfied.[44] With this concept, he follows the long line of Catholic and English writers who felt the connection between meditation and the sacrament of communion to be necessary and inevitable.

In this attitude, Mather anticipates Taylor's own concern for meditation, which he addresses as part of preparing to receive the sacrament. Preaching about the necessity of approaching the sacrament in a pure state, Taylor urged his congregation in 1694 to "Carry a sacramental frame along with thee. Stir up all sacramental graces; repentance, faith, love, humility, a discerning eye, hunger and thirst after communion with God in Christ" (*1694*, p. 168). In agreement ideally as well as verbally with Increase Mather, Taylor insists first upon cleanliness from sin: "Stand clear from sin. . . . O! abhor it, come not nigh it: fly from it; both in heart and life purge away this evil thing, both in heart, affections, and conversation." Moreover, he urges what must sum up his idea of imitating Christ as he continues: "Be much in the exercise of love, patience, meekness, faith, hope, joy in the Lord, repentance, self denial, prayer, meditation, and the like" (*1694*, p. 169). And finally, like Mather, Taylor closely identifies meditation with the examination of conscience.

Taylor would have the examination of conscience be twofold: first, of the worthiness of the soul, which includes a review of one's conviction and conversion; and secondly, of the merit of the person outwardly in one's visible holiness, personal reformation, and knowledge of the spiritual mystery of the sacrament. But examination itself can only be part of the preparation. "Examination cannot be without contemplation," says Taylor; and he therefore urges his congregation to meditate as well. In this directive he clearly reflects his own meditative concerns, and he appears to be urging others to follow his own example: "Meditate upon the feast, its causes, its nature, its guests, its dainties, its reason and ends, and its benefits, etc. For it carries in its nature the circumstances as umbrage, or epitomized draught of the whole grace of the Gospel. For our Saviour is set out in lively colors" *1694*, p. 172). These are also the major subjects of his own sermons—those he thought most worthy of preserving.

In greater detail Taylor presented the considerations proper to a full meditation of Christ in the sacrament. Men should meditate upon "Our utter and eternal ruin by sin" and upon Christ's death for it; the covenants of redemption and grace; and Christ's role in the covenants, including his asssumption of human nature, his fulfilling of the law in his human nature, and the application of this action to the elect (*1694*, p. 173 ff.). This catalogue describes almost exactly what Taylor presents in the "Christographia" sermons: a detailed picture of Christ, designed to show his excellence and loveliness by a dry and intellectual analysis of "Christ's Person, Natures, the Personal Union of the Natures, Qualifications, and Operations."[45]

The ratiocination called for by Richard Baxter—and, indeed, the initial acts of the memory, understanding, and reason that Loyola and most others made the rational cud-chewing part of the meditation—Taylor practiced himself as he pondered his sermon material and reduced it to method. His analysis yielded a full realization of Christ's excellence, which he in turn praised in song:

> Thou altogether lovely art, all bright.
> Thy loveliness attracts all love to thee.
> Yea all of thee and thine is fair and white
> Together or apart in highest degree.
> Thy person, natures, properties all thine,
> Thy offices and acts most lovely shine.
> (2.127)

Thus the song, addressed to Christ and called a "Preparatory Meditation" by Taylor, is not really complete in itself; but it marks what Loyola called the last stage of the formal meditation—the "colloquy with the Lord." And thus to be fully understood, the poem must be read with its accompanying sermon in which the intellectual analysis is carried out rigorously, in which the food of belief is chewed most finely between the grinders of faith and meditation.

III *Rapture*

Soon after the soul on its mystical quest awakens to the desirability of Christ, purges itself of carnality and sin, and militantly undertakes to discipline itself in virtues and through the mental exercise of meditation, it is frequently rewarded by visions, voices, and ecstatic raptures. Underhill describes these as encouragement to the novice to continue the mystic quest. Both she and Dean Inge insist that such "mystical phenomena" belong only to the beginning stages of the "unitive way,"[46] and the most recent student of the subject— R. C. Zaehner—joins both in making such experiences purely extrinsic, as quite unnecessary to the mystical experience.[47]

But when Inge adds that "Self-induced visions inflate us with pride, and do irreparable injury to health of mind and body,"[48] he does an injustice to the seventeenth-century practice of meditation. Taylor's meditations—the exercise of the rational faculties applied analytically to the nature of the Mediator—were designed especially to induce an exceptionally clear image of Christ's excellence and loveliness or, in effect, a vision. The difficulty of treating this subject of visions in the mystical process is complicated by the fact that we are studying a sensitive artist's expression. For example, Vaughan writes:

> I saw ETERNITY the other night
> Like a great *Ring* of pure and endless light,
>   All calm, as it was bright,
> And round beneath it, Time in hours, days, years
>   Driv'n by the spheres
> Like a vast shadow mov'd.[49]

Are we to take this as descriptive of an actual, though hallucinatory experience, or is it purely imagined symbol, a visual metaphor designed to give concrete vividness to a difficult abstraction? Was there a ring of light that Vaughan saw either with his eyes or in his imagination, or does he create the ring himself to embody in it his "sense" of eternity? The same questions occur in the study of Taylor.

The purpose of his meditations was to produce a vision, not perhaps for his eyes, but for the one of the soul that is the mirror or image of God in him. In highly conventional mystical language, Taylor expresses his desire to achieve a vision of the Lord in 1715:

> Lead me, my Lord, upon Mount Lebanon,
>   And shew me there an aspect bright of thee.
> Open the valving doors, when thereupon,
>   I mean the casements of thy faith in me.
>   And give my soul's clear eye of thee a sight,
>   As thou shin'st its bright looking glasses bright.
>
>   (2.125)

Once the divine spark of the soul is conceived to be an eye, visual imagery follows both naturally and appropriately; and it is difficult for this reason to be sure that Taylor describes an actual experience. What the soul's eye sees, of course, is Christ's incomparable beauty, which prompts the soul to desire Him:

> Thou court'st mine eyes in sparkling colors bright,
>   Most bright indeed, and soul enamoring,
> With the most shining sun, whose beams did smite
>   Me with delightful smiles to make me spring.
>
> .   .   .   .
>
> Shall not this lovely beauty, Lord, set out
>   In dazzling shining flashes 'fore mine eye,
> Enchant my heart, Love's golden mine, till't spout
>   Out streams of love refin'd that on thee lie?
>
>   (2.12)

Taylor's frequent use of terms like *ecstasy, enravishment, rapture,* and *rapt,* invites us to reason that he experienced heavenly visions quite often. But he seems to claim actual visions on very few occasions. One he describes very consciously as a daydream or a vision in the imagination. But Taylor does seem to suggest that it actually occurred:

> My shattered phancy stole away from me,
>   (Wits run a wooling over Eden's park)
> And in God's garden saw a golden tree,
>   Whose heart was all divine, and gold its bark.
>   Whose glorious limbs and fruitful branches strong
>   With saints and angels bright are richly hung.
>   (1.29)

Taylor identifies the tree as "The tree of life within God's Paradise," compared to which he finds himself "a withred twig." The remainder of the poem is devoted to an explanation "with careful analysis, [of] the exact relation of Man to God by developing the central image of a 'Grafft' upon that tree."[50] But the tree returns again as the central image of a "vision" in the second series of Meditations. Again the poet imagines himself in "Eden's park":

> Walking, my Lord, within thy Paradise,
>   I find a fruit whose beauty smites mine eye
> And tastes my tooth that had no core nor vice.
>   And honey sweet, that's never rotting, lie
>   Under a tree, which viewed, I knew to be
>   The tree of life whose bulk's Theanthropie.
>
> And looking up, I saw its boughs all bow
>   With clusters of this fruit that it doth bring,
> Nam'd greatest LOVE.   (2.33)

But from this point on there is no sense of actually seeing a tree, and Taylor attends in the rest of the poem to the implications of what he has seen.

Very early in the first series of meditations, however, Taylor alludes most clearly and significantly to a not uncommon visionary experience among mystics.[51] He describes this in "The Reflexion":

Once at thy feast, I saw thee pearl-like stand
  'Tween heaven, and earth, where heaven's bright glory all
In streams fell on thee, as a floodgate, and,
    Like sunbeams through thee on the world to fall.
    Oh! sugar sweet then! my dear sweet Lord, I see
    Saints' heavens-lost happiness restor'd by thee.

That this vision, which Taylor treats so matter-of-factly, should have occurred at the sacrament ("thy feast") is highly significant of the intense concentration Taylor brought to the Lord's Supper. But he does not treat the vision as an exceptional experience in its own right; for in the next stanza of "The Reflexion" he drops the floodgate vision and returns to the central image of the poem—Christ as the Rose-of-Sharon. This indicates that his "visions" are less actual than imaginary, and this interpretation seems valid since Loyola and Baxter and other guides to the spiritual life encourage the use of imagination to vivify the matter of their meditation. But visions and preternatural experiences aside, Taylor seeks, both as mystic and communicant, complete loss of his own identity in God, union with his Maker.

IV Union

Taylor's conception of this mystical union with the divine is perhaps the most significant in his thought and his writing. He discusses union in several ways: the "hypostatic" personal union in Christ, the mystical union between Christ and his church, the natural union of Christ with his human kinsmen, and the sacramental union which signifies all three. These are mutually related, but it is useful to consider them separately.

In the theology espoused by Taylor and his contemporaries, man depends utterly upon Christ for his salvation because only Christ—being human and divine at once—can mediate between sinful man and an angry God, plead man's case as advocate before the bar of an infinite and offended Divine Justice, and so redeem man's debt to his Landlord by His own suffering death. But the idea of a "theanthropos" or "God-man" is not an easy one to grasp, and New England ministers devoted a good part of their preaching to trying to make their congregations understand it. Centuries of heresy regarding the precise relationship of the human and divine in Christ also made it necessary to reason most exactly. Taylor writes that "human faculties are as much too low to contain adequate conceptions of the Godhead as the Godhead is too high to be grasped by the little hand of human understanding" (C, 2, p. 4), but he strives with his colleagues to close the gap. Most of the "Christographia" touches on the personal union of Christ's two natures, but the first three sermons speak about it most directly. The first points out that Christ's human nature was really human, although it was especially purified to be joined with the divine; the second demonstrates that Christ was also truly divine; and the third preaches the doctrine "That the divine nature and the human are personally united in Christ. Or, that the union between them is a personal union."

Unions are of different kinds, he reasons: physical or non-physical. Obviously the union of natures in Christ is not physical, but non-physical unions may be either "artificial" or "not artificial." He dismisses artificial unions (C, 3, p. 55), and explains the inartificial as those that bind the things united by some special relationship involving no essential change in the things themselves:

> And this sort of union is either common, as in a civil government and marriage compacts, or supernatural as to the institution of it, which is either visible, as our solemn and visible convenanting with God according to the rules of the covenant of grace . . . or it is invisible . . . an union of our nature special to the head, and this is the personal union, whereby the two natures in our Lord Christ are joined together (C, 3, pp. 55-56).

By virtue of this invisible, special union, "Christ is as truly flesh as spirit; as properly mortal as immortal. No more rightly styled God than man; infinite than finite; almighty than weak; unchangeable than changeable; omniscient than nescient; omnipresent than confined" (C, 3, p. 58). In other words, Christ has in his person all the properties of humanity and divinity together.

There is another kind of invisible union, not special but universal to "all members of the body of Christ mystical," the union between Christ and his church. Christ is to his elect as a head is to a body. The church and Christ make one eternal union: the body and head are mutually dependent; one without the other would be monstrous and unnatural. Taylor calls the elect saints the mystical body of Christ, and from this relationship springs the optimism in Taylor's theology: Christ is perfect only when all the members of his body are maintained together. "If Christ should have but one single child of God taken from him, he could not be complete or full." The fact that "Christ's body cannot lose its least member in its mystical nature" assures the saints that they will persevere in God's saving grace, for Christ hereby needs them as desperately as they need him. As long as any saint remains sinful, as long as any member of the mystical body remains corrupt, Christ must be unhealthy and his union with his body incomplete.

A third kind of union results from the personal one between Christ's human and divine natures, one Taylor calls "natural." In Christ himself, there is a transfer of divine properties to the human nature and of human properties to the divine. Were this not so, divinity could not suffer and die; and humanity could never acquire the spiritual and sanctifying influences necessary to carry on the work of prophet and priest. Christ would then be an inadequate Mediator. But Christ is not inadequate, the properties are transferable; and, furthermore, they may also be passed on to the saints, Christ's mystical body, through the church.

> The Spirit of God tells us, Eph. 5:30, that we are members of his body, of his flesh, and of his bones. His manhood is of our manhood. . . . He is our . . . near kinsman: so that there is a natural relation between his manhood and ours; and hence, so long as his human nature remains in personal union to the divine, there is this natural relation between Christ and his church (*C*, 3, pp. 60-61).

But of course this union is eternal, and so the saints eternally have access through the human nature they share with Christ to the divine properties of light and grace which Christ's human nature possesses through its hypostatic union with the Godhead. In Taylor's view, the purified saint is united with Christ, and with Christ he shares the divine wisdom of the Father.

Through these concepts of union, Taylor sees mankind most highly honored and advanced in glory. This idea seems most unusual in a Puritan, but it is reiterated in Taylor's prose and verse throughout his professional career. In one of the earliest of the *Preparatory Meditations* Taylor exults in the honor given to man over the angels:

> I'll claim my right: Give place ye angels bright.
> Ye further from the Godhead stand than I.
> My nature is your Lord, and doth unite
> Better than yours unto the Deity.
> God's throne is first and mine is next: to you
> Only the place of waiting-men is due.[52]

And the statement, the proud exultation, is even stronger in the prose intended for the public:

> Human nature is advanced as nigh to Deity, in its union unto the Deity in the person of the Son of God, as created nature can be. . . . Oh! admirable. Give place ye holy angels of light, ye sparkling stars of the morning. The brightest glory, the highest seat in the kingdom of glory, the fairest colors in the scutcheon of celestial honor, belong to my nature and not to yours. I cannot, I may not allow it to you, without injury to mine own nature, and indignity and ingratitude to my Lord, that hath assumed it into a personal conjunction with his divine nature and seated it in the trinity (*C, 1,* p. 44).

This statement is not simply a symptom of emotional enthusiasm; it is a reasoned conclusion based upon the soundest theological assumptions. Its orthodoxy may be appreciated when we find the concept in the writings of Increase Mather, who has long stood as the epitome of New England Puritanism. In *The Mystery of Christ,* a book so much like Taylor's "Christographia" that it may have served as a basis for

Taylor's sermons, Mather devotes the fourth sermon to the same doctrine—that Christ's union with God is a personal union—and he actually works with the same text as Taylor does in his third sermon: John 1:14: "The Word was made Flesh." Mather, too, reasons that, because of Christ's humanity, "we may be humbly familiar with the Lord Jesus, and with God through Him. . . . He is become our near Kinsman."[53] He likewise agrees with Taylor that "That which does belong properly to the Person of Christ is ascribed to either nature,"[54] and that, by virtue of the union of human and divine natures in the person of Christ, "Humane Nature is Dignifyed above any Created Nature."[55] But for Mather this conclusion does not yield the same intense joy it brings to Taylor. It is almost as if Mather were oblivious to the exciting implications of the idea; for Taylor the idea is charged with energy.

Indeed, Taylor carries the elevation of humankind so far as to see it "seated . . . in the trinity." This phrasing, which sounds as if Taylor were actually claiming to be deified or transformed into God, is common among the most noted mystics in the history of Christianity. To many it sounds like heresy; it is damnable because it represents the same kind of *hubris* or proud arrogance that led, in the first instance, to the fall of Adam and Eve; and it was described by Milton as the reason for Satan's banishment from heaven.[56] In the meditation accompanying Sermon III of the "Christographia" Taylor seems dangerously close to heresy in his proclamation:

> You holy angels, morning stars, bright sparks,
>   Give place: and lower your top gallants. Shew
> Your top-sail conjues to our slender barks:
>   The highest honor to our nature's due.
>   It's nearer Godhead by the Godhead made
>   Than yours in you that never from God stray'd.
>   (2.44)

But Taylor, neither ignorant of the danger in such statement nor careless in his wording, guards himself from heresy by making a careful distinction in the same poem:

> O! dignified humanity indeed:
>   Divinely person'd: almost deified.

Man is *almost* deified, but not quite; he is above the angels, but not yet God. Being created, he can never achieve Godhood, since God is by nature uncreated. Yet the honor accorded human nature in its union with Christ is greater than that accorded by any other nature: "Oh! then how is man's nature hereby advanced, when a body is prepared of it for the Son of God. Higher it cannot be, unless it could be deified. Created nature cannot be deified: but human nature is advanced as nigh to Deity, in its union unto the Deity in the person of the Son of God, as created nature can be" (*C, 1,* p. 44).

What distinguishes Taylor's expression of this concept from most of his contemporaries is, I think, his strong sense of personal involvement in what is, for others, only an abstract and relatively distant speculation. That is, Taylor conceived of "human nature" not as an abstraction but as the distinguishing quality of himself. He therefore, whether only metaphorically or actually, makes himself representative of the entire human race. This representation is especially clear in Meditation 77, where he traces the full cycle of man from original glory in Paradise to the fall into "this lowest pit more dark than night," to his eventual elevation upon Christ's "golden chain of grace" back into "Glory's happy place." He uses the first person throughout, presenting himself as a bird with "Gold-fincht angel feathers"; but there is no doubt that the bird represents all humanity:

> I once sat singing on the summit high
>   'Mong the celestial choir in music sweet
> On highest bough of Paradisal joy,
>   Glory and innocence did in me meet.
>   I, as a gold-finch nighting gale, tun'd o'er
>   Melodious songs 'fore glory's palace door.
>
> But on this bough I tuning pearcht not long:
>   Th'infernal foe shot out a shaft from hell,
> A fiery dart pil'd with sin's poison strong:
>   That struck my heart, and down I headlong fell.
>
>   (2.77)

Once we recognize this representative quality of Taylor's

first person pronoun, we can more accurately appraise his most significant way of talking about the union between man and God: their marriage.

With deification, the Spiritual Marriage is, in the history of mysticism, perhaps the most frequent mode of describing the consummate union of the soul with God.[57] Especially those mystics who emphasize the personal nature of God are "forced in the end to acknowledge that the perfect union of Lover and Beloved cannot be suggested in the precise and arid terms of religious philosophy."[58] Underhill further explains: "It was natural and inevitable that the imagery of human love and marriage should have seemed to the mystic the best of all images of his own 'fulfillment of life'; his soul's surrender, first to the call, finally to the embrace of Perfect Love. It lay ready to his hand: it was understood of all men: and moreover, it certainly does offer, upon lower levels, a strangely exact parallel to the sequence of states in which man's spiritual consciousness unfolds itself, and which form the consummation of the mystic life."[59] Taylor's choice, therefore, of images of love, courtship, and marriage are quite traditional; these not only offer the strongest support to his place in the literature of mysticism but also provide the strongest defense against the accusation that his sensual and erotic imagery is somehow in opposition to his Puritan faith.

In this heavenly romance the soul of man is feminine; and it is pursued by Christ, who—we must remember—needs as greatly as man to consummate the union. Taylor's description of the game of love begins when he casts a furtive glance at Christ, who is coming to woo him:

> I threw through Zion's lattice then an eye,
>   Which spi'd one like a lump of glory pure
> Nay, cloaths of gold, buttons with pearls do lie
>   Like rags or shooclouts unto his he wore.
>   Heaven's curtains blancht with sun and stars of light
>   Are black as sackcloath to his garments bright.
>   (1.12)

At this coy view of his coming Lover, Taylor bids his soul to "pine in love until this lovely one be thine."

> Pluck back the curtains, back the window shuts:
>> Through Zion's agate window take a view;
> How Christ in pinckted robes from Bozrah puts,
>> Comes glorious in's apparel forth to woo.
>> Oh, if his glory ever kiss thine eye,
>> Thy love will soon enchanted be thereby
>
> (1.12)

But his soul, ashamed of her own unworthiness, not only draws back from the encounter in fear but confesses her inadequacy in what is perhaps Taylor's most ardent passage:

> My lovely one, I fain would love thee much
>> But all my love is none at all, I see,
> Oh! let thy beauty give a glorious touch
>> Upon my heart, and melt to love all me.
>> Lord melt me all up into love for thee
>> Whose loveliness excells what love can be.
>
> (1.12)

At this point his soul, sensing the great distance between her capacity for love and the infinite love offered to it by Christ, is often thrown into dejection. Teased by the view of beauty she cannot possibly possess, she is simultaneously encouraged and denied at this point of her spiritual progress, which is common to many mystics, and plunged into the "dark night of the soul" as St. John of the Cross termed this stage. Taylor's soul cries in disappointment:

> And shall the spiritual eye be wholly dark,
>> In th'heart of love, as not belov'd, condole?
>> In th'midst of love's bright sun, and yet not see
>> A beam of love allow'd to lighten thee?
>
> (2.96)

But Taylor mollifies her anguish, pointing out that

> Christ loves to lay thy love under constraint.
>> He therefore lets not's love her candle light,
> To see her lovely arms that never faint
>> Circle thyself about, with great delight.
>
> (2.96)

The finite soul cannot expect, after all, to contain the infinite this side of heaven. Desiring all—Taylor tells her—

> Maybe thy measures are above thy might.
>   Desires crave more than thou canst hold by far:
> If thou shouldst have but what thou would, if right,
>   Thy pipkin soon would run o'er, break, or jar.
>
>   (2.96)

He assures the soul that the lack of "love's evidence" is no sign that the love is wanting.

For we know that the Divine Lover is relentless, even militant, as we see in *God's Determinations;* and, even if the soul wished to avoid his love, she could not. He turns his eye of love upon her, and she surrenders:

> Lord, let these charming glancing eyes of thine
>   Glance on my soul's bright eye its amorous beams
> To fetch as upon golden ladders fine
>   My heart and love to thee in hottest steams.
>   Which bosom'd in thy brightest beauty dear,
>   Shall tune the glances of thy eyes, Sweet Dear.
>
>   (2.119)

And thus is love exchanged through the eyes. The eyes of the soul follow the beauty of Christ in the scriptures, the "rich love letter" from God to man.

But this visual exchange between the lovers focuses finally in their marriage, a circumstance so astonishing that Taylor never tires of expressing his amazement. The very first of the Meditations introduces this as an image:

> What love is this of thine, that cannot be
>   In thine infinity, O Lord, confin'd,
> Unless it in thy very person see
>   Infinity, and finity conjoyn'd?
>   What! hath thy Godhead, as not satisfied,
>   Marri'd our manhood, making it its bride?

Just as in the union between Christ and God, there is an exchange of properties, and what may be predicated of one may also be claimed for the other; so it is in this marriage between Christ and the Soul:

> What strange appropriations hence arise?
> Thy person mine, mine thine, even weddenwise?
>
> Thine mine, mine thine, a mutual claim is made.
> Mine, thine are predicates unto us both.
>
> (2.79)

But always Taylor marvels at the miracle of his wedding to Christ:

> Oh! matchless love, laid out on such as he!
> Should gold wed dung, should stars woo lobster claws,
> It would no wonder, like this wonder, cause.
>
> (2.33)

As it is cause for wonder, so is it cause for celebration—a wedding feast to acknowledge the espousal of Christ and the soul. Preaching in 1694 on the text from Matthew 22, the parable of the feast, Taylor exhorts his congregation to attend to its message: "It calls you, it exhorts you, it salutes you with a fresh invitation unto the feast, saying unto you 'Come, Come. Come in, thou blessed of the Lord. Wherefore standest thou without it? Come, and welcome. I have prepared room for thee. . . . Oh, then come to the wedden'" (*1694*, p. 153). Over a period of about a year, Taylor preached about the same parable, interpreting the feast itself to be the Lord's Supper; but, from the very beginning of the *Preparatory Meditations* to at least 1720, this parable offered a source of feast and food imagery that Taylor plundered frequently. But in the poetry he never comes to describe the marriage itself. Its consummation, however, is another thing; it offers Taylor an unusual opportunity to describe the ecstasy of love. Fondling, kissing, embracing, Christ ravishes his bride: he is presented "to our love to hug and 'brace" (2.160), and Taylor exclaims:

> Oh! what love like this?
> This comes upon her, hugs her in its arms
> And warms her spirits. Oh! Celestial charms.

Thus is the soul ravished until she flies to Christ "upon the wings of extasies" (2.100), and is impregnated by her Lord. Suggestions of pregnancy range from the most general images —a box or cabinet or tabernacle in which something is placed —to somewhat more suggestive images—as of a bowl or vessel filled with some fluid:

> O let thy lovely streams of love distill
>   Upon myself and spout their spirits pure
> Into my vial, and my vessel fill
>   With liveliness. . . .   (2.32)

Taylor carries the sexual implications of the spiritual marriage considerably further than most writers who use it; and he does so consciously, for he takes full advantage of the conventional Christian ways of talking about the regeneration of the spirit, the birth of the New Man. Writing almost as a physician, Taylor explains:

> The soul's the womb. Christ is the spermadote,
>   And saving grace the seed cast thereinto;
> This life's the principal in grace's coat,
>   Making vitality in all things flow,
>   In heavenly verdure brisking holily
>   With sharp ey'd peartness of vivacity.
>   (2.80)

He concludes: "When of this life my soul with child doth spring, / The babe of life swath'd up in grace shall sing."[60]

Because the Divine Lover, husband to the soul, pledges an eternal marriage, the soul is greatly consoled. In very human terms, Taylor's soul warns off other hussies who seek to steal her bridegroom from her:

> Christ will not play the knave to shab me thus,
>   Though knavishness of such sort youths oft use:
> And youthful damsels to do so don't blush,
>   Yet shameful 't is and grossly to abuse.
>   Your virgin beauty will not taking be
>   Him by his eyes t'inchant his love from me.
>   (2.133)

Almost immediately, however, the image of a somewhat petty, jealous housewife is dropped; and the soul is seen as representative again. The spouse of Christ, about whom Taylor has been writing as if she were his own soul, is now identified for us in another way. Still addressing the "Daughters of Jerusalem," by whom he intends all unregenerate souls, Taylor reveals to them that:

> Whom Christ espouseth is his spouse indeed.
> His spouse or bride no single person, nay,
> She is an aggrigate so doth proceed
> And in it sure and can't be stole away.
> And if you thus be members made of me
> He'll be your bridegroom, you his spouse shall be.
>
> (2.133)

So we see in these last two lines that the soul of Taylor's spiritual marriage with Christ is at once both his own personal soul and the representative of all souls united in the Lord—the elect church.

In Meditation 133 Taylor is midway in a series of thirty-nine consecutive meditations upon his favorite book of the Old Testament—"The Song of Solomon"[61]—which he calls "Canticles." The most popular way to read "Canticles" was as an allegory of love between Christ and his church. Especially for mystical writers has this been a particularly attractive source of imagery; and among them was Saint Bernard, whose sermons on the "Cantica Canticorum" Taylor knew. Underhill suggests that "the mystic loved the Song of Songs because he there saw reflected, as in a mirror, the most secret experience of his soul."[62] We cannot, therefore, rely on Taylor's use of the first person pronoun as reference to himself alone. Even in those meditations where the representative quality is not obvious, we may not suppose that it is absent. What Taylor claims for his own experience is at the same time the collective experience of all the elect through all time.

Taylor becomes increasingly passionate in his poetry as he grows older. From the age of seventy on and when he is concentrating almost exclusively on the Song of Songs, he treats the spiritual marriage more and more amorously. His very last meditation begins, in fact, with the ardent "Heart sick, my Lord, heart sick of love to thee!" And he claims in 1714 to have been brought "up in a trance" by Christ's "amorous chains" (2.120).

The entranced mystic is most familiar to the popular mind through the frequent portrayals of Saint Teresa and Saint Francis frozen in ecstatic agony at the moment of union with Christ. The end of the mystic progress has come to be viewed as the complete loss of the senses—as absolute oblivion to the immediate world. And this view has been abetted by the great debate from the Middle Ages on between the advantages of the life of pure contemplation over that of action. But the most notable mystics were hardly perpetual solitaries: Saint Teresa, Saint Francis of Assisi, Saint Catherine of Siena, Saint Ignatius Loyola, George Fox, Saint Bernard of Clairvaux, Saint Joan of Arc—and for that matter, Saint John the Evangelist and Saint Paul—all were reformers, some on an international scale; founders of hospitals and religious orders; military leaders and teachers. Vigorously engaged in the business of living, they were men and women of superb energy, discipline, and efficiency who were unafraid of this world and who were distinguished by their attempts to grapple with it.[63] Except for some orientals and especially the Buddhist, the highest mystical attainment results in an active, though changed, worldly life.[64]

So with Taylor, building a world at the westernmost limit of the Massachusetts Bay Colony, there was not time, occasion, nor desire to withdraw from carrying out God's will in mundane affairs. Taylor assumed that the spiritual life and the natural life went together, that the transformation brought about by the birth of the New Man is evidenced "in holy conversation" or behavior:

> It doth saints' souls and conversation gild
>   With Godlike glory of a gracious shine:
> Brightens its superstructure where it builds
>   A lofty tower of holy life divine.
>
> (2.89)

Again and again in the "Christographia," Taylor tries to tell his frontier congregation what the unitive life means. He calls it, as Thomas à Kempis does, the Imitation of Christ. Through the mystical union—whether by the immediate elevation of one's own soul through the stages Taylor traces in his own writing, or through the more conventional admission to full membership in Christ's mystical body—one gains access to the properties of the Godhead. These properties—life, grace, truth, and wisdom—are reflected in the Christ-like life of he who attains them. The Godly gifts are not merely for man's appreciation but for his use.

The duty to "improve all the talents thus derived" is, then, the philosophical root of Taylor's entire life; and it was more fully revealed to Taylor's consciousness than the bases of lives usually are even to very alert and self-conscious men. But we have to view Taylor's concept as he understood it before we can judge its fruits, his poetry. It is a mystical root that proceeds through various stages so conventional that histories and descriptions of the mystical process seem to have been written with Taylor in mind. It proceeds from the awakening of the self to a real awareness of God, which is marked both by a conviction of personal sinfulness and by an illumination of his understanding regarding the nature of ultimate reality. Once converted, Taylor moves through almost ascetic self-struggle to reach a state of purification from sin; and he exercises his whole being in the arduous mental discipline of meditation. This exercise occasionally yields visions, or it at least results in the active use of the imagination that finds expression in his poetry. He passes beyond these, finally, to a state of complete mystical union with Christ—he is elevated above all created things, nearly deified. This union he can only describe in terms of holy wedlock; and he reflects this union, or strives to, in the imitation of Christ.

Yet the progress seems rather a confused one. The marriage imagery which opens the first of the *Meditations* supposes that the mystical union has already taken place; but thirty years later Taylor still bewails his "hide-bound heart" for re-sisting the loveliness of Christ and thereby suggests that the union has never been consummated. And in some poems in between, confessions of filthy sinfulness and exultation at his great elevation and near-deification occur side by side. This apparent confusion becomes somewhat clearer when we consider Dean Inge's statement that the mystic "strives to reach its end, but the end being an infinite one, no process can reach it."[65] The mystical process is a *progressus ad infinitum*;[66] and Taylor's expression of the process must, therefore, be repetitious and unending, and all the stages of it must be uttered throughout his entire life.

CHAPTER 3

From Mystic to Poet

BECAUSE the mystical attainment gives a new meaning and value to the active life, Taylor's activities as a pastor in the wilderness take on new significance. Had they been different, his poetry would not be what it is. His mysticism made him publicly a preacher just as it made him privately a poet. Furthermore, his preaching so influenced his poetry that the poems lose their full import if divorced from his sermons. Only twenty-five sermons—one in 1679, eight in 1694, two in 1713, and the fourteen of the "Christographia"— are extant of the nearly three thousand Taylor must have preached; but they give us another striking instance of the union between his teaching and his artistic life. In fact, the sermons stand as an indispensable commentary upon the poems, for they are in some cases like a poet's worksheets.

These sermons are typical of the New England Puritan: Taylor begins by citing a scriptural text, which he briefly explicates or "opens." What the explication reveals is summarized in a pithy proposition called the "Doctrine," which is the main truth inferred from a particular text. The body of the sermon—contrary to the practice of some of his comtemporaries—is an extensive proof of this doctrine, a fact which again underlines the intellectual emphasis of Taylor's faith.[1] He reduces his proofs to Ramist method, for he divides and subdivides and then numbers each head and subhead of his topic but seldom allows more than a page or two to each unit of thought. This method results in clear distinctions and in a fairly clear progress of thought, but it chops the sermon into such small units that graceful writing never extends beyond a page or two at a time.

Taylor spends anywhere from half to two-thirds of his sermon proving the doctrine, and he then applies or "improves" it for the congregation. In this application he observes a conventional division into a series of "Uses" to which the doctrinal truth may be put. These are ordinarily four: the use by way of information or inference, in which Taylor points out the consequences of the truth he has just demonstrated or draws corollary truths; the use by way of reproof, in which those who do not accept the doctrine are shown to jeopardize their salvation; the use by way of consolation, in which Taylor assures those who accept his proof that they have thereby climbed one more rung up the ladder to bliss; and, finally, the use by way of exhortation, where Taylor urges sinners to repent and saints to persevere in the acceptance of this doctrine.

Because these sermons allow us to see Taylor at work as a writer more clearly than does the poetry alone, they, generally, provide interesting insights into Taylor's style and thought; and, more particularly, they develop images and ideas that from time to time appear in the poems. Addressed to a single representative or collective soul (like the "I" of the *Meditations*), the sermons are a kind of extended soliloquies. They reflect Taylor's fondness for *exempla*, allegory, and illustrious providences; and they sometimes explain the symbolism of the poetry. In 1679, for example, his sermon "A Particular Church is God's House" uses the central image of a house in which God will dwell. Christ is the cornerstone; the saints are the stones of which the superstructure is built; and the church covenant cements them together. These are commonplace figures which need no explanation; but early in the sermon he considers the furnishings for this house and the utensils to be placed in it. These include golden candlesticks, altars, incense, and sacrificial fire—strange furniture for a Puritan temple. But Taylor clearly explains that the altar represents the person and merits of Christ; the incense, the prayers of the saints; and the fire, "the holy flame of heavenly affection" (*PC*, pp. 5-6). Taylor's use, then, of the details of the Old Testament ceremony in his poetry is no sign at all that, as some critics and historians have implied, he finds the high Anglican or the Catholic church service more attractive than the Congregational.

But the "Christographia" sermons most fully illustrate how Taylor's prose influenced his poetry. The "Christographia" is Taylor's only collection of sacrament-day sermons, which, besides being the most basic statement of his Christology, are also the most intimately related to his verse. He wrote them at about six-week intervals; and then, after completing each one but before delivering it, he composed the poetic meditation. The sermon is the dry, ratiocinative discourse which analytically demonstrates the great admirableness of Christ; the poem is Taylor's private response to his own exhortation, a statement of raised affections cast in the form of a colloquy with Christ.

The clue both to the order of composition of the sermon and poem and to the relationship of the two lies in the subtitle Taylor penned to the *Preparatory Meditations*. He says the poems are based "chiefly upon the doctrine preached upon the day of administration" and that they were written before his approach to the Lord's Supper. Now, if they were based upon the "doctrine" preached on that day, it must at least have been chosen before the poem was written; and this, by the way, obviates the problem of trying to relate the meditations to their scriptural texts. Many readers are disturbed by the fact that the poems often seem completely unrelated to the scriptural passages that function as epigraphs to the poems. Meditation 6, First Series, for example, begins with the text from Canticles, 2:1: "I am the lily of the valleys." But the central image of the poem concerns the minting of a gold coin, the poet's soul, upon which Taylor petitions the Lord's image to be stamped; and there is no flower imagery at all. The problem of explaining the apparent lack of connection would be solved, of course, if we had the sermon accompanying this poem; for then we should have the doctrine itself—the central proposition which Taylor proves in the sermon—and its relationship to the poem would presumably be quite clear. Usually, because the doctrine and the text of the sermons are so similar, this problem does not arise.

In the "Christographia," where sermons and poems do match, their relationship is inescapable. Not only does the sermon usually call the poem into being (ordinarily in the exhortation) but it also presents the subject, provides both the central and subordinate images, and sometimes even dictates the logical order in which the poem develops. Moreover, the sermon opens avenues of inference that the poem ignores completely; it restates more clearly what the compression of the poetry seems to overlook; and it supplies details necessary to a full, accurate understanding of the poem. And, most significantly, the sermon provides the larger contexts of Taylor's thought in which the poem belongs.[2]

This dependence of the poems upon the sermons probably holds for the majority of Taylor's 217 *Meditations*. Since we do not have most of the sermons for these poems, our understanding of them must remain something less than complete. And, consequently, our appreciation of Taylor's poetic workmanship is limited to the extent that we can apply what we know from the extant sermons to other poems. But because of the underlying unity springing from Taylor's mysticism and because the sermons we have are so crucial to his mystical thought, the extent to which they can be applied is great indeed. However, Taylor's teachings regarding the Lord's Supper and the direct influence of his preaching upon his poems do not indicate alone the influence of his mysticism in his poetic life; for his theory of poetry was derived from his mysticism.

The relationship of poetry—or, for that matter, any of the arts—to mysticism is traditionally close. The mystic, transcending the world of sense to achieve union with God, has had an actual experience for which his vocabulary—even his categories of understanding and discursive reason—are inadequate. The fullness of his experience is not only inexpressible in the propositions of literal language but also logically unthinkable. To reduce the ineffable experience to something tangible enough to be grasped and retained in the understanding, he must find a symbol or set of symbols to stand for that experience—some mechanism by which he can conceive and order his utterly new cognition and with which he can express and so communicate his experience to others.

For this reason, all discussions of mysticism become, at their most profound, symbolic; and always, because the whole human complex is involved in the experience, these symbols serve affectively or emotionally as well as intellectually. In fact, the symbolism is designed not so much to assist communication or discourse as it is to make possible the formulation of new concepts.

This describes exactly the function of symbols in poetry; for the problem facing the articulate mystic and the poet is identical. Poets, painters, musicians, sculptors, architects, and even mathematicians and scientists, when considering the creative act that brings them to new formulations or concepts or works, fall irresistibly into the language of search, vision or insight, and expression. The sociologist—tracing what the modern poet thinks he himself does or actually experiences in the act of creating a poem—also finds a pattern suspiciously parallel to that of the mystical experience. And the philosopher, working in most unmystical terms, comes likewise to the language of vision to explain artistic creativity.[3] Each sees the artist transcending somehow—by effort, by chance, by force—the world of normal sense and thought to a perception of something "beyond." This "beyond" is always expressed differently, but the expression always assumes that truth or reality lies ultimately outside the world of normal sense experience—or at least that area of experience covered by our vocabulary. It further assumes that through discipline the artist actually attains a "sight" or intuition of this ultimate reality and, finally, that the materials of the world of sense may be manipulated, shaped, and formed to express the new insight.

Behind these attempts to analyze creativity lies the faith that art involves a truly creative act; that this act is a way of truth independent of science and its disciplines, independent even of reason (though not inconsistent with reason); and that the act is, therefore, a most important human activity. Largely because of the conception of the artist as creator, recent books about the relationship of theology and literature have without fail devoted a chapter to mysticism, in which the author indicates the inescapableness of the connection.

Two points of connection have received considerable attention: one has been the theory that the artist is divinely inspired; the other, more amenable to modern critics, generally follows Coleridge and finds the creative faculty itself—the imagination—"a repetition in the finite mind of the eternal act of creation in the infinite I AM."[4]

Both notions of divine inspiration and the creative act entered Taylor's thought; but, not primarily interested in the speculative side of this problem and limited by the aesthetic principles of his own time, he never very systematically developed his theories. But throughout his prose and poetry he drops frequent judgments about art and nature; the art of creation; beauty; the function of poetry; the nature of language and metaphor; the limits of the imagination; and his own motives for writing. He even makes some criticism of his own poetic efforts. Assembled, these comments delineate a most useful, if not startlingly original, conception of the art of poetry. Since our present aim is to understand Taylor as a poet, we must examine his notion of what he was about.

In the first place, the writing of poetry was to Taylor a religious act in two ways: the first rather subtle, the second fairly obvious. The first begins with Taylor's understanding of the meaning of "reason," which he defined from the two "principles" inherent in it. The first of these is "internal," according to which reason is simply "the exercise of that faculty or power of the soul, discursively, which inseparably cleaves unto the mind of God: Hence it is in all men. This power doth from its very essence adhere to the mind of the Almighty, and wherein its exercise is not conformable to the mind of God, willingly, conscience accuseth, and wherein it fails thereof thrô ignorance, conscience excuses" (*1694*, p. 47). This congruity of the human with the divine mind is impossible while man is in a state of sin, and so there could be no reason if all depended upon this internal principle. God has therefore provided reason with an external principle, which Taylor explains: "Now the will of God is revealed unto us more obscurely, as in the law of nature and of the creation. For there stands imprinted upon the nature of the creature a declaration of the will of God in suitableness of one part unto another: and of one thing unto another. So also in the disposal and management of the whole, and of each part." Reason in this statement means consistency with natural order; but a second external principle is also presented: God also reveals his will "in the law of grace and Holy Scriptures. This is given out graciously, to regulate the principle internal in its exercise, now being blinded by sin, and that in order to his recovery from sin principally. So that reason is the exercise of that internal principle of adherence unto God's will discursively, according to the external rule revealing the same. Now where the discourse is not conformable to this rule (whether the discourse is mental or vocal), it is not reason, but unreasonableness and sophistry" (ibid.).

In Taylor's terms, one reasons correctly when he first sees things as God actually intended them to be seen and then applies the correct name to them. Correct naming of objects of experience is a sign of wisdom, Taylor argues; for he assumes that in the order of the universe the connection between words and the things they signify is a God-ordained, immutable one. His conception of the absolute nature of this relationship between language and nature is revealed in Taylor's description of Adam's wisdom in paradise.

"O the light with which Adam's soul was filled," exclaims Taylor. "It must needs be great, and the rectitude of his will answerable. Otherwise it could not have been according to the majesty of infinite wisdom to have left with him the giving of names to the creatures that were created by him [Christ]. For had not his light discovered their very natures, and his delight have been to name things according to their natures, he might have called light 'darkness' and darkness 'light'; life 'death,' and death 'life'; heat 'coldness,' and cold 'heat'; a man a 'brute,' and a brute a 'man,' etc." (C, 7, p. 153). He does not spell out what the consequences of this universal misnomer would have been, but he implies it would have been catastrophic.

Language is the symbol of thought to Taylor; and, if language is inaccurate or inadequate or unsuitable, it bespeaks a failure of thought and reason, or, in the last analysis, a want of wisdom. Simply to articulate sounds and put them together with stress and intonation is not, in itself, to speak. There must also be truth in the sounds:

> Words oral but thoughts whiffled in the wind.
> If written only inked paper be.
> Unless truth mantle, they bely the mind.
>
> (2.158)

This idea Taylor repeats several times, always emphasizing the necessary connection between words and thoughts.

> Words mental are syllabicated thoughts;
> Words oral but thoughts wiffled in the wind.
>
> (2.43)

Consequently the *Preparatory Meditations* frequently reiterate the want of words proceeding from a want of reason or wisdom or thought:

> My only dear, dear Lord, I search to find
> My golden ark of thought, thoughts fit and store:
> And search each till and drawer of my mind
> For thoughts full fit to deck thy kindness o'er,
> But find my forehead empty of such thoughts
> And so my words are simply ragged, nought.
>
> (2.141)

There are thus two reasons why Taylor so often laments his own failure of language in the meditations. The first is not because his vocabulary is particularly limited, but because the subject he has chosen to celebrate in language is beyond the ken of human reason. This limitation he makes explicit in both prose and poetry: "Human faculties are as much too low to contain adequate conceptions of the Godhead as the Godhead is too high to be grasped by the little hand of human understanding" (*C*, 2, p. 1). In another instance, writing of the all-fullness of the Godhead as it appears in Christ, he states: "It doth as far exceed understanding to produce any full answer thereto, as the all fullness of Godhead doth exceed the capacity of the created understanding to contain it" (*C*, 5, p. 106). Of the union of Christ's two natures in one person, Taylor preaches, "it is so singular a work, there is not so much as a shadow of it to be found in the creation to enlighten our conception in the same. Reason cannot portray out the same. All the light in the eye of reason is not so much as can make out a little glimmering thereof in the soul" (*C*, *1*, p. 43). It is, he concludes, a matter of faith, not of definition.

In poetry, the same attitude finds expression even more clearly:

> Things styled transcendent do transcend the style
>   Of reason. Reason's stairs ne'er reach so high.
> But Jacob's golden ladder rungs do foil
>   All reason's strides, wrought of THEANTHROPIE.
>
>   (2.44)

Even more explicitly in the poem just preceding this, he defines this difficulty:

> Nay, speech's bloomery can't from the ore
>   Of reason's mine, melt words for to define
> Thy deity, nor t'deck the reeks that soar
>   From love's rich vales, sweeter than honey rhymes.
> Words, though the finest twine of reason, are
>   Too coarse a web for deity to wear.
>
>   (2.43)

And the reason is pretty clear. Human reason, unaided by saving grace, is thoroughly confused and unreliable regarding things of this world, to say nothing of the transcendent truths of religion. Because human thoughts are "filthy fumes that smoke / From smutty huts," the hut itself must be purified before the poet can speak truth. And what makes the hut smutty in the first place we can easily imagine—sin: "Thou art a golden theme," Taylor says to his Lord,

>   but I am lean,
> A leaden orator upon the same.
> Thy golden web excells my dozy beam:
>   Whose linsey-woolsey loom deserves thy blame.
> It's all defiled, unbiassed too by sin.
>
>   (1.26)

The true poet, then, must be inspired in a sense—filled with
the spirit of the Lord—actually filled with saving grace. Without such gracious illumination of his intellectual faculty, his
judgment, his understanding, and his will, the poet can do no
more than darken the glory of his theme.

> What shall I say, my dear, dear Lord, most dear
>   Of thee? My choicest words, when spoke, are then
> Articulated breath, soon disappear.
>   If wrote, are but the drivel of my pen,
>   Beblacked with my ink, soon worn out unless
>   The Holy Spirit be their inward dress.
>
> (2.142)

As one might readily suspect, the poet only wastes his time
invoking the classical Muses. In one of his earliest poems—
written before he came to New England and when, as a
student of languages, he was deeply involved in classical literature—Taylor begins with an invocation to all nine Muses.
But when he observes the convention later, it is always to
contrast his Muse with the true source of inspiration, Christ.
"Fain would I brighten bright thy glory," he says to Christ,
"but / Do fear my Muse will thy bright glory smoot" (2.123B).
He naturally turns to Christ to correct his want of reason and
want of words:

> Lord, dub my tongue with a new tier of words
>   More comprehensive far than my dull speech,
> That I may dress thy excellency, Lord,
>   In language welted with emphatic reach.
>
> (2.19)

He petitions the Lord to inspire him most directly:

> Be thou my head, and act my tongue, whereby
> Its tittle-tattle may thee glorify.
>
> (2.37)

Sometimes he invokes inspiration by wishing that he had
for a pen a quill plucked from the wings of an angel (2.60B);
that he were enriched with "seraphic life" (2.72); or that

Christ would implant in his heart "Each sanctifying garden grace" (2.145). While he never banishes the Muses—nor supplants them with the heavenly Muse Urania, as Milton and many English writers did—Taylor seems to have felt them unnecessary, inappropriate, or perhaps only inefficacious.

Of course, what Taylor speculates to be the right relationship of words, reason, wisdom, and grace to the poet's divine subject is equally applicable to anyone—poet or not—who seeks to praise God. In one meditation, for example, Taylor joins the minister or divinity scholar and the poet together in the same task of celebrating the Lord's mysterious ways. This does not indicate that in Taylor's mind the poet and divine are confused, or that he thinks that one must be a divine in order to be a poet. But it does emphasize the similarity of their problems and their limitations, and it indicates his own full awareness of the fact that as a poet he writes largely to define and explain, as a minister would do.

This similarity of function is further affirmed in Taylor's frequent descriptions of himself in his poetry as an orator; and, in fact, most of his statements regarding reason and words and thoughts grow from this image. Taylor seems in this attitude to be in agreement with most of his contemporaries; for they, as Professor Miller says, were trained in the Ramist principles of rhetoric as well as logic, and they believed that "verse was simply a heightened form of eloquence, it was speech more plenteously ornamented with tropes and figures than prose, but still speech; like the oration, its function was to carry . . . arguments from man to man."[5] We have already seen Taylor call himself a lean and leaden orator upon a golden and transcendent theme. Elsewhere he describes his poetic function in much the same way:

> The orator from rhetoric gardens picks
>   His spangled flowers of sweet-breathed eloquence
> Wherewith his oratory brisk he tricks,
>   Whose spicy charms ear jewels do commence.
>   Shall bits of brains be candied thus for ears?
>   My theme claims sugar candied far more clear.
>   (2.44)

According to the theory of the times, the main body of oratory was "dialectic," including the acts of invention, of memory, and of disposition of matter. Rhetoric tended to include ornamentation and exornation, elocution, and delivery; its specific purpose was to ornament the oration, and this seems to agree with Taylor's conception, where, as in the poem quoted above, he seeks in poetry to decorate or ornament, tricking out the sense of his speech with jeweled earrings.

Ornamentation is largely the basis of Taylor's poetry, and Taylor frankly views it as a mode of decorating the transcendent truths of his faith.

> Thoughts, though the fairest blossoms of my mind,
>   Are things too loose and light t'strew at the gate
> Of thy bright palace. My words hence are wind
>   Moulded in print up thee to decorate.
>
>   (2.141)

And a few lines later he confesses that Christ's love for his spouse is beyond even the rhetorical power of angels to dress it out (11.21-22). Favorite among images of decoration or ornament for Taylor is that of a beautiful robe or gown with which Christ's truth is dressed or made more attractive. The notion of a poet as a weaver of a lovely cloth appears most early in Taylor; for sometime before 1668 probably, when Taylor was still living in England, he sent an affectionate letter in verse to one whom he identifies only as "my school-fellow, W. M." (no one with these initials was at Harvard between 1668 and 1671 while Taylor was there); and he concluded it with these lines:

> What though my Muse be not adorned so rare
> As Ovid's golden verses do declare
> My love: yet it is in the loom tied
> Where golden quills of love weave on the web.
> Which web I take out of my loom and send
> It, as a present unto you, my friend,
> But though I send the web, I keep the thrum
> To draw another web up in my loom.[6]

With somewhat different implications, the weaving image culminates finally in Taylor's best known poem "Huswifery," but it is a common figure of his thought. Nearing graduation from Harvard in 1671, the members of the senior class met in the College Hall on May 5 to present their final declamations. Taylor explains the proceedings: "Four declaimed in the praise of four languages, and five upon the five senses. Those upon the languages declaimed in the language they treated of, and hence mine ran in English." But it seems not to have been an unwelcome division of topics to Taylor, for he wrote 212 lines of heroic couplets with considerable gusto and with some of the heavy humor that marks Milton's "Prolusions." He begins with the hope that his auditors will not expect the sweetness of a heated fancy in his discourse; for, as he apologizes, "no such flowers grow / Within my garden; no such spirits flow / From mine alembick, neither have I skill / To rain such honey falls out of my still" (11.15-22). Then, as if concluding a dramatic scene, he recalls his main purpose:

> But why stand I thus rapping at the door?
> I'll draw the latch, and in, and rap no more.
> (11.33-34)

Once "in," he introduces the robe image almost immediately. Speech, "the crystal chariot where the mind in progress rides," is the holiday attire of human thought.

> Now that speech wealthiest is, whose curious web
> Of finest twine is wrought, not cumbered
> With knots, galls, ends, or thumbs, but doth obtain
> All golden rhetoric to trim the same.
> (11.49-52)

The yarn with which English is woven is distinguished for its grammatical simplicity—its lack of the encumbrances of a multiplicity of cases and declensions. Moreover, compounded of the most useful words and sounds of Hebrew, Latin, and Greek, woven together with the proverbs of all tongues to make a cloth of gold (11.55-140), it combines richly with other yarns. Rhetoric then appears to enhance the language:

> Our web thus wrought, rich rhetoric steps in
> As golden lace a silver web to trim.
> There's scarce a single thrid but doth entwine
> A trope or figure in't to make it fine.
> Here lies a metonymy; there doth skulk
> An irony; here underneath this bulk
> A metaphor; synecdoche doth rear
> And open publicly shop windows here.
> These and their offspring their affections spend
> Our Lady English to court and tend.
> Of swashy figures, too, there throngs in store
> Her dressing to emblanch and broider o'er,
> And first decks words and sounds where jiming feet
> Of measured steps with symphony run sweet,
> Clothing our English Muse in poetry
> Whose warbling melody let them descry,
> Whose light souls in their fingers' ends to caper
> And dance on ropes with curtsies to the quaver.
> (11.141-58)

Poetry as speech fancified seems to be Taylor's sole view. The next few lines enumerate particular decorations—the figures of sound and sense that poetry makes use of, all "set and spread / Like to mosaic work all o'er our web."

The web, woven of English yarn, intertwined with the borrowings from other languages, and decorated with poetry is a kind of "English huswifery," says Taylor, a satin cloth fit "to set / Forth majesty in ev'ry single jet." This last refers directly not to setting out the majesty of Christ but that of human thought. Since, however, the highest of human thoughts concern the mysteries of Christ, the union of natures, and the redemption, the robe of English seems to fit these as appropriately as it does thought in general. On the whole, though Taylor's may be a noble view of speech, it is rather a low view of poetry.

But Taylor's declamation is, after all, a college exercise; and it should not be surprising that it offers only a superficial view. In one way it has implications of significant scope; that is, the sartorial notion of speech as a cloth for thought necessarily in time brings Taylor to a sense of symbolism that enriches his poetic theory, though he never articulates that theory. And more directly, it offers him a ready metaphor to put to work in his own poetry.

> Had I angelic skill and on their wheel
>   Could spin the purest white silk into
> The finest twine and then the same should reel
>   And weave't a satin web therein also
>   Or finest taffity with shines like gold
>   And decked with precious stones, brightest to behold,
> And all inwrought with needle work most rich
>   Even of the Holy Ghost to lap up in,
> My heart full freight with love refined, the which
>   Up on thy glorious self I ever bring
>   And for thy sake thy all fair spouse should wear't.
> (2.147)

By 1718, when he wrote this poem, the web of speech functioned in a much more complex manner than it did at first: it covers Christ and then, because Christ and his spouse are one, it is made to drape the spouse—probably the church—but, because of the ambivalent meaning of the spouse as either the church or Taylor himself, it may also be a glorious robe for himself.

Had Taylor ever undertaken to compose an extended poetics, I think it doubtful that he would have produced a significant treatise. Certainly his intellectual capability would not have disqualified him, nor would his quickness of wit and obvious sensitivity to beauty have done so. But, accepting the basic Ramist view that rhetoric itself is the dressing of oratory and that poetry is the "tricking out" of that dressing, he could not, I think, have progressed from that position to the profound understanding of poetic symbolism that stretches from Plato through Coleridge and Emerson to modern theorists. In this sense, it is true that Puritanism impeded the development of a serious art and philosophy of poetry—not simply because religious sternness forbade exciting the affections, as many critics and historians have too easily said, but because the Puritans turned to an educator whose system removed poetry from a serious position to an adventitious one. Certainly the Puritans in their faith generally, and in their theology specifically, were not unsophisticated in their symbolic theory.

Basically, Taylor's view of symbols is twofold, as may be seen in his comments about metaphor. When his intention is humbly to compare the best he can do with the glory of his Lord, he minimizes the nature and function of metaphor; he makes it a tassel on the robe of speech:

> Thou glory darkning glory, with thy flame,
>   Should all quaint metaphors teem ev'ry bud
> Of sparkling eloquence upon the same,
>   It would appear as dawbing pearls with mud.
>   (1.13)

Even if he works as purely as it is possible for a human being to work, the gift of poetry he can present must be a poor one: a "pack of gilded nonsense," "dull tacklings tag'd / With ragged nonsense" (2.35, 36). This represents, however, only one view of metaphor; the other is more dignified.

The dignity arises, appropriately, from his consideration of the personal union of the divine and human natures in Christ. Contending that both natures are united in one person, he offers several arguments to the effect that anything one can say about one nature is equally applicable to the other (*C*, *4*, p. 93). In this fashion Taylor justifies a kind of anthropomorphizing of God and transcendent reality, which accounts in large part for his domesticating divine actions, for his reducing the most noble and magnificent metaphysical facts to kitchen images—the source of both surprise and delight in Taylor's poetry. Because the union is real and eternal, the individual soul—or the representative elected soul—which is Christ's spouse may be described most legitimately as carrying on the tasks of an ordinary human housewife; and the cleaning, spinning and weaving, and preparing meals are all metaphorically applicable to the relationship of Christ and the soul.

To conceive thus of the hypostatical union is not adequate to the fact of that union itself, he admits. But, he adds: "It is above the contemplation and reach of men or angels to describe this union as it is. That small account given of it is like unto our shallow and dark understandings, and though we conceive of it in some respect thus, yet we cannot come to it thereby" (*C, 3*, p. 75). To admit that metaphorical speech is not suitable to transcendent reality itself is not, however, to admit that it is a lie and should not be used. Some means must be found for grasping transcendent reality, and for this metaphor works. In the first place, "Words are used only to import the intent in the mind of the speaker. And all languages admit of metaphorical forms of speech. . . . And this sort of speech never was expected to be literally true, nor charged to be a lying form of speech, but a neat, rhetorical, and wise manner of speaking. Hence saith God's Spirit in the Psalmist, Ps. 49:3-4, 'I will open my mouth in wisdom: the meditation of my heart shall be of understanding. I will encline mine ear to a parable and open my dark saying upon my harp.' Hence then this form of speech is a truth-speaking form, conveying the thoughts of the heart of the speaker unto the hearers in such words as are apt to do it metaphorically and wisely" (*C, 9*, p. 201). This is certainly to give symbolic import to metaphors, which, as Yeats suggests, "are not profound enough to be moving, when they are not symbols, and when they are symbols, they are the most perfect of all. . . ."[7]

Taylor continues to defend this view elsewhere. He maintains that there is between worldly and spiritual things a correspondence that not only permits one to talk of spiritual matters in natural terms but is the only way some spiritual matters can be discussed. "Natural things are not unsuitable to illustrate supernatural things by. For Christ in his parables, doth illustrate supernatural things by natural, and if it were not thus, we could arrive at no knowledge of supernatural things. For we are not able to see above naturals. As God hath a sweet harmony of reason running the same throughout the whole creation, even through every distinct sort of creatures, hence Christ on this very account makes use of natural things to illustrate supernaturals by . . . and the Apostle argues invisible things from the visible . . ." (*1694*, p. 33). Thus Christ becomes a poet by reducing supernatural matters through metaphor to bring them within the scope of human understanding, thereby sanctioning Taylor's doing the same.

Christ as an artist appears with reasonable frequency in Taylor's poetry, but it is usually in His creative capacity. In Meditation 50 He carves a box out of pure pearl, so creating the first man; and, when the beautiful box falls and breaks, "The artist puts his glorious hand again / Out to the work." In Meditation 78, Christ, working out the plan of man's redemption, is described thus: "Yet in the upper room of paradise / An artist anvill'd out relief, sure good." But most significantly for Taylor's theory of poetry is Christ as the poet, who appears in two meditations. Both of these are among the last ones of Taylor's career, and both are about Taylor's favorite "Canticles." Meditation 151 comments on the allegory of Canticles 7:4, in which, as Taylor reads it, Christ is singing the praises of his spouse, comparing her neck to an ivory tower, her eyes to beautiful fish pools, and her nose to the alert tower of Lebanon as it "smells the actions of Christ's enemy." Each of these comparisons is a metaphor, says Taylor, after elaborately rehearsing them. What the reader must do is "spiritualize" and moralize the metaphors—see them symbolically, in other words, until the intent of the speaker, Christ the poet, is made clear. In this case, the metaphors designate that Christ's spouse is most dear but has enemies from whom she must be protected.

Taylor continues his view of Christ as distilling silver metaphors and tropes, divine rhetoric upon his spouse in Meditation 152:

> Thou gildest o'er with sparkling metaphors
> The object thy eternal love fell on,
> Which makes her glory shine 'bove brightest stars,
> Carbuncling of the sky's pavilion,
> That pave that crystal roof, the earth's canopy,
> With golden streaks, bordered with pomel high.
>
> The inward tackles and the outward traces
> Shine with the varnish of the Holy Ghost,
> Are th'habit and the exercise of graces,
> Sent out with glorifying a part an host.
> Yea, every part from leg to toe do shine,
> Or rather from the toe to th'top divine.
>
> (2.152)

In this poem the two views of metaphor seem to coalesce. That is, metaphor is treated as Taylor treats it rhetorically— a decoration, a shiny varnish used to beautify its object. But at the same time we know that the varnish has to be spiritualized and moralized, that it is a symbolic varnish used by the most glorious of poets to express what otherwise could not be accommodated to human understanding. Thus "Canticles" sanctions the writing of poetry. Moreover, since Taylor always preaches that the holy life is imitative of the life of Christ, here he has Christ the glorious orator to emulate in his poetry. In so emulating Christ, Taylor is, in a way, making the writing of poetry a religious act; he is repeating finitely "the eternal act of creation in the infinite I AM." This—plus the necessity of saving grace to the poet's intellectual faculty and of inspiration from Christ—constitutes, I think, the rather more subtle way in which poetry is a religious act to Taylor.

But on a far more obvious level, Taylor thought of his poetry as a religious duty, especially in his *Preparatory Meditations* in which he reasons that men owe honor to those who honor them most. No one has honored man more than Christ did in assuming a human nature and in elevating man above the angels. For this reason, man has the constant obligation literally to sing God's glory as the rest of nature does. In this sense, Taylor's motive was the same as Anne Bradstreet's in "Contemplations."[8] In a world where natural objects sing God's praises simply by being what they are, converted men and angels are obliged "to give the revenue of praise to God on the account of the works of creation. The whole creation doth bring all its shining glory as a sacrifice to be offered up to God from and upon the altar of the rational creature in sparkling songs of praise to God" (*C, 10*, pp. 230-31).

This conception of man as the singer of the creation was not only fairly popular but practiced a good deal. Jonathan Edwards makes bursting into song characteristic of a true Christian, and we know that he frequently roamed the fields and woods singing God's praises aloud. And Richard Baxter, who thought, "Sure there is somewhat of Heaven in Holy Poetry," remembered late in life that "It was not the least comfort that I had in the converse of my late dear Wife, that our first in the Morning, and last in Bed at Night, was a

Psalm of Praise (till the hearing of others interrupted it.)"⁹
When Taylor says of his poetry, "I'll bring unto thine altar
th'best of all / My flock affords" (1.21), he too indicates
clearly that his meditations are part of his religious duty and
a sacrificial offering to Christ.

This sacrifice to Christ is not always made easily; for devotional writers constantly called for devotees to shoot sighs,
groans, and tears to God—ejaculatory prayers expressing love,
sorrow, gratitude, or praise. These brief prayers were not performed at set times but whenever the soul was moved to such
expression. While such praises might flow abundantly at
times, too often the soul underwent periods of dryness, when,
if left to its own, it would give over its religious duty. To
compensate for these periods, Taylor set himself the task
of regular meditation; he forced himself to sing the Lord's
praises even when he would have preferred not to.

These were the periods when Christ's praises were wrung
from his Muse with great effort—when he could only sing
lamentations and not anthems.

> But duty raps upon her door for verse.
> That makes her bleed a poem through her searce.
>   (2.30)

Even when it would be preferable to be still, Taylor wrote
"But thus I force myself to speak of thee" (2.132); and it
seems clear that many of his meditations were the forced
product of this sense of duty.

Throughout forty-four years he complains over and over
again that his imagination is at fault, that he cannot invent
new ways of giving the subject of his meditations poetic body.
He would have agreed with Thomas H. Johnson's criticism
that the meditations are repetitious both in their ideas and
their images and that they are not, as a whole, impressively
inventive.¹⁰ Taylor actually made the same criticism of them—
and did it as he wrote—for he knew that these acts of devotion had to be written even when his imagination or
"phansy," as he usually refers to it, refused to work:

> My phansy's in a maze, my thoughts aghast,
>   Words in an ecstasy; my tell-tale tongue

> Is tongue-tied, and my lips are padlocked fast
> To see thy kingly glory in to throng.
> I can, yet cannot tell this glory just,
> In silence bury't must not, yet I must.
> (1.17)

His phansy was too often befogged and dark, coarse, shattered, puzzled, unspun, chilly, benumbed, tattered, rusty; and in his seventies he confessed:

> My muse's hermitage is grown so old
> Her spirits shiver do, her phansy's laws
> Are much transgressed. She sits so crampt with cold.
> Old age indeed hath find her, that she's grown
> Num'd. (2.122)

Partly by virtue of a darkened reason incapable of conceiving Christ's transcendent glories and partly because he composed poetry when his phansy was not up to the task, he wrote poorly, but he knew it.

For this reason, the apologetic openings of a sixth of his meditations are really more than a polite convention or a guise of humility. They are also often a critical reaction to his own limitations as a poet. The one characteristic about his own work that seems to have bothered him most frequently was—is—its roughness or harshness. At one level this concern is merely a sense of inelegance in comparison to the beauty he desired to express. That is, Taylor sees Christ as the great hero of his poems, and so describes his poetry as attempting "t'run on heroic golden feet" (1.21). He promises Christ, "I'll sing / And make thy praise on my heroics run"; but, too often all he could wring from his intentions was sorry verse. Occasionally his poetry excited him, but at other times the impossibility of the task and his own spiritual coldness prevented his writing well:

> Sometimes, my Lord, while that my soul enwarms
> Heroics to thy viol, I did find
> My heart enchanted with thy ambient charms,
> That like an angel agitate my mind,
> Soaring't as on seraphic wings on high.
> But now, like lead, I cold and heavy lie.
> (2.86)

Forcing his poetry in such a state of dullness, he says, "wrack my rhymes to pieces in thy praise" (1.10). He calls his rhymes ragged, and says his voice is rough, his tongue blunt (1.23). Everything he writes, it seems to him at times, he fouls with his pen's "harsh jar" (2.138).

The roughness or harshness, then, in Taylor is not, like Donne's, an intentional departure from the fluidity of Spenser's lines for the sake of dramatic, or at least conversational, reality. Taylor's roughness—part of what modern readers call his metaphysical quality—is, in his own eyes, a fault, which he attributes modestly to lack of ability. "I would do well, but have too little skill," he says, and he frequently offers his poetic devotions as poor and unworthy products, but as the best he has to offer:

> Hence I do humbly stand, and humbly pray,
>   Thee to accept my homely style, although
> It's too too hurden a bearing blanket, nay
>   For to lap up thy love in, it to show.
>
> (2.141)

"Homely" is the word modern critics, too, use to describe his style, and insofar as moderns see Taylor as a perfunctory rhymer, as a writer of harsh lines, as difficult of pronunciation, and as occasionally failing through weakness of diction or the dull repetition of almost stock metaphors, they really do no more than echo his own self-criticism. In fact, Taylor goes further than most critics in rejecting some of his rhymes, which he thinks "would choke the air with stinks" (2.67B).

But his shame with his poor, dull notes—as he calls them—and with his leaden metaphors of ragged nonsense, clumsy lines, feeble words, and awkward rhymes really springs from comparison of his own work with the most beautiful of all pictures of Christ's glory—the Gospel. He seems to see his own poems as a gloss upon the poetry of the Lord himself:

> Thy Spirit's pencil hath thy glory told,
>   And I do stut, commenting on the same.
>
> (2.123B)

By comparison with the inspired writing of the Bible Taylor sees, therefore, his own work as poor. For this reason he turns to the scriptures for texts and doctrines, hoping thereby to warm his benumbed "phansy," and to free his stubborn pen:

> Steep my stubborn quill
> In Zion's wine fat, mend my pen, and raise
> Thy right arm's vein, a drop of 't's blood distill
> Into mine inkhorn, make my paper tight
> That it mayn't blot. In Sacred Text I write.
>
> (2.58)

The one thing that Gospel language has for Taylor is power—the power to move admiration, love, gratitude, all the affections; and the force to re-frame the human heart, to make it congruent with God's will. Taylor also associates total power with beauty, for he reasons that a thing which is all-powerful can admit no defect or want and, therefore, must have a mighty and transcendent beauty (C, 7, p. 156). Taylor does not develop this notion of beauty himself, but it seems to lie behind much of his self-criticism and to add an aesthetic dimension to judgments which seem not to be concerned directly with the idea of beauty. The one word that he attaches most frequently to both his diction and his inventive ability is "feeble," which carries for him not only the meaning of weakness and powerlessness but, for that very reason, lack of beauty.

Thus through weakness of imagination and reason he finds himself capable of doing no more in his attempt to beautify Christ than to dirty, smut, and darken that most powerful of all beauties. Only through true and saving faith can the poet hope to write truly beautiful poetry. Saving faith is basic to all activity—physical, mental, even spiritual. It is the oil that permits the workings of grace to move smoothly; and, without it, all speech, even preaching, is like the chattering of magpies.

> It makes th'tongue tipt with it silver, the couch overspreads
> With Gospel pillows, sheets, and sweet perfumes,
> And sweetest tunes sings in the spirit halls,
> Sweet music on the spirit's virginals.

So Taylor's constant petition to be graced with saving grace; to have his candle lighted with Christ's illuminating grace; his mirror shined; his mental eye annointed with saving salve; his seed impregnated; and his reason, will, and understanding rectified—all this is a plea to be made a poet fit to sing heroics in praise of the Lord.

CHAPTER 4

Apprenticeship–the Early Poems

TAYLOR'S poetic theory yielded results only very slowly. His beginnings as a poet are both obscure and unflattering, for none of the early poems came to public attention until 1960. They reveal none of the exalted poetic purpose that we have just considered; for, as Donald Stanford, the editor of this juvenalia says, "The youthful Taylor does not show discriminating literary taste. His chief preoccupations were theological and political. He liked Robert Wild and George Wither and other second- or third-rate poets now forgotten; he liked them, apparently, for their subject matter and was probably not alive to their deficiencies of style."¹ This is a fair judgment, for what little light appears in these poems is generated less by saving grace than by political friction. Nonetheless, these early and occasional poems are significant to a study of Taylor's poetry: as apprentice work, they often anticipate his later and better efforts, and they always illuminate the process by which the poet comes into being.

Six poems, attributed to Taylor with fair certainty, probably date from before his arrival in New England. Two—a verse acrostic sent to his brother Joseph and his wife Alice and the verse compliment sent in a letter to his "schoolfellow, W. M."—are personal; the other four are attempts at controversy. Political and ecclesiastical warfare in the seventeenth century was as vicious when conducted on paper as on the battlefield. Scurrility, personal vilification, and gross raillery poured from the pens of some of England's most distinguished writers. Taylor, who was born at the very beginning of the

Puritan domination and who grew up during the Commonwealth and the Protectorate of Oliver Cromwell, was approaching maturity when King Charles II was recalled to the throne. Taylor's parents and their friends had undoubtedly known at first hand what Archbishop William Laud's persecution meant. Dissenting and non-conforming preachers who managed to elude Laud and make their way to New England were still, to certain elements in England, heroes of a sort. And so Taylor, in sympathy with the heroic exodus to America, tried several times to write a "Nipping epigram" that he remembered having seen by "some poetaster" who could not abide Laud, though Taylor could not have been older than three when Laud died.

Taylor's relishing this particular piece of doggerel is symbolic not only of the tenacity with which he held to the Independent position in England but of the hopelessness he must have felt when Charles returned there. By 1661 a largely pro-royalist Parliament was seated, and it succeeded within four or five years in completely reversing the political and ecclesiastical fortunes of the Puritans. Taylor saw a series of acts come into effect that strikingly altered the political face of the land and that put his ecclesiastical and theological polity to the test. The Municipal Corporations Act effectively eliminated conscientious Puritans from many public offices by requiring officeholders to take communion in the Anglican church. In 1662 the Act of Uniformity required subscribing to the prayer book, which, since Taylor could not bring himself to it, cost him, along with nearly two thousand others, positions in churches, universities, and schools. The Conventicle Act (1663) prohibited religious worship outside of an Anglican church; and the Five Mile Act (1665) ejected ministers from their congregations if they would not accept the Act of Uniformity, and it prohibited them from coming closer than five miles to their former congregations.[2]

The shoe of intolerance was back on the Puritan political foot now, and the Anglicans were determined to make it pinch. Taylor's reaction to the Act of Uniformity is a 208-line satire titled "The Layman's Lamentation upon the Civil Death of the Late Laborers in the Lord's Vineyard, by way of Dialogue between a Proud PRELATE and a Poor PROFESSOUR

Silenced on Bartholomew Day, 1662."[3] The decasyllabic couplets begin with the poet-layman, who is no doubt Taylor,
undertaking a mock elegy for the "civil death" of the silenced
ministers. Since they are as good as dead, the poor professor
of the true faith writes their final epitaph for the lawyers,
physicians, divines, soldiers, and builders of the true faith.
Echoing John Cotton, he laments, "There's not a sup / Of
milk for babes: our spiritual fathers thrust / Quite out of
doors; poor children, starve we must" (11.20-22). But the
proud prelate—who interrupts him with 'Leave these com-
plaints, you whining sectary!"—then explains that the change
brought about by the Act of Uniformity is certainly no dis-
aster; it will prove a blessed change even for the layman,
whom he describes as a "Foolish, fanatic, silly schismatic, /
Round-headed fury, crack-brained lunatic" (11.39-40).

The layman answers that the change will be desperate indeed, that in place of dignified and worthy ministers of the
gospel—"We'll not hyperbolize, and yet we'll call / Them
next to Christ, our very all in all"—simple scholars of religion
will have priests whose character he proceeds to draw, as he
calls heaven his witness that he speaks neither in passion
nor prejudice, but calmly:

> Some few amongst them (hardly one in seven)
> May possibly be found without the leaven
> Of ignorance or scandal; led awry;
> And did conform in heart's simplicity.
> Some (I conjecture) ventur'd to conform,
> Not being furnished to endure a storm.
> Some wanted courage, and some wanted coin,
> Which made them daub and dodge, and so purloin.
> Take out these few, and every one o' th' rest
> Call you not parish priest, but parish pest,
> Locust from hell, fit journey-men for Rome,
> The very nation's plague, and church's doom,
> Wells without water, clouds that have no rain,
> Merely self-seekers, gapers after gain,
> Ill beasts, dumb dogs, blind leaders of the blind,
> Foes to the church of Christ, and to mankind:

> (I know not what to say) They are a tribe
> My ink's not black enough for to describe.
>
> (11.119-36)

Nonetheless, he continues to blacken his character of a priest under the new law; eventually he declares that the loss of good ministers will only be fully measured in time and tears.

Politically, the new law was adroit and effective but hardly subtle; and Taylor's layman describes the critical issue pointedly:

> This sad dilemma that new law did bring—
> Displease your God or else displease your King,
> And men of conscience need not long to muse,
> What in this case to leave, and what to choose.
>
> (11.171-74)

With mock politeness he requests that another law be enacted to prohibit priests from their cups, carousings, and rantings, at which point the exasperated prelate exclaims:

> We have got power now. How dare you prate.
> We'll gag you if you prattle at this rate.
>
> (11.189-90)

So the poor professor, tongue-tied, resolves to weep secretly for the pride of the new ecclesiastical order, the confusion of which he ardently expects from the Lord's hand by the end of the poem.

Another dialogue—this time between a writer and a Maypole dresser—occupies Taylor's attention for some ninety-four lines of undistinguished decasyllabic couplets. He makes no attempt to capture, either by vigorous dialogue or by narrative, a dramatic situation for the poem, though the writer has presumably arrested a gamester in the act of decorating a Maypole. He accuses the gamester of setting up Dagon in God's place by dressing the Maypole, but the gamester can not see how this is so: "What though we do make fine the fine Maypole?" he argues, "We love God's Ark and Dagon we control." But the writer answers that one can not have it

both ways; for Maypoles are a pagan celebration of the
Goddess Flora. Jeremiah has warned men not to follow the
ways of the heathen, and so the writer reminds the gamester.
But the gamester refuses to forego his recreations, taking license in the writer's explanation that

> he that doth Flora hate, each one
> Allows a lawfull recreation.
> Yet doth he not of any sin permit,
> But will severely jerk men home for it.
> (11.61-64)

Jolly blades may make this their excuse for calling their sinful
defections from godliness lawful recreations, but Taylor
makes it clear that

> There is no man that sets his heart upon
> These wicked May-games, that loves God alone.
> (11.75-76)

The poem is interesting because it indicates that sterner
side of Taylor—his steady view because he is so stiff-necked.
He is in it not only Puritan, but puritanical; and he is quite
different from the poet of mysticism which he becomes in the
New World. The two facets of his personality are not, however, completely separate; for in many of the later meditations
the image of sinfulness as a playground of the devil dominates.
The "Dialogue between the Writer and a Maypole Dresser"
anticipates, therefore, one of his favorite later devices.

Similarly in his last poem of controversy, an answer to a
"Popish Pamphlet cast in London streets not long after the
city was burned," Taylor anticipates another less wholesome
aspect. The pamphlet interprets the London fire as a sign
of God's anger with Protestantism and as a kind of pre-
figuration of the day of doom. London is equated with
Babylon, and its destruction is God's warning to Protestants
to return to the Church of Rome to avoid eternal fires:

> But if you would avoid the hap,
> Return into your mother's lap,

Taylor answers the pamphlet's couplets with his own octo-syllabics and with a brand of vulgar sexuality that the Popish publication hardly warrants:

> The devil rode (as it appears)
> Your mother hackney as thousands years.
> She's yet his hag without control,
> For he and she sit cheek by jowl.
> His seed within her lap is sown,
> As testifies your dad, Pope Joan.
> Let bastards, then, and all such crew
> Lie in your mother's lap with you.
> You known't your father's house, therefore
> Your Holy Mother is a whore.
> And bastard like you do retain
> Your mother's, not your father's name.
> We have a Father dear at home,
> Who favors us when so're we come,
> Whose name we do retain, to wit,
> Christian, not Roman Catholic.
> Shall we to scape your mother's snap
> Then turn into her whorish lap?
> If we do so we prove, I'm sure,
> That we are bastards, she's a whore.
> We loathe it, let her frown or fawn,
> Because it scents of Satan's spawn.
>
> (11.35-36)

Common though it was among Puritans to consider the Church of Rome as the Antichrist and the Whore of Babylon and for Taylor to denounce Catholicism in his sermons—particularly in the "Christographia"—there is more to this nasty rejoinder than doctrinal rejection. Taylor enjoys this kind of verbal infighting; he seems postively to have delighted in the invective of whoredom.

The allusion to Pope Joan is especially significant in this regard, for Taylor, who attempted to versify the bawdy legend, left five drafts—or partial ones—among his manuscripts; and the most complete one was "probably composed when Taylor was over eighty years of age."[4] Originating in the Middle

Ages, the story of the English girl who became Pope and died after giving birth to a monstrous bastard during a Papal procession enjoyed widespread popularity. In Taylor's own time Dryden mentions the legend in his "Prologue at Oxford, 1680," and apparently refers to Elkanah Settle's *The Female Prelate: Being the History of the Life and Death of Pope Joan*, a London play of 1679. The legend peeks into John Trumbull's *M'Fingal* in American literature; and, for that matter, it received full dramatic treatment as recently as 1930 in Arthur Porter's *Pope Joan*. Taylor finds the coarse story a kind of "jokery," as typical of Papal actions, and as splendid fuel with which to feed the scurrilous fires of the times.

But, to return to the juvenile poems, though they are all three in dialogue or debate form, none has a real dramatic setting; only "The Layman's Lamentation" approximates dramatic conflict in the abruptness with which speeches are interrupted and passions raised. Even in it, however, the two speakers receive only the broadest of characterizations—humble sincerity opposed to proud authority—and they speak rather than act. Moreover, Taylor's early poetry is the product of wit rather than of the later realization that power comes from beauty, as well as from reason and vituperation. As a satirist he belongs among the railing rhymers, scorned by Dryden, who wield their satirical wit more like a bludgeon than a rapier.

The other two poems, poetically as inept as these satirical sallies, are both greeting-card compliments. In the one which he sends his love to his brother Joseph and his wife after visiting them, he expresses such sentiments as

> The which I trust will find your health as sound } E
> As (blest be Israel's God) mine doth abound. }

He exercises his wit to double the effect of his sentiments by spelling them out acrostically. That is, the first letters of each line and the last letters of each line spell out "EDWARD TAYLOR TO HIS BROTHER AND HIS SISTER JOSEPH AND ALICE TAYLOR." The habit of acrostics was a widespread Puritan vice and one which Addison damned as "false wit" along with shaped poetry—but Taylor used it with more complication in his later elegies than any other New England Puritan.

The other poem, which Taylor says he included "in a letter I sent to my schoolfellow, W. M.," echoes the one to his brother and sister-in-law. Not an acrostic itself, it begins by offering his love to one from whom he is separated by fortune's bustling wind and "the cloudy time," by asking after his health, and by promising to include a code or alphabet of love. Once decoded, it presumably reaffirms his love for his friend; he urges W. M. to take up the game:

> From which, as in a book there may arise
> All syllables of love you can devise,
> Of which all words are made, and so you may
> Imagine what an alphabet doth say,
> From which a new language of love doth rise
> And I present it here before your eyes.

His complex love letter to Elizabeth Fitch employs the same device of an alphabet, but this time it is employed as a kind of acrostic, the letters running down as the first letters of each line. This is certainly his most quaint and complicated form, for the lines are so arranged that within the general acrostic two figures are described—a ring inside a triangle, tangential with the triangle at three points. By carefully displacing the lines of his alphabet acrostic, Taylor allows certain letters to fall within the triangle; and, read separately, these letters yield the message: "The ring of love my pleasant heart must be, Truely confin'd within the trinity." The ring within the triangle uses the same letters at points of tangent, spelling out "Love's ring I send, that hath no end." The whole is delightfully confused, and must have afforded Miss Fitch plenteous enjoyment. Most astonishing is the fact that Taylor makes poetry out of the entire business—not very good poetry, but respectable nonetheless.

Puritans seem to have been irresistibly drawn to such exercises of wit in commending the persons of others, especially at the time of their death. Thus the funeral elegy nailed to the hearse of the deceased, passed about at the funeral gathering, or even sent in letters as a way of publicly announcing a death employed the acrostic and anagram abundantly. The inappropriateness modern readers find in the anagram-acrostic for a funeral sentiment was apparently not felt by the Puritan; for example, the honored Thomas Dudley, Anne Bradstreet's father and one of John Winthrop's most energetic rivals for the governorship of Massachusetts, met with the letters of his name rearranged to spell out the edifying message, "ah! old, must dye," reflecting the tough-minded quality so often attributed to the Puritans before sentimentality crept into their elegies around the end of the seventeenth century. The poem explains the anagram and works it into its explanation in lines three, five, and seven:

> A deaths head on your hand you neede not weare
> a dying hand you on your shoulders beare
> you need not one to minde you, you must dye
> you in your name may spell mortalitye
> younge men may dye, but old men these dye must
> t'will not be long before you turne to dust.
> before you turne to dust! ah! must; old! dye!
> what shall younge doe, when old in dust do lye?
> when old in dust lye, what N. England doe?
> when old in dust doe lye, it's best dye too.[5]

This subtle and clever weaving of the anagram through the poem is called the contrapuntal method by Harold S. Jantz.[6] One wonders really how Mr. Dudley reacted when he saw this poem. But from the verses found in his own pocket when he died, we can be fairly certain the anagram was no shock to him.

Another example involves William Tompson, father of the Boston poet of King Philip's War, who went to Virginia in 1642 to preach the Congregational system to the Anglicans. Arousing the ire of the governor, he and his cohorts were invited to leave Virginia almost at once, but weather forced them to winter there. During that winter his wife Abigail died; and John Wilson, pastor of the first Church at Boston and an incorrigible rhymer, undertook to inform the absent preacher of his loss with a verse elegy. Wilson rearranged Abigail's full name to yield the message "i am gon to al blis."

New England's major contribution to the conventional elegy was, perhaps, introducing the deceased as the speaker of the poem; and William Tompson found himself, therefore, reading a bit of doggerel sent him from his wife in heaven. "Thy bride i was, a most unworthy one," she tells him, "But to a better bridegroom i am gon." Perhaps it is no wonder that for years afterwards William Tompson so suffered from nervous disorders and religious doubts that his contemporaries thought him insane.

Taylor, who believed that names really revealed God's providence by permitting such anagram messages as these, would not have been surprised to find other members of the Tompson family so tortured in other poems. Elizabeth Tompson becomes "o i am blest on top" and the indomitable John Wilson twice wrenched William Tompson's name into edifying texts for funeral verses: "Lo my ionah slumpt" and "most holy paule mine." Wilson's son commended his father's "fluent strain in Poetry, (oh how excellent was the matter contained in the same, being full of Direction, Correction, and Consolation, senting much unto spiritual Edification. . . . He was another sweet singer of Israel, whose heavenly Verses passed like to the hankerchief carryed from Paul to help and uphold disconsolate ones, and to heal their wracked Souls, by the effectual priscence of Gods holy Spirit.)"[7]

These very qualities also mark Taylor's elegies, and they indicate the kind of elegist he was. Even as early as 1647, Samuel Danforth—John Wilson's son-in-law—employed nymphs, Phoebus, and a variety of literary and classical poses and allusions in his poetry; from then on they abound in one tradition of American elegies, as in the one in which John Norton's learned tears dropped on the grave of America's Tenth Muse, or the excellent elegy about Thomas Shepard by Urian Oakes:

Oh! that I were a Poet now in grain!
How would I invoke the Muses all
To deign their presence, lend their flowing Vein,
And help to grace dear *Shepard's* Funeral!
　　How would I paint our griefs, and succours borrow
　　From Art and Fancy, to limn out our sorrow!

Taylor avoids this manner of elegy, perhaps because he was writing for an audience that would look, as Kenneth B. Murdock says, primarily for what the elegist's "verses had to say and not often at the manner of their saying it. Those readers were, he must know, deaf to the nuances of verse. They . . . relished a pious poem because it was pious, liked ballad metre because it was familiar, and offered to an author none of the stimulation of an audience ready to appreciate all that he could give."[8]

Taylor wrote eight elegies in the New England mode; and, just as his meditations excel any lyric poetry attempted in the first century of American settlement, so are his elegies the best of their kind. Three of them were written in his senior year at Harvard; and they may have been composed at the request of the college since there is no other record of Taylor's connection with these persons, all three of whom were eminent New Englanders or at least closely connected with Harvard. The first elegy—"upon the death of that holy man of God Mr. Sims, late Pastor of the Church of Christ at Charlestown"—opens with this general lament:

> Ah me! Ah me! Could grief but make a poet,
> Surge after surge of sorrow sure would do it,

And it becomes hardly more specific in tracing the virtues of Zechariah Symmes. Comparing the earliest New Englanders to the Nazarites driven into the wilderness, Taylor commends Symmes as both a builder and a pillar of God's house in New England, which, since he had been pastor at Charlestown from 1636, is an appropriate figure to describe him. But Taylor seems not to have known him personally, for he can only say of him that he "wrought hard" in the quarry of hard hearts "with pickaxe, wedge, and maul, God's Word." In fact, the main reason for Taylor's lament seems to be that Symmes's loss represents the thinning of "Israel's glory" from what it was in the first half-century. Surges of sorrow have followed the loss of dozens of the founders of the colony:

> When death supplants our plants and planters so,
> The whole plantation drinks a cup of woe,

he rhymes; and he echoes the fear of the Mathers that the loss of the New England dream might accompany that of the first dreamers.

Two months after Symmes's death another plant was taken from New England soil "and set in glory's flowering pot." Though no more personally acquainted with Francis Willoughby, then deputy governor of Massachusetts, than with Symmes, Taylor constructed a much more elaborate elegy. Grief causes him to surrender his studies:

> Begone, begone, my books, start from my hand,
> Stand off, or offer verse up as you stand.
> Bleed tears, mine eyes; weep blood, my pen; my heart,
> Beat up for volunteers in every part
> To march in sorrow's regimental plot,
> For Willoughby, Oh! Willoughby IS NOT.

The fact stated, Taylor calls the country, court, churches, and college to acknowledge its woe:

> Rise, Harvard, rise; stand up with wat'ry eyes,
> Until a second Willoughby arise.

The second part of this elegy is a very interesting acrostic. Taylor runs the letters "FRANCIS WILLOUGHBY" vertically as the first and the last letters of each of thirty-four decasyllabic lines. This would spell out the name four times, but Taylor complicates the trick by placing the couplets side by side, thereby cutting the thirty-four lines to seventeen doubled lines. The first line, for example, thus reads "F ull fraught with grace, well fit for glory's shel F irmly in glory now enrich thysel F." The middle "F" functions portmanteau-like as both the last sound of the first rhyme word, and the first sound of the second line of the couplet. This cuts the number of times the name is actually spelled out to three.

Unlike the acrostic letter to his brother Joseph, this elegy exploits much more successfully the poetic possibilities of the occasion for which it was written. Ignoring the acrostic, we find the idea that a noble gem deserves a weighty and worthy setting. Likewise,

No man gets weeds a palace to adorn,
No weeds as posies in our hands are borne,
Counting these sweet enameled knots from whence
Conspire perfumed gales not worth the scents.
If so, no marvel Christ, when his bright eye
Enthralled in dust his shining rosies spy,
Stoops down, up picks them: for hereby he gets
Sweet slips of grace that he in glory sets.
We may assure ourselves that blessed shew
Within Christ's garden for Christ's garment grew,
In which his garden flowers may clearly spy,
Intails of all their happiness do lie.
Lo, for the flowers in grace's garden shall
Leap into bliss to garnish glory's hall.

We notice that Willoughby is not mentioned and that his public or private virtues are not sung even indirectly. Taylor's compliment is even greater because he states a general proposition about those raised to glory by Christ with his figures of shining roses in a garden; and Willoughby is subsumed as a kind of minor premise only by virtue of the acrostic. But Taylor is unwilling to rely utterly upon this subtle relationship of form and content; he drives the conclusion of his syllogism home plainly, if prettily:

God, spying Willoughby here on our string
Glister so bright, fitter for glory's ring,
Hath called him out, and caught him here beneath,
Hath wrapt his brows about with glory's wreath.

These images, their order, and the idea they disclose are repeated again in "The Glory of and Grace in the Church Set Out," one of the final lyrics and one of the best in *God's Determinations*. The contrast between these two versions of essentially the same idea turns on the acrostic itself. The rhyming and spelling game Taylor plays in the elegy forces him to pad both lines and ideas, and the application directly to Willoughby is like the explanation of a joke. But the elegy shows the forming of Taylor's techniques, and it stands as a kind of experiment in false wit that he profitably relinquished.

A third and last section, which is more directly concerned with Willoughby, again raises the lament for New England, Christ's seed plot, the waning of which Taylor fears. If the Lord takes these fairest of New England blossoms, where will the seeds come from to raise future blooms for glory's hall? Morbidly, he concludes:

> When fruits do drop, it plainly doth appear
> That summer is well spent, and winter's near.

With this dreary thought he writes Willoughby's epitaph, which shows him bidding farewell to the world and the grave, for he expects to *fare well* at the day of judgment.

Four months later another pillar crumbled into New England's dust; Taylor's voice again joined the general mourning for John Allen of Dedham, who had been overseer at Harvard from 1654 until his death in August, 1671. Once more Taylor really says nothing about the deceased, and he devotes the main part of his poem to the development of three similes. His soul, he claims, sitting on the "lippit" of his ear for news, has been quelled by a puff of sorry words; like a watchman most exposed to the foe, it is most easily dropped by a bullet; or—clumsily anticipating Emily Dickinson's frostbeheaded flower—like a rose open to receive the sun, the soul is shriveled by a barbed lightning flash. So the thunderclap of bad news strikes the ear, and the soul is sunk by grief to a point beyond hope, even beyond fear.

At this point a second speaker is introduced:

> "But, what's the matter? Sir, shew what is done.
> Pluck out the plug and let the causes run."

In spite of the bathetic pun, the first speaker explains that the very air's tumult tells the cause, carrying "the echoes of our griefs . . . far and near." He condescends,

> To anagrammatize, the case is this:
> The GRACES ALL ON ALLen showing bright
> Are call'd ALL IN to bed and bid good night.

Not yet satisfied, he wrings the anagram-pun into the last line: "ALL ENd in ALLEN by a paragog."

His main interest in the poem, however, is his continued astonishment at the steady loss of the church fathers. In the most elegant image of spiritual conflict ever to appear in his verse, he describes Allen as having laid down "His Gospel hilts, and's gone out of the ring." The next lines develop the image of a fencing school where spiritual gamesters lay at sin:

> How are our spiritual gamesters slipt away?
> Crossing their hilts and leaving off their play?
> Leaving the ring to us who'd need, before
> We take up hilts, the fencing school implore.

The gamesters—John Norton; Samuel Newman; Samuel Stone; William Tompson; John Wilson, the anagrammatist; Samuel Shepard; Henry Flint; Jonathan Mitchel; John Eliot, son of the Indian converter; Richard and Eleazar Mather; Benjamin Bunker; William Woodward; John Raynor; John Davenport; Symmes; John Warham; and one Gray—all have preceded Allen into bliss. As Taylor reminds his auditors of their deaths, there lurks behind his list the phantom of uncertainty.

> Shall none
> Be left behind to tell's the quondam story
> Of this plantation?

In November, 1671, Taylor, too, withdrew from the major arena of spiritual fencing in New England; for he had decided after some serious self-examination and consultation to make "the desperatest journey that ever Connecticut men undertook" to Westfield in the dead of winter. President Chauncy had at first been reluctant to let his student get away to the frontier, but now he changed his mind. Taylor writes of his good-bye to Chauncy on November 26, the night before he set out, in his diary: "I went to take my leave of our honored President, whose mind was changed, and his love was so much expressed that I could scarce leave him, and well it might be so, for he told me in plain words that he *knew not how to part with me*."[9] Before that winter ended, Charles Chauncy died; and Edward Taylor had written another elegy.

Perhaps because of Chauncy's love for him Taylor decided to compose the most elaborate elegy he had yet undertaken. The poem falls into three parts. Part I, set in "A Double Acrostic," is a lament that sorrow should surge so soon again after the death of John Allen. Like the other elegies, this is in decasyllabic couplets. Read vertically down the left margin, it spells out the first part of the deceased Chauncy's name; the rhyme sounds, read vertically down the right margin, complete the acrostic:

> C Come weep with me, alas! alas! that dew } V
> H Hung on our eyes by Allen's funeral new }

Part II is "A quadruble acrostic whose trible is an anagram." That is, as in the elegy on Francis Willoughby, the couplets are arranged side by side instead of one under another; the end of the first rhyme word acts as the beginning of the first word of the second line. But this time Taylor does not merely spell out his subject's name. Reading down the left margin we find "PRESIDENT DYED" and down between the two sets of lines an anagram of the President's name, "A CAL IN CHURCHES." The anagram thus also begins the second line of each couplet and ends it, the first and last letters of second lines being the same.

P eace, sobbing Muse, come sum thy loss defra^y	A fter that's done, the debts are to Pa^y A
R are learning's gone, a polyglotta choic^e	C uriously printed in a silver voic^e C
E xtract of Greek and Hebrew Rabbins la^y	A ptly inshrined in his temples gra^y A
S cutcheons of arts and artificial skill	L ay boxed in his memory, at will L

Again, because he knew Chauncy fairly closely, Taylor can portray him as an individual person, though he restricts himself to general characteristics. Symmes, Willoughby, and Allen were vague, if eminent, personages; Chauncy's eminence is detailed for us—learned, particularly in languages, his speech is not crabbed and pedantic, but smooth, silver; disdaining nothing except evil, he, a storehouse of learning, was able to unravel the difficulties of scholastic theology and to enlighten the dustiest of questions and the dimmest of minds; worthy of emulation in piety of prayer and practice, he was a zealous and courageous preacher, many seeing him give "a call in churches." Having worked the anagram into the text of this section, Taylor stops.

Part III plays a number game with the occasion, for the opening letters of each of its forty-six lines is a roman numeral in this order:

MCLVLVCLCVVIIIIIIIIVLVIVVVVVVLVIIIIIVVVVVVVVII.

When added, they represent the year of Chauncy's death, 1671. In this section, which Taylor calls "An acrostic Chronogram," the churches are depicted as swimming in tears; but it ends with Chauncy swimming in bliss. Taylor commands Harvard men to think about Chauncy's incomparable virtues. They would willingly plunge across the Jordan of death to follow him, but they find their lives "too rich a gift to leave behind." Chauncy cries out to them:

> Who'd fear a tomb, such glory to enjoy?
> Who'd fear the grave? Death's but the golden door
> Wherein we must unto bright glory's shore.

And they sink back in sorrow, judgment, and darkness, imploring at the end of the poem, "Inable us, oh Lord, to shine as he."

Had Taylor made poetry out of this hodgepodge of spelling and counting puzzles, we might admire his cleverness; but poetically the verse succumbs to so many conventions that we can not commend it. Not even the better characterization if its subject saves the elegy as poetry; for, though the drab New England winter sat like a cosmic *memento mori* over Taylor, he seems to write with no really personal sense of loss or awareness of death. The form, content, and attitude are merely conventions; they are not infused with the personal involvement that might have converted even so artificial a form as the New England elegy into fine poetry.

Within ten years, however, after the red death that was King Philip's War had strutted across the frontier, after the responsibility for the lives of his community must have weighed as heavily upon him as upon any young wilderness physician, and after he had lost two of his own children, Taylor's personal involvement appears in his poetry. His poetic reflections about death gain in depth, and he forsakes the artifices of acrostic, anagram, and chronogram.

Representative of this change is his fine "Upon Wedlock, and Death of Children," composed probably late in 1682, since it seems to have been occasioned by the death of his daughter Abigail in August of that year. The poem is not technically an elegy, since its purpose is not to commemorate the death of Abigail herself, but it is certainly related to the elegies as Taylor writes them subsequently. Coming in the same year as the first of his *Preparatory Meditations,* these reflections avoid decasyllabic couplets and fall into the stanzaic pattern of the *Meditations*—iambic pentameter lines rhyming *ababcc.* The stanza provides units of thought and image that structure his reflections much more rigidly than the elegiac couplets did. The result is an almost classical restraint, similar to Ben Jonson's, against which the personal anguish of the experience Taylor describes creates a tension he rarely matches. The sense of strain and tension produces a powerful statement, but it is controlled by the strength of the poet's religious faith and by his compliance with God's demanding will.

In this attitude Taylor steps midway between Donne and Herbert. Donne, who solves his spiritual conflicts by fiat, leaves one feeling that the solution provided has not actually resolved the question in his soul. Herbert echoes Donne's struggles vociferously, as in "Love" and "The Collar"; but, when he submits to God's will at the end of the poem, we realize that the sound and the fury have been merely a rhetorical device to accentuate the final, child-like submission. In "Upon Wedlock, and Death of Children," Taylor submits to the Lord's will as fully as Herbert; but Taylor's struggle, while not so loud in expostulation as Donne's, is no mere rhetorical or intellectual quibble but an intensely personal and human one.

The poem opens easily and prettily. God ties a curious knot in paradise. The knot, a true-love's knot, a wedding knot, suggests a plot of flowers; and it occasions flower, slip, plant, sprout, seed, and perfume imagery throughout the rest of the poem. He compares the knot to that of Gordius which the baffled Alexander the Great could untie only with his sword.

But "No Alexander's sword can it divide," he says. The sword allusion forms the only image contrary to the prettiness of the knot of flowers, though it occurs only to be dismissed. Flowers planted in this knot grow "gay and glorious," continues Taylor, "Unless an hellish breath do singe their plumes." Like the sword of the first stanza, this is the only image which contrasts with the flowers; and it represents, of course, sin and death. With Elizabethan taste he continues to describe the knot:

> Here primrose, cowslips, roses, lillies blow,
>> With violets and pinks that void perfumes,
> Whose beauteous leaves o'er laid with honey-dew,
>> And chanting birds cherp out sweet music true.

In the third stanza Taylor relates himself to the marriage knot:

> When in this knot I planted was, my stock
>> Soon knotted, and a manly flower out brake.

He refers to his first-born, Samuel; and, in the next line a second child, his daughter Elizabeth is born:

> And after it my branch again did knot,
>> Brought out another flower, its sweet-breathed mate.

Still the images are pleasant, the two flowers smiling, sweet, and perfumed. Besides the natural meaning of perfume as the fragrance of flowers, the term usually means for Taylor some kind of satisfaction. The most frequent use of perfume in his poetry is as a pillar of incense rising to please the Lord, and it is a familiar metaphor for prayer. It probably represents in this poem the satisfaction the children bring him. There is no utterly contrary image in this stanza, but the word *knot* takes on a sense inherent in it from the beginning, but not emphasized—a sense of hardness and tightness, stress, and effort, consistent with the strain of childbirth.

Elizabeth died almost exactly a year after her birth, apparently quickly and suddenly, in an "unlookt for, dolesome, darksome hour." The "glorious hand from glory" that cropped

this flower "almost tore the root up of the same," he confesses, recalling the sword of the first stanza, in the word
"crop." Yet, in this stanza the images are not all dark; and,
though nearly uprooted himself, Taylor consoles himself with
the knowledge that his daughter is attended to heaven by
angels. In fact, he reconciles his loss stoically in the next
stanza: he offers his child to Christ as a pledge or assurance
that he will follow, as a sacrifice of part of himself.

> But pausing on't, this sweet perfum'd my thought,
>   Christ would in glory have a flower, choice, prime,
> And having choice, chose this my branch forth brought.
>   Lord, take't. I thank thee, thou tak'st ought of mine.

Thus reconciled, he has another child, a boy again, and in
1681 "another sweet," a daughter Abigail. Again, almost a
year after her birth, "The former hand" took her away. But
this time the child's death was not an easy one, and his consolation came only with tremendous effort:

> But oh! the tortures, vomit, screechings, groans,
> And six weeks' fever would pierce hearts like stones.

Unlike Taylor's imagined golden door of death swinging
easily to let President Chauncy swim through, Abigail's passage is a bramble of undecorated, unvarnished vomit, groans,
and fever.
 This time, when Taylor submits to God's will, his submission
is not so witty. He doesn't even invent a new figure to express
it, and the last stanza echoes none of the self-satisfied thanks
of the fifth stanza.

> Grief o'er doth flow: and nature fault would find,
>   Were not thy will my spell, charm, joy, and gem,
> That as I said, I say, take, Lord, they're thine.
>   I piecemeal pass to glory bright in them.
>   I joy, may I sweet flowers for glory breed,
>   Whether thou getst them green, or lets them seed.

Reconciliation to grief through obedience to God's will is
attained with joy, but a clouded joy. Unlike Taylor's *Medi-*

tations, this last stanza has no dizzying rhetoric. Not sullen, yet it does not sing. And we are aware that Taylor has learned Job's lesson: he is not to speak from the bitterness of his heart.

"Upon Wedlock, and Death of Children" belongs among Taylor's finest accomplishments. Among them it stands unique; for it is the only poem prompted by no specific occasion as were the elegies, by no sense of regular duty like the *Meditations,* and by no literary motive like *God's Determinations.* The "I" of the poem is not the representative soul or the church as it so often seems to be in the larger poems; it speaks for Edward Taylor, frontier minister and physician who has lost two children and who seeks relief from his sorrow in poetry. The intense personal involvement and the universality of his problem elevate the poem from among his elegiac verse. The poet-physician touches the open wound in his spirit with a salty finger, but only to apply a healing balm. He never again writes elegies exactly as he did before.

Between 1682 and 1689 Taylor lost three more children, none of whom survived the first year; and, in midsummer of 1689, his wife followed them. Again the image of the "weddens knot" recurs:

> Some deem death doth the true-love knot untie:
> But I do find it harder tied thereby.
> My heart is in't and will be squeezed therefore
> To pieces, if thou draw the ends much more.
> Oh! strange untying! It ti'th harder: what?
> Can anything untie a true love knot?
> Five babes thou tookst from me before this stroke.
> Thine arrows then into my bowels broke,
> But now they pierce into my bosom smart,
> Do strike and stob me in the very heart.

But he relinquishes her to the Lord as he had formerly committed the flowers from this knot; and again, like Donne, he turns to poetry to ease his grief:

> Grief swelling, girds the heart strings, where it's purst;
> Unless it vent, the vessel sure will burst.

> My gracious Lord, grant that my bitter grief
> Breathe through this little vent hole for relief.

Like the earlier elegies, this one about his wife is divided into three sections—the first identifies the occasion and sets the mood; the second introduces Elizabeth as a speaker and constitutes a defense of the elegy; and the third rehearses her virtues. But both the second and third sections differ from their counterparts in their earlier elegies, as does the first, because of his personal involvement. Elizabeth chides him for singing:

> My dear, dear love, reflect thou no such thing,
> Will grief permit you at my grave to sing?

He agrees that songs and sorrows do not belong together, but he compares his dirge to the groans that grief wrings from his heart. Remembering his elaborate love letter sent her in 1674, he pleads that she impute it no crime to grace her with a poem:

> What, shall my preface to our true love knot
> Frisk in acrostic rhyme? And may I not
> Now at our parting, with poetic knocks
> Break a salt tear to pieces as it drops?
> Did David's bitter sorrow at the dusts
> Of Jonathan raise such poetic gusts?
> Do emperors interr'd in verses lie?
> And mayn't such feet run from my weeping eye?
> Nay, duty lies upon me much; and shall
> I in thy coffin nail thy virtues all?
> How shall thy babes, and theirs, thy virtuous shine
> Know or pursue unless I them define?

Out of this combination of motives—to preserve her memory, to instruct his children and grandchildren, to release his grief by giving it voice, and to raise for her a monument of neither marble nor stone, but of powerful and immortalizing rhyme— he approaches logically the third section. The connection between parts is, therefore, closer than in the other elegies.

Resolved not to abuse Elizabeth's modesty by hyperbole,

Taylor described her generally as he considers her various rôles in life—child, neighbor, mistress of her household, mother, wife, and finally Christian and church member. Some details are specific—the fact that her mother was dead, that she had experienced conversion at home, that she enjoyed Michael Wigglesworth's *Day of Doom*, and that she reconciled herself to misfortune with the words, "An all-wise God doth this"—but the virtues displayed are obedience, tenderness, meekness, courtesy, compassion, prudence, dutifulness, humility, modesty, patience, and piety. In short, Taylor draws an idealized portrait of the Puritan wife—one to be emulated rather than known. Lacking figure and illustration, the poem mourns moderately; it is a very self-conscious and restrained performance, which is not without tenderness and warmth on Taylor's part, but which was designed for the eyes of others, and so expressed discreetly.

His most ambitious elegy—"Upon the Death of that Holy and Reverend Man of God, Mr. Samuel Hooker"—was written in 1697. Unlike the poem to his wife, which, though it ends with the statement that "she fear'd not death," seems somehow unfinished, this one about Hooker's death is the most polished, rounded poem of its type. This accomplishment is due in part to its division into five sections: each is directed to a different group of mourners, which creates a sense of completeness—the feeling that all parties have been accounted for. And partly its success is due to the fact that the gnawing uneasiness of the earliest elegies about the thinning of Israel's glory becomes its major concern. In fact, Hooker's death is really used to preach a verse Jeremiad against apostasy in New England. Hooker himself is merely a point of focus—an occasion for Taylor to declare his deepest ecclesiastical concerns, or an eminence from which he can descry and rout the enemies of Congregationalism. Partly because it is not basically an elegy but a public edict, it shows Taylor speaking publicly at his best.

In the opening section, after a conventional statement of grief, Taylor mentions Hooker's death briefly and then introduces the main issue. Taylor is less concerned with Samuel Hooker himself then with his "choice name," for Samuel was the son of Thomas Hooker, the famed founder of the Hartford colony. Now that this brave Jonathan is dead, Taylor asks, will no David arise to avenge him? These are times

> When birds new hatcht wear, as in nest they lie,
> Presbytick down, pinfeathered prelacy
> (Young cockerils, whose combs soar up like spires,
> That force their dams, and crow against their sires)

Where, he inquires, apparently addressing all of New England,

> Where hast thou left thy strength and potency?
> And Congregational artillery?
> We need the same and need it more and more.
> For Babel's canons 'gainst our bulwarks roar.

Just as his concern for the problem of apostasy had appeared most pointedly and most directly in his preaching about the Lord's Supper in 1693 and 1694, so here again he aims fire at the problem of Presbyterianism, and, by implication, at its leader Solomon Stoddard. At the time of the loss of Symmes, Allen, Willoughby, and Chauncy, Taylor's fear of the trend was uncertain; but, by the year of Hooker's death, the direction in which New England was wavering had become quite clear.

The second movement of the dirge is directed "To New England," and begins,

> Alas! Alas! New England, go weep.
> Thy loss is great in him.

and it then engraves a character of a good Puritan preacher, which is related generally to the one in "The Layman's Lament" but which is more complete and precise with Hooker as its model. Taylor describes his wisdom, inventiveness, and excellent rhetoric; his habit of witty maxims; and his strength and sturdiness in carrying out God's will, whether as peacemaker or as corrosive rebuker. The one quality to emerge most visibly from this category of traits is his steadiness; because of it, Taylor implies, New England would do well to emulate him. This is really his point in the poem, and the remarks he makes about Hooker as a rich divine, a preacher never "notion sick," and a pious father and husband move quickly to Hooker's death. At this point Taylor raises the main question—"But art thou gone, brave Hooker, hence? and why?" His answer to his own question seems to be that "the country's sins" brought Hooker's death to pass, and hereupon he turns to diagnose the ills of New England, whose brains are giddied by false preachers and false Gospel. The terseness of his prognosis—"Such symptoms say, if nothing else will ease, / Thy sickness soon will cure thy sad disease"— speaks no good for New England. If it continues to decline, Taylor indicates where it must end:

> Apostasy, wherewith thou art thus driven
> Unto the tents of Presbyterianism
> (Which is refined Prelacy at best),
> Will not stay long here in her tents, and rest,
> But o'er this bridge will carry thee apace
> Into the realm of Prelate's arch, the place
> Where open sinners, vile, unmasked indeed,
> Are welcome guests (if they can say the Creed)
> Unto Christ's table, while they can their sins
> Atone in courts by offering silverlings.

Only one cure can save the country, and that Taylor prescribes:

> Watch, watch thou then: reform thy life: refine
> Thyself from thy declensions. Tend thy line.

In part three, "To Connecticut," Taylor reminds the colony of its "Foundation Stone," the elder Hooker; and he asserts that now no one is left to help the colony recover from its ills. And in part four he turns to Farmington, the town where Hooker presided as minister; in a series of paradoxes, he calls her to lament:

> Alas, poor Farmington, of all the rest
> Most happy and unhappy, blesst, unblesst:
> Most happy having such an happiness:
> And most unhappy losing of no less.

At this point Taylor uses Hooker's death as a prophecy both made and fulfilled by the Farmington minister—as an *exemplum* of Farmington's and all New England's dire prospects. Hooker had preached, five days before he died, on a text from Jeremiah 6:26, which Taylor very skillfully metaphrases:

> Oh! Daughter of my people, (that last text)
> Gird thee with sackcloth, wallow thee perplext
> In ashes. Mourn thou lamentably
> As for an only son: weep bitterly,
> For lo, the Spoiler suddenly shall come
> Upon us.

Then he recalls for Farmington that "the prophesy / Had an accomplishment before your eye," for, resting while they sang a Psalm, Hooker blessed them and collapsed. The Spoiler had come, and Taylor draws the moral clearly:

> Lord, grant it ben't an omen of our fate,
> Foreshewing our apostate-following state.

Again he prescribes the bitter purgation:

> Search into thy sin,
> Repent and grieve that ere thou grievedst him,
> Or rather God in him, lest suddenly
> The Spoiler still should on thee come and stroy.

What if they reject the pill and refuse the physic?

> Shall angling cease? And no more fish be took,
> That thou callst home thy Hooker with his hook?

With this comparatively dignified pun Taylor ends part four.

The final section, "To the Family Relict," which addresses Samuel Hooker's widow and children, contains the finest touches of Taylor's artistry. For what consolation it may offer, Taylor personifies New England in assuring the widow's "Poor bleeding soul" that "New England lays her head / To thine, to weep with thee over thy dead." He then most adroitly manipulates his consolation so as to have the departed Hooker speak to his wife from bliss:

> Christ's napkin take, grace's green taffity,
> And wipe therewith thy weeping, wat'ry eye,
> And thou shalt see thy Hooker all o'er gay
> With Christ in bliss, adorn'd with glory's ray,
> And putting out his shining hand to thee,
> Saying, "My Honey, mourn no more for me."

The vision of Hooker encourages his wife to obey patiently the will of God until she joins him in salvation.

When Hooker's speech is ended, Taylor turns to the children to urge them to accept the spirit of their father and grandfather and to admonish them not to be like some ungrateful offspring who pull out their fathers' brains, make wassail bowls of their skulls, and stuff their eyes with folly. The great name of Hooker must endure no apostasy; for the dead Samuel was a cabinet of virtue and a treasury of grace; a bright temple of piety in print; and a stage of war, a golden pulpit, and an oratory of prayer. He compounds this list of conventional metaphors, takes leave of the body, and adds a feeble cliché as epitaph to the whole.

This commemoration of Samuel Hooker is Taylor's finest elegy, and it is also one of the finest in the New England metaphysical style.[10] It is, therefore, an excellent representative of all the devices of the elegy, except for the classical allusion, which Taylor prefers to avoid. It also represents the summation and refinement of his abilities in the form—puns and biblical allusion; the speech of the deceased and the *exemplum;* the personification of country, colony, and town; the carefully inwrought text from Jeremiah to support his own Jeremiad; and the fully accomplished organization of the whole.

His later elegy about Increase Mather (1723) is interesting for being not only a statement about New England's foremost intellectual leader for more than a quarter of a century and Taylor's close friend but also an echo of his dialogue with Maypole dressers who seem now to have moved to New England and to have displaced Mather, who chose rather to play at "Gospel games, which is an heavenly race." And his elegy on Mehetable Woodbridge, his sister-in-law (1698), has been given the honor of having sketched "the most effective death scene" in the form. Neither is equal to the Hooker elegy; but these and the six other elegies form a minor theme in Taylor's developing skill as a poet. They are also a kind of sketchbook in which he practiced initially the celebration of his golden theme in the *Meditations*, and they reflect his growing skill in verse. Finally, they represent Taylor's growing concern with the state of God's cause in the New World, and his progressive fear and discouragement with the ecclesiastical and social decline there.

CHAPTER 5

Accomplishment

I *Preparatory Meditations*

PRECISELY why Taylor began writing and collecting
his *Preparatory Meditations* in 1682 is a moot question,
but his growing concern for the Congregational way may
have had something to do with it. In his illuminating study
of "the Transfiguration of Eucharist Symbols in Seventeenth
Century English Poetry," Professor Malcolm Mackenzie Ross
suggests most broadly that disenchantment with the actuali-
ties of state and church in Herbert, Crashaw, Vaughan, and
Milton largely propelled them to the creation of new—and
different—worlds into which they retreated poetically.[1] Something of this reaction may lurk behind Taylor's poetic mysticism, but his preaching and controversies after he began the
meditations argue no surrender of the New England vision.

Two American publications of 1682 may have offered both
encouragement and precedent for Taylor's poems. One, Increase Mather's *Practical Truths Tending to Promote Godliness*,[2] urged meditation as a means of attaining a transforming, mystical vision of the Lord; and it also emphasized that
a sense of duty should accompany the exercise. The other
was the third printing of a book of *Daily Meditations* by a
young seaman named Philip Pain.[3] Although Pain's ama-
teurish attempts at a stanza similar to Taylor's frequently echo
the sentiments and manner of George Herbert, Pain's main
concern, unlike Taylor's, was entirely with the imminence of
death and with the transitoriness of all earthly things. From
Loyola to Cotton Mather the injunction to the reader to
imagine himself at the point of death to increase the im-

mediacy and urgency of the act of devotion was traditional. Furthermore, Pain's six-line stanza is merely a grouping of three couplets.

Although the specific reason for Taylor's *Meditations* remains entirely unknown, there is little question about Professor Martz's judgment that "Taylor's standing as a poet must be measured by a full and careful reading of the *Meditations*."[4] Much of what I have said about Taylor depends upon the *Meditations* seen as a whole, but I have so far approached them only thematically.

Considered formally, they appear more similar than dissimilar. While tracing the elements of uniformity—as Martz has done—is a very valuable way to come to a total appraisal, it tends to neglect the variations within the *Meditations* as a whole; a look, therefore, at the different things Taylor undertakes in the poems and at the different characteristics they possess may also be illuminating. First, there is uniformity, for all 217 poems use the same versatile stanzaic form: iambic pentameter lines rhyming *ababcc*. Occasionally Taylor allows his thought, image, and syntax to run from one stanza to the next; but, usually, the six-line unit marks the structural limit of his statement. This structural limitation gives a regularity to the cadence of his verse beyond that imposed by the decasyllabics themselves, and it also provides a kind of angularity and steadiness to the development of both thoughts and images. Against this formal regularity, Taylor's roughness—sometimes intentional, usually not—is even more striking that it would be in a freer form.

The main disadvantage of the stanzaic method lies in its limitations for a long poem, where it inhibits dramatic changes of pace; interrupts development; and, for want of emphasis, slips too easily into tediousness. This monotony is especially evident in Meditation 58, the longest and one of the dullest of the poems, though length alone is not responsible. The shortest poems, like Meditation 1 of the first series, on the other hand, breed no weariness; its three stanzas are, in fact, most inconspicuous; and the brevity emphasizes rather than impairs the unity of the whole poem. At least for Taylor, then, the form works most successfully when restricted to less than ten stanzas; and this he seems to have realized, for most of his *Meditations* fall within this limit.

The structure of each of the poems is likewise similar. They begin with a question—"My Blessed Lord, art thou a lily flower?" or "Am I thy gold? or purse, Lord, for thy wealth?" —or a statement of fact, which usually, like the question, presents a metaphor: "My silver chest a spark of love up locks," or "Like to the Marigold, I blushing close," or some exclamation. The exclamation is usually a series of epithets— "Oh! Leaden heel'd," "Oh! Golden rose," "A crown of glory, Oh!" "My Lord, my life, can envy ever be," "Oh! Wealthy theme! Oh! Feeble," "A king, a king, a king indeed, a king." Sometimes it functions as the opening of a longer sentence: "Raptures of love, surprising loveliness / That burst through heavens all, in rapid flashes." Occasionally it is self-admonishing: "Astonished stand, my Soul: why dost thou start," or "My sin! my sin, my God, these cursed dregs." These opening lines, or the remainder of the stanzas they open, set the subject of the meditation.

From this point, the poems develop the opening idea or image. Usually Taylor develops the idea or the underlying logic rather than the image itself, but there are some notable exceptions. As a result of this concentration upon ideas, however, there is very little to be said about the central development of the poems, where diversity predominates. As Stanford points out, Taylor's development is at times grossly inconsistent. Meditation 20, for example, begins with Christ's soaring to heaven swifter than angels. The second stanza shows him seated in "His bright sedan," an azure cloud that acts as his chariot. Stanza three denies the chariot image and insists Christ rises by the rungs of Jacob's Ladder. But by the end of that stanza the ladder image is altered to one of "golden stepping stones" to the throne of Deity.

If the second part of the poems is diverse—sometimes reduced to a single stanza, sometimes developed through several —the final part is uniformly the same. These *Meditations* are a form, we must remember, of secret prayer; and prayer combines both praise and petition. The logic of the poems is designed to bring the poet to the final stanza of petition, which ordinarily applies the consideration of the preceding two parts of the poem to his own condition; usually this stanza combines the personal application with his personal request: "Lord, make my soul thy plate; thine image bright / Within the circle of the same enfoil"; "Pare off, my Lord, from me, I pray, my pelf"; "Lord, make me to the Pentecost repair, / Make me thy guest too at this feast." It ends with the promise to praise and give thanks if the petition is granted: "Yet thy rich grace save me from sin and death? / And I will tune thy praise with holy breath"; "I'll sing / And make thy praise on my heroics ring."

This threefold pattern governs all the *Meditations,* and it tends to make each poem a discrete unit—an entirely separate effort, structurally, from the others, yet one exactly like them. I think this tendency argues against Martz's suggestion that "the *Meditations* are written in sequences, sometimes with tight links between the poems."[5] The linking is certainly there, but the sequence is quite accidental. Meditation 3, for example, is built up primarily from images of odors, and the last stanza petitions:

> My spirits let with thy perfume be fed
> And make thy odors, Lord, my nostrils fare.

The following poem, "The Experience," begins as if it remembered the preceding experience:

> Oh! that I always breath'd in such an air
> As I suck't in, feeding on sweet content.

Meditation 4, which centers upon the Rose of Sharon image, is followed by "The Reflexion," which opens with the same image in the first two stanzas.

In the second series, Meditation 20 ends with the lines "And I will, as I walk herein, / Thy glory thee in temple music bring." The first line of the following meditation is "Rich temple! Fair! Rich festivals, my Lord." Meditation 58, which is long and dull, petitions the Lord in the third stanza:

> Christen mine eyeballs with thine eye-salve then,
>   Mine eyes will spy how Isra'l's journeying
> Into, and out of Egypt's bondage den,
>   A glass thy visage was imbellisht in.

The eye-mirror image does not recur in the following eighteen stanzas, but in the opening of Meditation 59 it is the basis of the first stanza:

> Wilt thou enoculate within mine eye
> Thy image bright, my Lord, that bright doth shine
> Forth in the cloudy-fiery pillar high,
> Thy tabernacle's looking-glass divine?
> What glorious rooms are then mine eyeholes made,
> Thine image on my window's glass portray'd?

And in Meditation 60A again the scriptures are described as "a shining glass, wherein thy face, / My Lord, as bread of life, is clearly seen." Immediately following is a meditation that again, though very incidentally, uses eye-imagery; it concludes with the lament, "I'm sick." Meditation 61 introduces Christ as a healer, and Meditation 62 presents him with the herbs and remedies to supply his "doctor's shop." The herbs of purification come from a garden, which contributes centrally to the images of the next three meditations. Such a cluster of related and interlocking images serves to unite eight poems; and similar clusters in other poems seem to add support to Martz's suggestion.

But in refutation of Martz's suggestion, Taylor has pointed out that the poems are chiefly upon the doctrines he preached, and it was still popular in this period to prepare a plan for sermons—as in his "Christographia" ones—and to carry the plan through for three years or more. Babette Levy points out that often the Puritan preacher "lingered on a favorite or meaty passage, as John Warham did for twenty-seven sermons on Romans 1:5. With equal fervor of spirit, Thomas Hooker spent nearly a year on Acts 2:37, and Thomas Shepard, after four years on Matthew 25:1-13, congratulated himself that he had not, after the fashion of Papist commentators, squeezed the last bit of meaning out of it."[6] Taylor's Meditations 115-153, which cite texts from Canticles 5:10 to 7:6, cover a span of six years. Because they were based upon his sermons, we know that he must have been preaching a series of sermons based on Canticles over the same length of time. Whether in the case of these poems, or in the twenty-odd

poems on typology that begin the second series, or the interlocking images, or the image clusters, each of the poems is
separately conceived and developed. Their sequential relationship is an accident of the sermon sequence, and not a
poetic intention, though certainly Martz is right in concluding
that individual poems gain in strength and richness, and are,
in a very real way, sustained by the sequence in which they
occur.[7]

Because the motive and the general subject of the poems
are uniform, their attitude and tone never vary; and they
support the structural uniformity of the *Meditations.* Unlike
Herbert's *Temple* or Traherne's *Poems of Felicity,* Taylor
played very little with verse technique within the general
structure. Why he avoided such experiments is not clear, but
his avoidance is regrettable; for, when he does experiment a
few times, the results are excellent. In "The Return," for example, he converts the couplet at the end of each stanza into a
refrain, with minor incremental changes to fit the refrain to
the thought of each stanza. Meditation 16 resorts to a device
used successfully by Sir Thomas Wyatt in "Disdain Me Not"
and by Spenser in his first *Amoretti* sonnet. Spenser opens
his first quatrain with "Happy ye leaves," the second with
"And happy lines," the third with "And happy rymes"; all
three terms are then summed up in the first line of the concluding couplet: "Leaves, lines, and rymes, seeke her to please
alone." Taylor's second stanza begins:

> I cannot see, nor will thy will aright.
>> Not see to wail my woe, my loss and hew
> Nor all the shine in all the sun can light
>> My candle, nor its heat my heart renew.

The next line sums up these terms:

>> See, wail, and will thy will I must, or must
>> From heaven's sweet shine to hell's hot flame be thrust.

This is the only occasion when he tries such a technique.
Rarely he turns to some form of refrain, as he does most
successfully in Meditation 40, where he seems to echo Her-

bert's "Was ever grief like mine?" in "The Sacrifice." But in Taylor's eleven stanzas the question is put only five times, and he varies its position in the stanza and in the line very effectively. Only one other time does he use a refrain-like device, which is structurally reminiscent of many of Wyatt's lyrics, but ideologically most like Donne's "A Hymne to God the Father" with its punning refrain on his own name:

> When thou hast done, thou hast not done,
> For, I have more.

In Meditation 95, stanzas five, six, and seven begin with "But that's not all"; and the seventh concludes the series with these last words:

> *But that's not all.* Leaving these doleful rooms
> Thou com'st and tak'st them by the hand, most high,
> Dost them translate out from their death bed tombs,
> To th'rooms prepar'd, fill'd with eternal joy.
> Them crown'st and thron'st there, there their lips be shall
> Pearld with eternal praises, *that's but all.*

But the refrain is not a major device in the poem. It is rather absorbed into the total structure, where it perhaps functions more subtly than Donne's, but not so effectively.

For variety within the total structure, Taylor preferred less obvious devices of rhyme, meter, and repetition. A list of Taylor's rhymes turns up some unexpected combinations, brought about by a variety of rhyming tricks. The surprise is that he rarely rhymes multisyllabic words; there are, therefore, few feminine rhymes and no double or triple rhymes. Limiting himself to stressed monosyllables, he turns frequently to forms of off or slant rhyme to increase the number of words from which he can choose. Often identical vowel sounds satisfy his ear, regardless of their accompanying consonants: *sweet/reech; keep/sweet; breathes/leaves; like/light.* Identical vowels plus *r* and different terminal consonants also satisfy him: *heart/spark; curb/spur'd.* And often the final *r* is enough alone to constitute a rhyme: *where/here; restore/cure; flower/pour. Clear* can therefore be rhymed with *ere, there,* and *were.* Occasionally the terminal consonant, especially a stopped consonant, makes the rhyme: *bread/had; broad/God; deckt/fret.*

He exercises greater license with nasals, terminal *g*, and terminal *s*. In the first place, he apparently makes no distinction between the terminal nasals themselves: *slime/chalybdine; in/him; resume/tune; grain/same.* When he combines the nasal with another consonant, he still seems to make no distinction, though what happens when that extra consonant is *g* is not clear; *shine/climb; strong/hung; rank/cramp.* It seems at times that Professor Warren's conclusion that "he did not sound terminal *g*"[8] is borne out—*bin/spring; thing/brim*—but it is doubtful that Taylor ignored the final *g* at other times, as in *tongue/throng; run/tongue; king/fling;* he seems, in fact, to sound it or not as the situation demands. This last combination exemplifies the freedom he gains through the terminal *s*, which, whether for plurality or possession, he adds freely to rhymes such as *should/folds; stand/hands; doors/o'er.* He also rhymes voiced and unvoiced *s—lies/sacrifice; pass/was; is/this*—and matches the unvoiced *s* freely with *sh* as in *afresh/deliciousness; this/dish.* Sometimes the voiced *s* alone is adequate for the rhyme as in *seas/rays. Th* and *f* are also frequent: *goeth/loaf; wealth/self.*

Other rhymes, slightly unusual, are commonplace in his verse: *confin'd/conjoyn'd; choice/price; would/cold; word/hoard; wave/have; convays/says; key/day;* the words *to* and *do* rhyme with *flow, below,* and *know.* Ordinarily Taylor drops the *-ed* ending on adjectives and past tenses, but sometimes he maintains them solely for the sake of rhyme as in these cases: *polishèd/head; lessenèd/fed.* In the case of multisyllabic words, this often wrenches the natural meter to allow the final stress to fall on the rhymed syllable: Taylor can thus rhyme *jar* with *scribener* once and again with *pottinger.* On the other hand, instead of lengthening words by that third syllable, he frequently cuts a two- or three-syllable word down or combines two words into one by elision: *in it* becomes *in't* to rhyme with *ink, o'er* for *over* rhymes with *doors;* and *drown us* becomes *drounds* to rhyme with *ground.* As outrageous and artificial as the devices are, one rarely feels that Taylor has turned to them in desperation. They seem rather a natural means for him to increase his rhyming vocabulary, and he often uses them so well that they are unobtrusively absorbed into the stanza. Unlike Emily Dickinson, whose slant and off rhymes are intended to catch, startle, and please the reader by their effects, Taylor's seem intended to disappear into the folds of the stanzaic pattern.

Taylor's extending and truncating words for the sake of rhyme inevitably results in some roughness and often an excellent compactness as these tricks impinge on the metrics of the verse: lines like

To th'rooms prepar'd, fill'd with eternal joy.
Them crown'st and thron'st there, there their lips be shall,

are impossibly bad; and the last part sounds like an echo of the worst of the *Bay Psalm Book*. Usually Taylor does better than this, and his roughness becomes part of his idiom rather than the accidental aftermath of an unsuccessful struggle to squeeze a thought into ten syllables. Since the roughness is characteristic, the means by which he secures it are easily analyzed.

In his elegy about Hooker, Taylor points out that under the force of emotion, a man does not speak easily, fluently, smoothly, but stutters, "Cutting off sentences by enterjections / Made by the force of hard beset affections" (11.3-4). In his sermons he exhorts his listeners to let their affections be moved, and in the poems he tries to utter his praise already beset by his own moved affections. Therefore, he cuts off his sentence and interjects exclamations, parenthetical phrases or clauses, and appositions. The result is a line broken into two, three, and sometimes even more parts. Meditation 1, as a case in point, ends with a stanza made up of half lines rather than whole ones:

Oh! that thy love might overflow my heart!
    To fire the same with love: for love I would.
But! oh! my streight'ned breast! my lifeless spark!
    My fireless flame! What! chilly love and cold?
In measure small! In manner chilly! See.
Lord, blow the coal: thy love enflame in me.

Not a single line reads smoothly, and four of them are broken by two pauses. In this instance, each line is also end-stopped, accentuating the brevity of the phrases. The three parallel phrases—"my streightn'd breast! my lifeless spark! my fireless flame!" also act appositively. The total result is choppy, curt.

In the stanza preceding the one quoted, the effect is much better, for Taylor does not stop his sense at the end of the line. The second line reads "O'er running it: all running o'er beside," and for the sense could end there, but it does not; it continues two monosyllables into the next line, where it ends with an exclamation. The effect is very similar to what Gerard Manley Hopkins achieves; for Taylor writes:

> O'er running it: all running o'er beside
> This world! Nay overflowing hell; wherein
> For thine elect, there rose a mighty tide!

The technique makes what would ordinarily be a rigid form quite flexible. By shifting the pauses or caesurae or by omitting them entirely, he can write abruptly or fairly smoothly, as he chooses. Characteristically, however, he chooses to be curt, and rarely runs more than two lines without some interruption. For intentional harshness he exaggerates the number of interruptions, mainly by running single words in series, as in Meditation 39, where he most successfully uses harshness to create a sense of dramatic struggle:

> My sin! My sin, my God, these cursed dregs.
> Green, yellow, blue-streakt poison, hellish, rank,
> Bubs hatcht in nature's nest on serpent's eggs,
> Yelp, cherp, and cry: they set my soul acramp.
> I frown, chide, strike, and fight them, mourn and cry
> To conquer them, but cannot them destroy.

The verse is as cramped as his soul, and it is undoubtedly meant to be so. The inversion of the last two words, also characteristic of his poetry, offers a problem: too often it is the necessary result of straining after rhymes, but many times it appears completely unprovoked. Taylor apparently felt inversion to be a legitimate mode of poetic expression.

Using the same devices as in Meditation 39, but beginning with two stressed monosyllables instead of the two iambs of "My sin! My sin," Taylor manages in Meditation 69 to slow the cadence from the opening words. Partly because of the diction, but primarily because of fewer interruptives, the roughness of this stanza is conversational rather than intensely dramatic, as in the former example:

> Dull! Dull! my Lord, as if I eaten had
> A peck of melancholy: or my soul
> Was lockt up by a poppy key, black, sad:
> Or had been fuddled with an henbane bowl.
> Oh, leaden temper! My rich thesis would
> Try metal to the back, sharp, it t'unfold.

It would be interesting to know at what point the inversion "eaten had" of the first line was adopted. Perhaps it is a revision of an initial syntax to fit the word "sad" of the third line, but the third line hardly seems important enough to have merited such a change.

By removing most of the interjections, he achieves rhythmic effects that sound most modern, as in these lines from Meditation 80:

> And if you say, What then is life? I say
> I cannot tell you what it is, yet know
> That various kinds of life lodge in my clay.
> (11.7-9)

The tone is mildly argumentative and without tangible imagery, bringing Taylor's love letters to the Lord under the same censure that befell Donne's legalistic love poems; Dryden accused Donne of perplexing "the minds of the fair sex with nice speculations of philosophy, when he should engage their hearts, and entertain them with the softness of love." But even when, as Taylor usually does, he concentrates on images, the brevity of phrase and the ruggedness of his verses keep him from attaining the mellifluence of—to choose extreme examples—a Milton or a Dylan Thomas. His poetry rarely sings.

Taylor often counteracts the asperity of his lines by manipulating images of sound within the line. Thus, though a line may be interrupted and almost broken into two half-lines, he maintains a connection between the two parts in the manner of Old English alliterative verse.

> Such *r*ugged looks, // and *r*agged *r*obes I wear
> (2.62)

. . . .

> The *c*louds to rend, // and *s*kies their *c*rystal door
> (2.92)

. . . .

> My *r*avisht hea*r*t / on *r*apture's wings would fly
> (2.93)

. . . .

> *Wi*ll ki*ll* the *w*orms / that *w*orm ho*l*e do my heart.
> (2.84)

Put together in consecutive lines, the alliterative sounds interlock to minimize the effect of the punctuation; in the following example, the *e, m,* and *p* sounds link four lines:

> What! shall a *m*ote up to a *m*onarch rise?
>   An *emm*et *m*atch an *emp*eror in *m*ight?
> If *p*rinces make their *p*ersonal exercise
>   Betri*mm*ing *m*ouse holes, *p*ainting with delight
> (2.95)

Often, I think, the alliterative effect is accidental; it is the simple result of repeating key words for which, in Taylor's theological reasoning, there could be no cognates or substitutes.

But intentional repetition of words for the sake of their sound is not only characteristic of his verse but is also one of the rhetorical devices Taylor would have learned at school. Technically, he favors two figures: *ploce* and *polyptoton.* Ploce is repetition of the same word in different contexts or functioning as different parts of speech; polyptoton is the repretition of the core or base of a word modified by various affixes. Words like *love, life, Lord,* and *grace* are most successfully treated this way, as with the word *glory* in the following passage, where it occurs thirteen times in nine lines:

> The greatest *glory glory* doth enjoy,
>   Lies in her hanging upon thee, wherein
> *Glory* that *glorifies* thee mightily
>   Is far more *glorified*. Hence *glories* spring.
> Now grace's *glory*, heaven's *glory*, and
>   *Glories* of saints and angels gild thy hand.
>
> A *glorious* palace, a bright crown of *glory*,
>   A *glorious* train of saints and angels' shine
> And *glorious* exercise as sweetest posy.
>
> (2.73)

And the fine ecstatic passage of Meditation 12 slips from one meaning and form of the word *love* without appearing to "torture one poor word ten thousand ways":

> My *lovely* one, I fain would *love* thee much
>   But all my *love* is none at all I see,
> Oh! let thy beauty give a glorious touch
>   Upon my heart, and melt to *love* all me,
>   Lord melt me all up into *love* for thee,
>   Whose *loveliness* excells what *love* can be.

Here the one word links three stanzas together and demonstrates the possibilities of ploce and polyptoton in connection with the favorite seventeenth-century witty exercises in paradox and oxymoron, the use of incongruous words. Thus the entire "Preface" to *God's Determinations* turns primarily on the repetition of the words *all* and *nothing*.[9]

In these "doublers," as Puttenham describes the ploce, or in his frequent "Grieve, grieve, my soul," "My sin! My sin!" or "Dull! Dull!" which Puttenham finds "not commendable,"[10] and in his exclamatory "Oh!" and parenthetical "Lord," Taylor uses repetitive means to a varied end; for all serve to vary the cadence and arrest attention at often unexpected intervals. As a result—and in combination with appositive phrases, subordinate clauses, and suspended grammatical connection—Taylor makes difficult reading. But the compactness produced

by these short phrases makes Taylor's line packed or strong.
Yet never, as with many exponents of the strong line, does he
fall into the Senecan fallacy of seeming to say more than he
actually does simply because the line is difficult to read. The
obscurity of many seventeenth-century poets is often equat-
able with their unexpected abruptness, but I think Taylor
never intended obscurity. Allowing for his grammatical license, his unusual punctuation, and his inversions, the sentence structure in Taylor's poetry is simpler than that in his
sermons, primarily because he rarely runs a sentence longer
than four lines.

What surprises modern readers of Taylor are not these tricks
of sound, but the *inharmonious harmony* of his images. Not
merely because of the actual or imagined distance between
elements yoked together fiercely by metaphor, but because
one of these elements is divine, modern readers react to the
quaintness of Taylor's *inappropriately* homely comparisons
much as did Samuel Johnson, who decried "that familiarity
with religious images, and that light allusion to sacred things,
by which readers far short of sanctity are frequently offended;
and which would not be borne in the present age, when, devotion, perhaps not more fervent, is more delicate." Using
the same figure Taylor does, Johnson describes the principles
of decorum:

> language is the dress of thought: and as the noblest mien
> or most graceful action would be degraded and obscured by
> a garb appropriated to the gross employments of rustics or
> mechanics, so the most heroic sentiments will lose their
> efficacy, and the most splendid ideas drop their magnifi-
> cence, if they are conveyed by words used commonly upon
> low and trivial occasions, debased by vulgar mouths and
> contaminated by inelegant applications.[11]

Taylor knew the principle, since his copy of John Weemes's
The Christian Synagogue clearly advises against drawing comparisons from "things altogether different" or "unfit," and also
points out specifically:

> If thou wouldst praise a thing, take the Comparison from
> stately things, as in the Canticles.
> If thou wouldst dispraise, take your comparison from
> base things.[12]

But another theory seems to have predominated in the English meditative tradition. George Herbert calls attention to the Bible's sanction of "base things," since the Holy Ghost there "condescends to the naming of a plough, a hatchet, a bushell, leaven, boyes piping and dancing; shewing that things of ordinary use are not only to serve in the way of drudgery, but to be washed, and cleansed, and serve for lights even of Heavenly Truths."[13] Bishop Hall turns the fact to precept by commenting that what "we are wont to say of fine wits, we may as truly affirm of the Christian heart, that it can make use of any thing."[14] And Richard Baxter urges even more strongly that "we might have a fuller tast of Christ and Heaven, in every bit of bread that we eat, and in every draught of Beer that we drink, then most men have in the use of the sacrament."[15] Surprisingly, Baxter anticipates Taylor's excited identification of the sacramental wine: "It's beer! No nectar like it," a beer "Wrought in the Spirit's brew house." And so, regarding the most elevated of subjects, Taylor's poems abound in cockle-shells, tobacco and tinder boxes, leather coats, trenchers, bowling balls, tents, needles, yarn and spinning wheels, canoes, bullets, and lobster claws.

Strangely, Taylor's use of the entire realm of nature never results in any fresh look at nature itself; and he is, therefore, less a poet of nature than Bradstreet. Furthermore, there is a tendency among mystical writers to make nature sacramental; to find a sacredness in natural objects because of God's imprint there; and to fall, in fact, into pantheism; and the absence of this characteristic in Taylor is rather surprising. "Every little ice-cycle is the workmanship of God," says Cotton Mather, wonderingly; Jonathan Edwards describes the new joy in nature after his conversion as ecstatically, if not as well, as Wordsworth; and John Woolman's descriptions reveal a sympathy for natural things unmatched to that time in American writing. But in spite of Taylor's stated preference for natural over artificial things, the nature of his *Meditations* exists as if it were in an allegorical tapestry. Its objects are purely symbolic, isolated from all natural environment, and interesting primarily as an illustration of some moral.[16]

Only once, in fact, does Taylor describe a natural phe-

nomenon as if he wished to capture its nature rather than
to apply it to some other use:

> This pale-fac'd moon that silver snowball like,
> > That walks in'ts silver glory, paints the skies,
> The tester of the bed, where day and night,
> > Each creature cover'd o'er with glory lies,
> > She with her silver rays envarnish doth
> > In silver paint, the skies as out she go'th.
> > > (2.99)

The description's porcelain brittleness might have appeared
in an Elizabethan sonnet; but, where Sidney's moon mounts
with sad steps, Taylor's merely walks, paints, and varnishes
the skies with silver. The actions become human actions without the moon's being personified. And in the next stanza
the moon's prettiness fades in the glory of the Sun of Righteousness, whose beams are "her tapestry / Which gilds the
heavens o'er, hung out on high."

Taylor's descriptions of the sky contain this same quality:
it is a bowling alley, golden battlements, the "paintice" of a
tent, "Heav'ns whelm'd-down crystal meal bowl," heaven's
curtains, a lantern holding a candle, a crystal roof, the earth's
canopy, or some other very tangible stage backdrop for divine
actions. Always the metaphor is either scriptural or in terms
of household objects: curtains, lanterns, roofs, bowls. The
effect of this is, on one hand, to elevate and dignify "base"
objects; on the other, to steal magnificence and sublimity
from the subject.

Although Taylor ranges widely for details, five general
classes of images recur with notable frequency. The first
class—writing images, including remarks on rhetoric, metaphor, and duty—we have already discussed.[17] Although such
images commonly open *Meditations*—just as the gamut of
musical instruments closes them—they often function as
central images around which Taylor structures the argument
of a whole poem. The second group of images is of warfare;
and most often Taylor employs the assault of the fort of life—
as in a Spenserian allegory—replete with soldiers, scouts, gen-
erals, bombardments, mortars, bullets. The attack may be

engineered by Satan or by Christ, Taylor may picture himself enlisted under Christ's standard, or the shepherd's crook may become a mace. These images of combat are closely related to the third class: those of metallurgy, mining, trying ore or distilling, and minting. These all suggest purification, testing, or trying for purity; the removal of impurities; or the alchemical transformation from one state to another. Alembics and try-pots, anvils, the face of Christ printed on the pure gold of the poet's coin, the conversion of lead to gold—all these belong under this category; and they identify Taylor with the Hermetic—or magical—sources of mystical imagery.[18] The monetary image leads naturally to images of treasures and purses, betting, and commerce; and the commercial imagery prepares the ground for the legal action and the advocates and the judges which are common in seventeenth-century lyrics. The categories tend, therefore, to extend themselves beyond neat limits.

But two classes of images predominate—gardens and feasts. Gardens flourish throughout mystical literature,[19] for they are an imaginative extension of the Garden of Eden. Taylor's garden images vary widely—formal knots, individual flowers, herbs, seeds, slips and cuttings, grafts, vines and trees, blossoms and fruits. And any of these may suggest new lines of imagery. Herbs, for example, being medicinal, often lead Taylor quickly from the garden to the apothecary's shop. His gardens almost always suggest the one of John's Revelations, but it is curiously removed to New England, where grains as well as flowers abound. The saints are the choice grain compared to which Taylor often feels himself to be the bran, chaff, husk, or shell. Related to the grain image is a series of images about the processes of grinding, kneading, and baking that turn the grain into the bread of life to be served at the Lord's Supper; or those about the pressing, distilling, and brewing procedures that convert the garden's grapes to sacramental brew. In this way the garden imagery moves naturally to the second major class, the images of the feast.

The surprising extent and the nature of Taylor's feast imagery are among the most striking features of the *Meditations*. The wedding feast celebrating the union of man and God was, as we have noted abundantly, the nexus of Taylor's

faith. Since it was also the occasion and the reason for the
Meditations themselves, it seems not unusual that images of
eating and drinking should occur plenteously. But again
Taylor's trick of converting the spiritual proceedings to domestic naturalism has a startling effect:

> Here is a feast indeed! in ev'ry dish
>   A whole redeemer, cooked up bravely, good,
> Is served up in holy sauce that is
>   A mess of delicates made of his blood.
>   Adorn'd with grace's sippits: rich sweet-meats.
>   Comfort and comforts sweeten whom them eats.
>   (2.108)

Grace personified does the honors: carves, rolls the meat
in the sauce, and fattens the souls of the partakers. Taylor
takes extreme advantage of cannibalistic ritual: "What!" he
exclaims, "feed on human flesh and blood? Strange mess!"
Nature calls this custom barbarous, and scripture finds
it inadmissable; therefore, it must be interpreted symbolically,
metaphorically. But once the symbol is introduced, he takes
complete license with the metaphor: Christ's body is heaven's
sugar cake, sweet junkets, Zion's pastry, griddle-cakes baked
in God's bake-house, roast meat or plum cake. Christ's blood
is wine, beer, nectar, or the drippings from the roast, into
which the saints dip holy biscuits.

As shocking and tasteless as this image appears to modern
readers, it is really almost commonplace in Renaissance and
earlier devotional writing. In it—and for that matter in St.
Augustine—appear the grinding of divine flour, the baking
of bread for Communion, and the wine-press as a symbol
of the breaking and converting of Christ's body. The following
passage from Taylor is, therefore, really less quaint in writing
of its kind than it appears to us. He is considering Christ
as the True Vine:

> Her grapes when pounded and presst hard (hard fare)
>   Bleed out both blood and spirit, leaving none,
>   Which too much took, the brain doth too much toll,
>   Tho't smacks the palate, merry makes the soul.
>   (2.98)

In this quotation it is not the wine-press figure that is unusual with Taylor; it is the gustatory smacking and the titillation of the soul.

Like the images of the banquet, bread, and the wine press, all of Taylor's symbols are conventional in devotional literature. Only his strange eye for peculiar details, his going one step beyond the convention, and his domesticating his symbols with kitchen details give his symbolism a quaint, sometimes grotesque, individual quality. But even Taylor's manner of treating his imagery indicates the specific source from which it was drawn. For, from the time of the publication of Geoffrey Whitney's *A Choice of Emblemes* (1586), the emblem as a formal, semi-literary device became influential in English literature. Emblem books proper consisted of collections of engravings or woodcuts of moral symbols; and attached to each picture was a motto or *sententia* explicating the drawn symbol. Each picture was also accompanied by a short poem or prose passage interpreting and moralizing from the picture and its motto.[20] The symbols pictured were largely medieval— a skeleton or skull or headstone representing death, an anchor for hope, a wheel for occasion or fortune—and they appeared either singly or related to other symbols. The more complex the relationship of symbols, the more necessary became the accompanying prose or poetry. Likewise, the poem so required the picture that it was often unintelligible without it.

By the time of Taylor's youth the emblem books had been fully exploited in the interests of religious devotion. Francis Quarles and George Wither, both highly respected among New Englanders and generally among middle-class Puritan groups, published books of this kind. Quarles's *Emblemes* (1635) and *Hieroglyphikes of the Life of Man* (1638), which were extremely popular, offer some close resemblances to Taylor's later practice. For, while Quarles changes his form and even his manner from narrative to dialogue to personal lyric, the basis of most of his poems is—like Taylor's—the soul aspiring to heaven; or, more particularly, the soul is personified as Anima seeking and being sought by Divine Love.

The pictures accompanying Quarles's poems make it most obvious that an earlier emblem subject, the adventures of Cupid, has been transmogrified to religious ends. Rosemary

Freeman describes the change most clearly: "By a simple transference the whole idiom was absorbed into a devotional framework: Cupid became the infant Jesus or Divine Love seeking the human soul, personified in Anima, a young maiden."[21] These are the major figures of Quarles's pictures, and around them are associated the symbolic devices—anchors, skeletons, lilies, roses, arrows piercing hearts, and so on. Consequently, Quarles often assumes—as in the following—the female rôle in the poems, very much as Taylor does:

> Nor Time, nor Place, nor Chance, nor Death can bow
> My least desires unto the least remove;
> He's firmly mine by oath; I his by vow;
> He's mine by faith; and I am his by love;
> He's mine by water; I am his by wine;
> Thus I my best-beloved's am; thus he is mine.[22]

But what Quarles gains in smoothness he lacks in fervor and intensity; he never attains the ardent personal feelings Taylor infuses into his best *Meditations.*

In another way, however, the emblems of Quarles are most important. They are based on two of the many such books sponsored by Jesuits,[23] who were not only ultimately responsible for Taylor's meditative method but for distributing emblem books designed primarily to assist exercitants in that method.[24] In these books appear the hearts, gardens, alembics, lilies, roses, candles, lanterns, sweeping of rooms, weapons, trees, and Old Testament "types" which Taylor employs and which served as a body of conventional images from which the emblem writer worked. Protestants, turning these Catholic devices to their own use, retained the pictures from Catholic books that were not too inimical to their own theology and then wrote new accompanying poems.

In this way the habit of emblematic thought became significantly widespread among English religious poets. Donne's famed compass image derives from the emblem books. George Herbert's manner of treating physical objects such as the church floor, the windows, the pulleys—which was so congenial to Crashaw, Vaughan, and Traherne—is also the fashion of the emblematists; and it is, therefore, less surprising that

Taylor often reminds readers of these poets. But emblems were not only a part of the study of rhetoric; they were also a prominent feature of the decorative arts generally in the England of Taylor's youth. Jewelry, domestic decorations, architectural ornaments, and, most significantly for Taylor, needlework and tapestry—all habitually used emblems as subjects or motifs.[25] Taylor could not have escaped these symbols.

In two ways the emblem manner influenced Taylor's poetry: one is the analytical approach to the allegorical symbols; the other, visualization. Quarles, for example, presents an engraving depicting a shipwreck. Only the stern and one mast of a vessel remain above water, poised for their final plunge; and, in the background, a vicious dart of lightning snakes its way into a stormy sea. In the foreground a smiling survivor swims toward a rocky haven where a winged and radiant figure leans forward to save the swimmer. In spite of the storm and darkness, the smile on the face of the survivor and the imminence of salvation turn the mood from violent desperation to calm assurance.[26] The accompanying poem, based on a text from Psalms 69:15, "Let not the water-flood overflow me, neither let the deeps swallow me up," actually supplies many physical details not evident in the engraving itself and it traces a point-by-point meaning of the symbolism:

> The world's a Sea; my flesh a ship that's mann'd
> With lab'ring Thoughts, and steer'd by Reason's hand:
> My Heart's the Sea-man's Card, whereby she sails;
> My loose Affections are the greater Sails:
> The Top-sail is my Fancie, and the Gusts
> That fill these wanton sheets are worldly Lusts.
> Pray'r is the Cable, at whose end appears
> The Anchor Hope, nev'r slipt but in our fears:
> My Will's th'unconstant Pilot, that commands
> The stagg'ring Keel; my sinnes are like the Sands:
> Repentance is the Bucket, and mine Eye
> The Pump, unus'd (but in extremes) and dry.[27]

Quarles continues to identify the details for several lines; then, repeating the catalogue, he indicates that each of the details—cable, anchor, pilot—is somehow faulty; and finally, going through the list a third time, he petitions the Lord to correct each where it fails:

> Make strong my Cable; bind my Anchor faster;
> Direct my Pilot, and be thou his Master;
> Object the Sands to my more serious view,
> Make sound my Bucket, bore my Pump anew:
> (Ibid., ll. 33-36)

Especially in this last section of the poem, but even its earlier two, we find the technique of extending a conceit by an analytic comparison of its parts; and this is precisely what we also find in a number of Taylor's *Preparatory Meditations*[28] and in "Huswifery" in particular:

> Make me, O Lord, thy spinning wheel complete.
> Thy Holy Word my distaff make for me.
> Make mine affections thy swift flyers neat
> And make my soul thy holy spool to be.
> My conversation make to be thy reel
> And reel the yarn thereon spun of thy wheel.

But the point-by-point anatomy of a central image is not so common in Taylor's poetry as "Huswifery" suggests. Taylor's concern is with anatomizing ideas rather than images; and the abrupt shift from one image to another quite disparate one is more characteristic of his verse. But the emblematic quality of visualization marks the poems even when this other method is dropped. He seems to imagine not only particulars clearly but also the peculiar allegorical relation they fell into so naturally in emblem drawings. This characteristic obviates the difficulty Professor Warren finds in such lines as the following where the Rose apparently "at once invites and repels visualization."[29]

> Shall heaven and earth's bright glory all up lie
> Like sunbeams bundles in the sun in thee?
> Dost thou sit Rose at table head, where I
> Do sit, and carv'st no morsel sweet for me?

The idea of the Rose of Sharon carving at table repels visualization only if conceived naturalistically; it is unnatural and illogical at first appearance. Seen, however, as an emblematist would see it, the rose at the head of a feast-laden table, surrounded by carving utensils, and radiating lines like sunbeams from the sun, is most plausible symbolically. And it is in this way that Taylor's *Meditations* are emblematic: they depend upon an imaginary drawing which is perfectly clear in Taylor's imagination; but, because understanding his images involves a mode of thought unfamiliar to modern readers, they are difficult for us to picture.[30] His most conventional emblems—the paintings of death which he describes in Meditations 1.34 and 2.112 as complete with skeleton, hourglass, and spade—offer no such difficulty because of their perpetual appropriateness.

Taylor transcends the emblem tradition at the same time that he uses it to full advantage in *Meditations;* and he achieves this transcendence not only by his individual visualization of highly traditional allegorical symbols, but also by his joining the visual with other senses. I know of no other poet who so fully resorts to other than visual imagery, for Taylor runs the full range. His feast not only looks like bread and wine or roast and sauce, but smells and tastes like it. Tactile sensations of snarled and ragged cloth and of a host of irritants—chaffing, grinding, pricking—contribute to his poetic texture. Incense, flowers, and pillars of perfumes reek heavily through the *Meditations*—and far more prominently than in other poets. Crashaw's fluid images of milk, blood, and tears are almost matched by Taylor. Birds, saints, angels, and a symphony of musical instruments swell his verse with twangs and tweedles, hymns, carols, and songs of praise, as his tabor stick drums at the company of ears. And kinesthetic sensations of wallowing, submersion, elevation, careening through the air, soaring, and even bouncing like a tennis ball round out Taylor's sensory world. The fullness of this feature of Taylor's verse is, however, less obvious in single poems; but a sustained reading of the *Meditations* makes it fully apparent.

The world of the *Meditations* storms constantly with an impressive variety of shapes, colors, odors, and feelings.

The effect is rich and ornate; but, like stained glass or medieval illuminations, it is strangely two-dimensional. Foreground and background are treated with equal attention, given equal scope. The perspective is unnatural, for earth and heaven impinge one upon another with a boldness at once medieval and cubistic or surrealistic. The *Meditations* become a tapestry-like setting, antique and modern at the same time, which makes a most suitable backdrop for the miracle play enacted before it.

II *God's Determinations*

In Taylor's one extended attempt to imbue this poetic world with life, he quite naturally drew from his meditative experience to present the drama of grace through characters derived from his entire devotional and literary experience. *God's Determinations Touching his Elect: and the Elect's Combat in their Conversion and Coming up to God in Christ, together with the Comfortable Effects thereof* has been dismissed as "a labor of versified doctrine,"[31] but it has also been applauded for its lyric demonstrations that elevate the piece "far beyond anything achieved by Americans until long after Taylor's day."[32] Probably both judgments are valid, for the work may be approached and appraised three or four distinct ways—a multiplicity which accounts for both its excellences and its defects.

God's Determinations may be profitably examined in these four ways: as a collection of separate but related lyrics, like the sonnets in a loosely conceived cycle; as a versified theological disquisition or sermon; as a morality play of the sort Taylor might have observed as a youth in Leicestershire; or even as a fully developed literary meditation of the Ignatian kind, an expanded version of Taylor's *Preparatory Meditations*. But much of the interest of *God's Determinations* arises from the fact that it is all these four literary kinds at the same time. There is, consequently, a diffusion of focus about the work that produces exciting effects; at the same time, however, this characteristic makes it impossible to consider seriously the work as any one of these genres.

Thomas Johnson speculates that *God's Determinations* was

composed around 1685, because of its position in the manuscript and because of the quality of the lyrics themselves.[33] Certainly the thirty-five poems illustrate all that Taylor accomplished in his other verse. The iambic pentameter couplets of the elegies appear in them with considerably more vividness and excitement than elsewhere, and they are varied occasionally by division into *aabb* quatrains as a vehicle for dialogue. The couplets are offset by six-line stanzaic verse rhymed *ababcc*, as in the *Meditations;* but these stanzas are sometimes altered metrically.[34] In all, Taylor makes use of eleven different verse forms; and he plays with unifying devices of refrain, incremental repetition, and rhyme to pull poems, or parts of poems, closely together.

"A Dialogue between Justice and Mercy," which is near the beginning of the work, is an exchange of stanzas between the two speakers which illustrates Taylor's use of repetition and interlocking to give continuity to the poem. Stanza IV, spoken by Justice, begins: "My essence is ingag'd, I cannot 'bate, / Justice not done no justice is." Mercy matches Justice in the next stanza: "My essence is engag'd pity to show. / Mercy not done no mercy is"; but Mercy counters Justice from there on. Stanza IX ends with Justice's challenge to Mercy:

> Then stand away, and let me strike at first:
> For better now, than when he's at the worst.

Mercy, who ends the next stanza with the same words, turns them against Justice:

> Then stand away, and strike not at the first.
> He'll better grow when he is at the worst.

The next two stanzas are linked the same way, but with different couplets:

JUSTICE
Nay, this ten thousand times as much can still
    Confer no honey to the sinner's hive.
For man, though shrived thoroughly from all ill,
    His righteousness is merely negative.

> Though none be damned but such as sin imbrace:
> Yet none are saved without Inherent Grace.
> MERCY
> What though ten thousand times too little be?
> I will ten thousand times more do.
> I will not only from his sin him free,
> But fill him with Inherent Grace also.
> Though none are saved that wickedness imbrace,
> Yet none are damned that have Inherent Grace.

Stanzas XIII and XIV are similarly linked, but by the first two verses only. The interlocking is made rigid here by also picking up the fifth verse of stanza XIII—"Then though he's spared at first, at last he'll fall"—and echoing it as the last line of stanza XIV—"Spare him at first, then he'll not fall at last." But these devices are never related one to another; they unify only parts of the dialogue, but not all, or even a major part of it. In this way the dialogue demonstrates, moreover, the erratic structure and inconsistencies of the entire work.

An incremental refrain begins the first of the concluding six lyrics, but it peters out in the last three stanzas. Like Meditation 95, the poem titled "The Glory of and Grace in the Church Set Out" ends the first four stanzas with the Donne-like refrain, "Yet that's not all," and it clinches the series in the final stanza with "And that's but all." In this poem Taylor sustains the refrain much more neatly throughout; and he also most successfully uses a two-verse incremental refrain to weave the final poem of *God's Determinations* together. But these stylistic reminders of the *Meditations* are insignificant in *God's Determinations* as a whole; for in the latter the individuality of the separate poems remains a far more distinct feature of a work which is primarily lyric in structure rather than narrative or dramatic. It is almost as if Taylor anticipated the romantic theories of Coleridge and Poe that there can be no such thing as a long poem—or that even the *Iliad* is "a series of lyrics."

One excuse for these breaks in the continuity of the whole is that the verse variations represent a change either in mode or in speaker. Couplets are his normal vehicle for exposition or narrative, and he interlards his dialogues with them quite unconventionally. Satan speaks couplets, as do the harassed souls who address him; and so does the Saint but, as his arguments grow more convincing, he speaks in the meditation-stanza form. Christ, who speaks only twice, uses two varieties of a stanza rhymed *aabccb*. And finally, as the three ranks of elect souls accept their fellowship in Christ, they utter six songs; each one is structurally different, and the last— "The Joy of Church Fellowship Rightly Attended"—returns to the same familiar six-line form that begins the entire work —"The Preface." But the neatness of this principle, which Miss Wright suggests Taylor grasped from the morality plays without actually adopting their practice,[35] is offset by the formality of the speeches; for it offers very little chance for dramatic exchange. The greatest energy comes, in fact, from the narrative passages.

Yet the development through speeches calls for dramatic analysis. Miss Wright finds a four-part plot: a prologue; man's fall (poems 2-6); the dialogue on salvation (poems 7-29); and a choral epilogue (the last six poems).[36] But viewed another way, *God's Determinations* assumes the general structure of a five-act drama. Act I sets man's predicament; it traces the Creation and the Fall and then digresses to enact the covenant of redemption in the "Dialogue between Justice and Mercy." In a sense this dialogue interrupts the action of the play like a flashback, since it expresses God's eternal will, which existed prior to the action of the Creation in *God's Determinations*.[37] But Taylor violates the theological reality to achieve dramatic continuity. In the two scenes that follow, man—unable to answer for his faults—is banished from God's favor; divided into two groups, one is invited to climb into a royal coach (at once Christ and his mystical body, the church) to be carried to a glorious banquet (the Lord's Supper); the other, the rejected, sculls to eternal woe in one line. The act ends as Justice, Mercy, and Grace put into action their plan to redeem man.

Man is a peculiar problem dramatically. In the beginning, he is one person, obviously Adam; and he remains so until Taylor's description of "The Frowardness of the Elect in the Work of Conversion," where he fractures into four kinds of men: (1) the Saints who surrender at once to Grace, and

enter the coach; (2) the elect souls—the first rank—who resist
at first but yield when pressed by God's Mercy; (3) elect
souls—the second rank—who are persuaded only by the as-
saults of God's Justice; and (4) the elect souls—the third rank—
who capitulate only to the combined forces of Mercy and
Justice. Because each of these four is part of "man" at the
beginning, the problem is to maintain identity and relationship at the same time. All four give in, as they must; for God's
grace is irresistible. The first act may be said, therefore, to
end with the conclusion of this conflict.

Act II introduces a new antagonist and a new conflict, for
Satan roars out to undo the work of conversion. In the first
scene—from "Satan's Rage at them in their Conversion" to "The
Effect of this Reply"—four poems trace Satan's violent accusation that all three reluctant saints are traitors, cowards, and
feeblehearted; then all three ranks, joined together in the
speaker "Soul," question Christ; Christ's stirring assurance
follows; and the effect of Christ's reply is delineated—it cheers
the souls saved by Mercy (the first rank) but leaves the
other two drooping. Satan turns his attack rather subtly not
against these weaker ranks but against the first; in Scene 2,
he accuses the inward temptations, the outward sinfulness,
and even the selfish motives behind the first rank's worship
of God. The badgered Soul (now limited to the first rank)
withstands Satan firmly, but he petitions Christ in Scene 3—
"The Soul's Groan to Christ for Succour"—to rid him of the
tempter. Christ replies soothingly; and the scene ends with
the Soul's ecstatic expression of joy—with what is really a
series of contrasts between what the soul can do and what
to Christ is due:

> Had I ten thousand times ten thousand hearts:
> And every heart ten thousand tongues
> To praise, I should but stutt odd parts
> Of what to thee belongs.

A second conflict concluded, the second act also ends.

In Act III Satan abruptly accuses the second and third
ranks since his plan to weaken them further by troubling
the first rank has been spoiled. He argues entirely from the

point of their failings and the justice of their destruction. After a lengthy threnody, they reject Satan's temptation to justify themselves, and they throw themselves into the sea of God's Mercy. This tactic sustains them temporarily; and they decide, at the end of Act III, to search Mercy's golden stacks of remedies, "and of the pious wise some council take."

In Act IV the Saints who entered the royal coach immediately upon Grace's urging return to the center of the action. The act begins as the Soul (still representing the combined second and third ranks) confesses its spiritual disturbance because of the doubts Satan has suggested about its worthiness of receiving God's favor from the hand of either Justice or Mercy. The Saint confutes all of Satan's arguments and describes his devious and sophistical tricks; and he then calls attention to the difficulties that arise from the ill behavior of Christians. As the Saint lapses into the verse form of the *Meditations,* the second and third ranks are moved to rapturous resolutions:

> Oh! let us then sing praise! methinks I soar
> Above the stars, and stand at heaven's door.

But this is not the end of the act, for in the next poem the two ranks join voices in singing "Our Insufficiency to Praise God Suitably for His Mercy." We must remember that this is precisely the effect conversion has upon the first rank of reluctant saints at the end of Act II, for the response of Act IV exactly parallels the earlier one:

> Nay, had each song as many tunes most sweet,
>   Or one intwisting in't as many,
>   As all these tongues have songs most meet
>   Unparalleled by any?
> Each tongue would tune a world of praise, we guess,
> Whose songs in number would be numberless.

> Now should all these conspire in us that we
>   Could breathe such praise to thee, most high?
>   Should we thy sounding organs be
>   To ring such melody?

Our music would the world of worlds outring,
Yet be unfit within thine ears to sing.

(ll. 25-36)

This poem functions as both the conclusion to Act IV and the opening movement of the choral epilogue—as Wright terms it—that is Act V. In the poem which follows—"The Soul Seeking Church-Fellowship"—Taylor shifts back to the narrative point of view of the first act. The Soul, who is the subject of this poem, is once again representative of all four kinds of elect souls, who now shyly accept their selection among the favored of God. As in the *Meditations*, the object of their desire—fellowship with saints and angels in the church—shifts unexpectedly from a garden to a city before the original image of the royal coach reappears; the soul first timorously and then joyously enters it, and it sings Christ's praises as it soars up to its banquet of love in heaven.

But a dramatic analysis—satisfying and informative though it may be—belies the basic fact that *God's Determinations* is not a play. It could not conceivably be acted: narrative and dialogue are jumbled together; Taylor depends too much upon the titles of the individual poems; the central character "man" assumes a constantly shifting rôle; and the speeches are tediously long. All the dramatic elements necessary for a play are present, but Taylor did not take advantage of them. Had his intention been to write a play, his neglect of dramatic techniques would legitimately leave him open for criticism, but this was almost certainly not his intention. The key to a much more accurate analysis of *God's Determinations* lies in the last six poems of the work.

If we view these last six poems as a single unit, we discover that they describe the general threefold pattern of the individual *Preparatory Meditations*: (1) statement or question, (2) development, and (3) final petition or praise. It is as if each of these poems were a single stanza in a long *Meditation*. As in so many of the *Meditations*, this one begins by asserting the soul's "Insufficiency to Praise God Suitably for His Mercy." The souls are described as mould and nettles, anticipating the garden imagery of the first poem of the development section, "The Soul Seeking Church-Fellowship." Also, as in the de-

velopment section of the *Meditations*, the central image shifts;
from the garden of "The Soul Seeking Church-Fellowship"
it becomes the glorious city of "The Soul Admiring the Grace
of the Church"; and it then goes back to the garden knot of
"The Glory of and Grace in the Church Set Out." Though the
image shifts, the argument is single: the soul, torn between
its fear of unworthiness and its desire for marriage with Christ,
uncertainly enters the "coach of God's decree" and so supplants fear with joy. This conflict between uncertainty and
longing is the emotional basis of most of the *Meditations*.

Even after the soul of *God's Determinations* enters the
church, her misgivings about her own weaknesses ("The Soul's
Admiration Hereupon") continue to plague her. As Taylor
does in the *Meditations*, the soul here continues her self-
deprecation in terms of an unskilled musician or an untuned
musical instrument. "The Soul's Admiration Hereupon" and
the final "Joy of Church Fellowship Rightly Attended" function like the last stanza of a *Meditation*, but in these poems
the hypothetical element is removed. In the *Meditations*, the
soul promises to sing God's praises *if* he helps her; the final
poem of *God's Determinations* describes both God's help and
God's praises as accomplished facts. The souls are "encoacht
for heaven," wheeling there melodiously; and, in their mystical union with the body of Christ, they have fully attained
the unitive life:

> In all their acts, public and private, nay,
> And secret, too, they praise impart.
> But in their acts divine and worship, they
> With hymns do offer up their heart.
> (ll. 19-22)

These last six poems, then, make up a statement of moved
affections, a response to the convincing truth of the arguments
presented by the Saint in Act IV and implicit in the total
action of *God's Determinations*, which is a drama of conflict
within the soul. As a unit these last six poems relate to the
rest of the work just as Taylor's individual *Meditations* do
to their preceding sermons. *God's Determinations* is thus
most usefully viewed as a formal Ignatian meditation: the

opening act corresponds to Loyola's historical prelude and composition of place, vividly imagined, particularly described; the debates with Satan and the advice of the Saint are Loyola's "points of consideration" and Baxter's "Discourse of Minde"; and the final poems are the colloquy or response of moved affections.[38]

The advantage of this view of *God's Determinations* is that it minimizes the dramatic demands of the work as a whole; justifies to some extent the theological argumentation; and relates the work, in spirit as in form, with the primary effort of Taylor's life and writing. If *God's Determinations* is viewed as a formal meditation rather than as a play—even a morality play—there need be no surprise that it does not take full advantage of its dramatic form. Conversely, the dramatic images give a vivacity to the meditation that otherwise it would lack, which is why several Renaissance devotional books turn to dialogue. Meditation also permits the arrangement of theological considerations very similar to that of Taylor's sermons. When the Saint turns to advise troubled souls in Act IV, he really comes to apply the doctrine of grace as in the application of the sermon, commending them to watch themselves, fear not, and be forward in the service of God.

But most significantly, *God's Determinations* is really—no matter how its structure is viewed—an extended literary effort; it is neither spontaneous nor duty-motivated, as were the *Meditations*. Their pull, however, was irresistible to Taylor; and, as I have shown, they are reflected in both the ideas, versification and the movement of *God's Determinations* as a whole. Identical images and wording, similar methods of development, and parallel structures all reflect the dependence of *God's Determinations* upon the *Meditations*. In the last work we also find Taylor's progress of the soul from its crippled, lapsed estate to the heavenly banquet; the necessity of allegorical reading; the self-deprecation and continual fear of hypocrisy; the anatomy of the soul in self-examination; the insistence upon purity before admission to the church; the mystical marriage; and even the anti-Stoddardean arguments about the assurance with which the Lord's Supper should be approached. And since the supper itself is never described but anticipated, *God's Determinations,* like Taylor's *Meditations,* is "preparatory." At the same time, the poem is the culmination of all Taylor wrote; and in this sense it may well be considered a core or summary—as an entirely representative work.

But as *God's Determinations* epitomizes Taylor's concerns and techniques, it also represents his general weaknesses as a writer. For *God's Determinations,* regarded as a sustained literary effort, even as a meditation, may be judged a success only if that judgment is buttressed with many qualifications. Taylor's favorite devices are admirably suited to the short lyric, but they occur at too distant intervals in the 2,107 verses of *God's Determinations* to effect the results achieved in the *Meditations.* Imaginative and didactic purposes cross too frequently, and tempt Taylor into unpardonable preachiness. The simultaneous pull in several directions—narrative, dramatic, lyric, and hortatory—and the division of the work into short poems make the poem angular and stuttering. The weaknesses of versification—excusable in the *Meditations* where personal piety rather than poetry is the main end but in which they coalesce frequently enough to succeed beautifully—are beyond excuse in a work motivated directly by literary aims. Taylor, like many modern poets, simply never acquired the staying power to sustain a work of any length.

Peculiarly, this inability to write a good long poem acts in two ways: first, it rules Taylor out of that class including Spenser and Milton, the sheer length of whose works permitted them to achieve a sublimity never within Taylor's reach; secondly, it ranks him among the religious lyricists of his day, and calls for his comparison with Donne and Herbert, in whom modern poets and critics have found much to admire. So long as the "metaphysical poets" remain in high esteem, readers will react favorably to Taylor; so long as T. S. Eliot, Gerard Manley Hopkins, Dylan Thomas, and others who have adopted the qualities of seventeenth-century poetry are read with interest and admiration, so long will Taylor's verse be experienced with enjoyment.

Taylor inevitably reminds critics of the metaphysical poets; and the names of Donne, Herbert, Crashaw, Quarles, and Vaughan appear with understandable regularity in remarks about Taylor. As W. C. Brown and Emma L. Shepherd have demonstrated, Taylor used all their stylistic devices—*discordia concors,* violent juxtapositions of terms and images, paradox, oxymoron, the apparently light treatment of religious matters, developed conceits, quaintness, and shocking or surprising acts of wit. Taylor has also their surprising range of imagery from the most obscure and learned to the most homely and mundane.[39] If he belongs with any class or group of poets, it is certainly with the metaphysicals.

Stylistic devices alone, however, are not the indication of Taylor's position in the history of English verse. And the group most frequently called to mind within the large and various class of poets called "metaphysical" is really very small: Donne, Herbert, Crashaw, Quarles, Wither, and perhaps Vaughan. With these Taylor shares many characteristics, but not equally. With Donne, for example, the relationship is almost entirely stylistic, and it is largely in terms of the *Songs and Sonnets,* not of the *Divine Poems.* Helen Gardner clearly, though not intentionally, differentiates Donne's religious verse from Taylor's in her description of the *Divine Poems* as "poems of faith, not of vision. Donne goes by a road which is not lit by any flashes of ecstasy. . . . The absence of ecstasy makes his divine poems so different from his love poems. There is an ecstasy of joy and an ecstasy of grief in his love poetry; in his divine poetry we are conscious almost only of an effort of will."[40] Miss Gardner explains this change in Donne's poetry as a difference between the truths of imagination and the somewhat restricting truths of revelation; and she concludes her study with this perceptive remark:

> Some religious poetry, Herbert's perhaps, can be regarded as a species of love poetry; but Donne's is not of that kind. The image of Christ as Lover appears in only two of his poems—both written soon after the death of his wife. The image which dominates his divine poetry is the image of Christ as Savior, the victor over sin and death. The strength with which his imagination presents this figure is the measure of his need, and that need is the subject of the finest of his religious poems.[41]

This extremely basic difference sets Donne, as a religious poet, apart not only from Herbert but also from Taylor. And all the poets we have mentioned owed more to George Herbert than they did to the learned Dean of St. Paul's. While comparing Taylor with Herbert reveals numerous similarities of method and mind, a number of significant differences also come to light. Meditative patterns, emblematic manner, verse form, even the tricks of shaped poems and anagrams unite the two poets; but Professor Martz points up Taylor's limited metrical skill, his much wider range of diction, and his freer use of homely comparisons.[42] Malcolm Ross's thesis that "the traditional Christian symbols in Anglican poets like Donne or Herbert sometimes function in contradiction to the tradition which bore them and that because of significant revisions of central Christian dogma, the actual aesthetic effect of such symbols must be searched and felt in terms of a subtle contrapuntal tension between tradition and innovation within dogma itself,"[43] is borne out by Professor Stanford, who shows that Taylor's theological and dogmatic differences from Herbert lead him to quite contrary aesthetic results— and this in spite of strong superficial similarities.[44]

With Richard Crashaw, whose debt to Herbert was perhaps strongest, there is this same theological difference. Similarity of images, high sensuousness, and extreme rapture— wanting in Donne's religious verse but characteristic of Crashaw's *Steps to the Temple*—find their counterparts in Taylor; but Crashaw's steps led straight to Rome, which was for Taylor the Antichrist, or the whorish Mother of Error. Even when Crashaw and Taylor work most identically, their meaning is quite diverse. Henry Vaughan, whose reliance upon Donne and Herbert is somewhat less, is more like Taylor in his mysticism than in his style; but he lacks Taylor's intensity and fervor, although he is often a better poet.

Francis Quarles's relationship to Taylor has been considered before, but we may state here that, essentially less poetic, Quarles was nonetheless far more skillful and versatile a verse maker than Taylor. While Taylor may have garnered his devices from Quarles's popular *Emblemes,* he far transcended his teacher in his personal effort to portray religious experience with vivid symbolic expression. Apparently Taylor liked George Wither's politics, and his satires; but though he refers to Wither several times, he never mentions him as a poet.

Surprisingly, Taylor's work most resembles that of a poet whom he is least likely to have known. Neither Thomas Traherne nor Edward Taylor very likely influenced one another, and yet the parallels between their thought and work is so striking that we must conclude the two men to have been formed in the same intellectual and poetic mold. Both, for example, relied heavily for their interpretation of history upon the *Magdeburgentian Centuries,* one of the outstanding achievements of Renaissance historical scholarship. Traherne used the work as a basic source for *The Roman Forgeries* (a copy of which Taylor owned); Taylor not only used the *Magdeburgentian Centuries* in composing his sermons, but actually versified sections of it in his ultra-pedestrian "Metrical History of Christianity." Between 1669—the year after Taylor left for America—and 1674, Traherne voluminously wrote poems and prose meditations not published for the most part until the twentieth century. Significantly, Traherne's prose *Centuries of Meditations* constantly resound with sentiments and language that cry for comparison with Taylor's sermon prose and the *Preparatory Meditations.* Whole paragraphs from Taylor's "Christographia" might just as easily have been composed by Traherne in his prose *Centuries.* Diction, figures of speech, sentence structure, and even habits of punctuation are similar, and a study of their rhymes shows the two men—born about eighty miles apart—to have spoken a related dialect.

The most telling parallel between Taylor and Traherne, however, is their mysticism. Traherne reveals the quality of his mysticism most beautifully in the *Centuries,* a quality exactly like Taylor's. This quality is meditative, for Traherne's *Centuries of Meditations* are not only related to his poems very much as Taylor's sermons relate to his *Meditations,* but John Wallace has traced the Ignatian method of meditation in Traherne's poems, too.[45] Indeed, in spite of the many echoes of Herbert and Donne in Taylor, Taylor seems spiritually and devotionally closer to Traherne than to any other metaphysical poet. This may not be entirely to Taylor's advantage if Professor Warren's dismissal of Traherne as "an overrated discovery" is valid.[46] But the work of neither man has received all the study it deserves; when it does, the proximities of their neighborhoods in the realm of English poetry must become clearer.

If Taylor were only an American metaphysical poet, however, his work would be far less interesting than it is. Whatever value there is in considering the metaphysicals as conspicuously in opposition to the smooth sweetness of Spenser and his followers is vitiated by Taylor; for he joins Spenser not only in emblematic manner but in his allegorical mode of thought. None of the metaphysicals relies so heavily on allegory as Taylor does; and, as a result, his poetry is rooted as firmly in the Middle Ages as it is in his own century. But beyond his era, his method with images anticipates Emily Dickinson, Gerard Manley Hopkins, and a number of more recent writers. God's grandeur gathers to a greatness "like the ooze of oil crushed" in Taylor as it does in Hopkins (2.66); and Hopkins's "Caged Skylark," like Taylor's Bird of Paradise in a wicker cage, also tweedles "sometimes the sweetest, sweetest spells."[47] And like Dickinson's inebriate of dew, Taylor's bird leans tipsy against a sun—the sun of righteousness (2.64). One time we find him sticking a feather in his cap like Yankee Doodle; another, we detect sin, which, hatched in his heart, hisses out like Hawthorne's bosomed serpent (2.16); but still another time we catch him preaching an Emersonian doctrine of polarities (1.35). His strange ability to remind readers of others—from Clement of Alexandria to Walt Whitman—frees Taylor from the narrow designation "metaphysical" and associates him with major writers in the entire stream of Christian, English, and American literature.

Taylor's relation to the mainstream of American literature raises an important issue. Some critics would have it that Taylor was merely a transplanted and "fossilized" Englishman or that his works might have been written anywhere in the world Taylor happened to be. But though in spirit and in form his work recalls writers of all times and many places, in motive and subject it belongs inescapably to seventeenth-century America. The Christ Taylor celebrated and imitated in his poems; the doctrines of his faith; the people and activities he valued; the terms he used and the concepts they held—all were defined and distinguished by the accumulated experience of colonial New England. Nowhere in the world did the Congregational system and Federal theology work out their implications and ideals so freely and fully as in Connecticut and Massachusetts. Admittedly, Taylor rarely treats his American situation directly; when he does, as in the elegies, the results are generally poor. The history of the New World was too recent and too little to provide the "stuff" of poetry. And his major poems almost never allude to his American locale. But these facts in no way minimize the influence of his American experience. Taylor transcended his frontier circumstances not by leaving them behind, but by transforming them into intellectual, aesthetic, and spiritual universals.

The curious thing about Taylor is that this transcendence resulted from no cosmopolitan ambition, but from his mystical introversion; his inward exploration of soul led him, deserving and fortunate, as Conrad would say, to speak like other artists "to our capacity for delight and wonder, to the sense of mystery surrounding our lives; to our sense of pity, and beauty, and pain; to the latent feeling of fellowship with all creation. . . ." Taylor's theology, his intense faith, and the American spiritual community in which he lived, combined to give a structure or form to his rapturous experience of reality; and they also provided a way of talking about it that is as valid now as it was for Taylor or for Plato. But the mystical experience, unfortunately, does not yield to the test of other experience at all. By tracing it, describing it, reacting to it, and praising it, Taylor limited his poetry; but he never relegated his verses to a minor activity. Unlike Milton, he could not have written poetry left-handed for fifteen years; for his poetry was to him a living act, his most prominent sign of the unitive life attained over a half century of painful endeavor and devotion. From time to time his writing moved him to think himself soaring above the stars to stand at heaven's door. But that mystical door always opened into the meetinghouse at Westfield, admitting him to the society of Christ to whom he had a special calling in the suburbs of glory in America.

Notes and References

Chapter One

1. John Hoyt Lockwood, *Westfield and Its Historic Influences* (Springfield, Mass., 1922), I, 138.

2. Actually Taylor forbade the publication of any of his writing, though this fact tends to be overlooked by critics wishing to further the myth that Taylor's poetry would have been considered evil by his contemporaries. See, for example, Kenneth B. Murdock, *Literature and Theology in Colonial New England* (Cambridge, Mass., 1949), p. 167, and Quinn, Murdock, *et al.*, *The Literature of the American People* (New York, 1951), p. 57; Perry Miller, *The American Puritans: Their Prose and Poetry* (New York, 1956), p. 301, and *The New England Mind: From Colony to Province* (Cambridge, Mass., 1953), p. 31; and Richard D. Altick, *The Scholar Adventurers* (New York, 1950), p. 307.

3. Taylor's birth date has been estimated anywhere from 1642 to 1645. 1642 raises several problems, but Professor Stanford, whose short biography is the most accurate in all other respects establishes this date with authority in *The Poems of Edward Taylor* (New Haven, 1960), p. xxxix. The description of Taylor's conversion is from Taylor's "Relation" (1679) in the manuscript "Public Records of the Church at Westfield" at the Westfield Athenaeum, p. 81. See Lockwood, I, pp. 113-15.

4. William T. Costello, S. J., *The Scholastic Curriculum at Early Seventeenth-Century Cambridge* (Cambridge, Mass., 1958), p. 147. Professor Costello's analysis of a college disputation (pp. 19-25) illuminates Taylor's later practice.

5. Professor Walter J. Ong's judgments that "Edward Taylor . . . is the least Puritan and least Ramist of all New England writers" are simply not borne out by a close study, especially of Taylor's sermons. *Ramus: Method and the Decay of Dialogue from the Art of Discourse to the Art of Reason* (Cambridge, Mass., 1958), p. 287.

6. *Ibid.*, p. 12 *et passim;* Costello, pp. 33, 146; Samuel Eliot Morison, *Harvard College in the Seventeenth Century* (Cambridge, Mass., 1936), I, 165.

7. "Diary of Edward Taylor," *Proceedings of the Mass. Hist. Soc.*, XVIII (1880-1881), 8.

8. Thomas H. Johnson, *The Poetical Works of Edward Taylor* (New York, 1939), pp. 11-12.

9. "Diary," p. 15.

10. Lockwood, I, 151.

11. See the letter urging Increase Mather to assist the publication of Daniel Denton's "A Divine Soliloquy," *Collections of the Mass. Hist. Soc.*, Fourth ser., VIII (1868), 629-31.

12. Johnson lists these volumes by title, *Poetical Works*, pp. 201-20.

13. Item 22 of the Taylor commonplace book in the possession of the Massachusetts Historical Society.

14. *Ibid.*, Items 2 and 3.

15. *Ibid.*, Item 5.

16. William B. Goodman, "Edward Taylor Writes His Love," *New England Quarterly*, XXVII (December, 1954), 510-15.

17. Donald E. Stanford, "An Edition of the Complete Poetical Works of Edward Taylor" (Unpublished dissertation, Stanford University, 1953), pp. 18-19.

18. "Public Records of the Church," p. 1; Lockwood, I, 218.

19. "Public Records of the Church," p. 1.

20. These "heads"—some developed at length later; others still blank—occupy pp. 5-74 of the "Public Records of the Church."

21. *Ibid.*, p. 101; Lockwood, I, 117-18.

22. Samuel Sewall records hearing Taylor preach excellently at the Old South Church "upon short warning." "The Letter Book of Samuel Sewall," *Collections of the Mass. Hist. Soc.*, Sixth ser., II (1886-1888), 274.

23. *Collections of the Mass. Hist. Soc.*, Fourth ser., VIII (1868), 629-31. See also Item 3 in "China's Description," a commonplace book in the Yale University Library.

24. Meditation 2.110.

25. Miller, *From Colony to Province*, p. 227.

26. Solomon Stoddard, *An Appeal to the Learned . . . Against the Exceptions of Mr. Mather* (Boston, 1709), p. 70. I have treated Taylor's argument and the entire controversy in greater detail in "Edward Taylor on the Lord's Supper," *Boston Public Library Quarterly*, XII (January, 1960), 22-36.

27. Solomon Stoddard, *The Doctrine of Instituted Churches Explained and Proved from the Word of God* (London, 1700), p. 27.

28. Williston Walker says the proceedings "awakened no debate of consequence," *A History of the Congregational Churches in the United States* (New York, 1894), pp. 189-90.

29. Miller, *From Colony to Province*, p. 232.

30. The entire correspondence is published in Norman S. Grabo, "The Poet to the Pope: Edward Taylor to Solomon Stoddard," *American Literature*, XXXII (May, 1960), 197-201.

31. These sermons are in the Prince Collection in the Boston Public Library. The manuscript is described in *Extracts*, Item 5 in *The Prince Library: A Catalogue of the Collection of Books and Manuscripts which formerly belonged to the Reverend Thomas Prince* (Boston, 1870), p. 159. Subsequent references are to *1694*. Taylor makes this statement on p. 105.

32. Stoddard, *An Appeal*, p. 53.

33. *An Appeal, of Some of the Unlearned, both to the Learned and Unlearned* (Boston, 1709), p. 28.

34. John L. Sibley, *Biographical Sketches of Graduates of Harvard University* (Boston, 1881), V, 342-43.

35. These sermons are bound with the *1694* sermons in the Prince Collection. Taylor reviews the fight on pp. 64-69.

36. Henry W. Taylor, "Edward Taylor," in William B. Sprague, *Annals of the American Pulpit* (New York, 1857), I, 178.

Chapter Two

1. Evelyn Underhill, *Mysticism: A Study in the Nature and Development of Man's Spiritual Consciousness* (New York, 1955), p. xiv. Although there are numerous studies of mysticism, Miss Underhill's book, first published in 1910, offers the most convenient, thorough, and sympathetic analysis of Christian mystical traditions. It makes an illuminating companion to Taylor's poetry.

2. John Frederick Nims, trans., *The Poems of St. John of the Cross* (New York, 1959), p. 119.

3. Underhill, p. 169 ff.

4. "Public Records of the Church," p. 81. Lockwood, I, 114.

5. "Public Records of the Church," p. 81. Lockwood, I, 113.

6. Jonathan Edwards, "Personal Narrative," *Jonathan Edwards: Representative Selections*, eds. Clarence H. Faust and Thomas H. Johnson (New York, 1935), pp. 60-61.

7. Underhill's term.

8. William Ralph Inge, *Christian Mysticism* (New York, 1956), pp. 156-59.

9. This is a continuation of the practice popular among Renaissance neo-Platonists from Ficino to Tayor's contemporaries, the Cambridge Platonists.

10. Taylor's "Christographia" sermons (1701-1703) are in the manuscript collection of the Yale University Library. Subsequent references appear in parentheses in the text, as *C*, followed by the number of the sermon in italics. This quote is from *C, 4*.

Notes and References

11. I Corinthians 1: 19-27.

12. H. M. Margoliouth, ed. *Thomas Traherne: Centuries, Poems, and Thanksgivings* (Oxford, 1958), I, iv: 3, p. 169.

13. *Ibid.*, iv: 4, p. 170.

14. The fifth poem in *God's Determinations* is titled "God's Selecting Love in the Decree."

15. *God's Determinations*, "God's Selecting Love in the Decree," ll. 23-24.

16. The best discussions of this ecclesiastical problem may be found in Perry Miller, "The Marrow of Puritan Divinity," in *Errand into the Wilderness* (Cambridge, Mass., 1956), pp. 48-98; in chapters XII and XV of his *The New England Mind: The Seventeenth Century* (Cambridge, Mass., 1939); and in his *From Colony to Province*, pp. 68-118, 210-47. The theological aspects of the problem are emphasized in Peter Y. De Jong's *The Covenant Idea in New England Theology, 1620-1847* (Grand Rapids, 1945).

17. "A Particular Church is God's House" (1679), p. 14. A manuscript copy of this sermon is in the Prince Collection of the Boston Public Library. Subsequent references will be made in parentheses in the text as *PC*.

18. Cited in Inge, p. 23.

19. Underhill, p. 204.

20. The full title of this work points up this struggle: *God's Determinations Touching His Elect: and the Elect's Combat in their Conversion and Coming up to God in Christ, together with the Comfortable Effects Thereof.*

21. "The Frowardness of the Elect in the Work of Conversion," ll. 3-4.

22. Damon S. Foster, review of "The Poetical Works of Edward Taylor," *New England Quarterly*, XII (December, 1939), p. 780.

23. John Calvin, *Institutes of the Christian Religion*, ed. and trans. John Allen, 7th ed., rev. (Philadelphia, n. d.), Book II, chapt. I, par. VIII.

24. *Ibid.*, par. VII.

25. *C, 1*, pp. 33-36. Professor Miller points out that two theories prevailed about this matter in New England. It is interesting to note that Taylor followed Augustine and Calvin rather than his New England colleagues. See Perry Miller, *Jonathan Edwards* (New York, 1949), p. 277.

26. "Public Records of the Church," p. 81. Lockwood, I, 114-15.

27. Ola E. Winslow, *Meetinghouse Hill: 1630-1783* (New York, 1952), pp. 31-49.

28. *God's Determinations,* "The Effects of Man's Apostacy," ll. 7-20.

29. *Ibid.,* "The Third Rank Accused," l. 64.

30. Underhill, pp. 222-27.

31. *Ibid.,* p. 310 ff.

32. Louis L. Martz, *The Poetry of Meditation* (New Haven, 1954), pp. 14-15.

33. Underhill, p. 46.

34. Martz, p. 16.

35. See above, p. 29.

36. Martz, p. 154.

37. Richard Baxter, *The Saints Everlasting Rest: or, a Treatise of the Blessed State of the Saints in their enjoyment of God in Glory. Wherein is showed its Excellency and Certainty; the Misery of those that lose it, the way to Attain it, and assurance of it; and how to live in the continual delightful Foretastes of it, by the help of Meditation.* . . . (London, 1649 [1650]), pp. 691-92.

38. *Ibid.,* p. 662.

39. *Ibid.,* p. 719.

40. *Ibid.,* p. 662.

41. *Ibid.,* pp. 749-51.

42. Martz, p. 174. But Catholic devotional books gave the same advice much earlier. Translations of two books by Luis de Granados—*An Excellent Treatise of Consideration and Prayer* (p. 6), bound with *Of Prayer and Meditation* (London, 1592), sig. l₉v—clearly indicate the affinity of the meditation with the sermon. And Gaspar Loarte's *The Exercise of a Christian Life* (Paris, 1579), which Baxter made a main cause of his own conversion, established the same relationship (p. 66).

43. Increase Mather, *Practical Truths Tending to Promote the Power of Godliness* (Boston, 1682), p. 79.

44. *Ibid.,* p. 135.

45. The full subtitle to the "Christographia" is "A Discourse touching Christ's Person, Natures, the Personal Union of the Natures, Qualifications, and Operations Opened, Confirmed, and Practically Improved in Several Sermons Delivered upon Certain Sacrament Days unto the Church and People of God in Westfield."

46. Underhill, p. 240; Inge, p. 16.

47. R. C. Zaehner, *Mysticism Sacred and Profane: An Inquiry into some Varieties of Praeternatural Experience* (Oxford, 1957), p. 32.

48. Inge, p. 17.

49. Henry Vaughan, "The World," *The Works of Henry Vaughan,* ed. L. C. Martin, 2d ed. (Oxford, 1957), p. 466.

50. Louis L. Martz, "Foreword," *The Poems of Edward Taylor,* ed. Donald E. Stanford (New Haven, 1960), p. xxxii.

51. Underhill, p. 288.

52. "The Experience," 11.19-24.

53. Increase Mather, *The Mystery of Christ opened and applyed in Several Sermons, Concerning the Person, Office, and Glory of Jesus Christ* (Boston, 1685), pp. 88-89.

54. *Ibid.,* p. 98.

55. *Ibid.,* p. 110.

56. John Milton, "Paradise Lost," I. 36-40.

57. Underhill, p. 415.

58. *Ibid.,* p. 425.

59. *Ibid.,* pp. 136-37.

60. Lines 47-48, cf. 2.89.

61. Meditations 2.115-53.

62. Underhill, p. 137.

63. *Ibid.,* p. 173.

64. Zaehner, p. 187 f.

65. Inge, p. 33.

66. *Ibid.,* p. 191.

Chapter Three

1. Most preachers emphasized the application rather than the doctrinal proof. See Babette May Levy, *Preaching in the First Half Century of New England History* (Hartford: American Society of Church History, "Studies in Church History," VI, 1945), p. 94.

2. I demonstrate this relationship in detail in my introduction to the forthcoming Yale edition of Taylor's "Christographia."

3. For the creators themselves, see Brewster Ghiselin, *The Creative Process: A Symposium* (New York, 1952); for the sociologist, Robert N. Wilson, *Man Made Plain: The Poet in Contemporary Society* (Cleveland, 1958); and for the philosopher, Susanne K. Langer, *Feeling and Form* (New York, 1957). Also see Underhill, pp. 74-80.

4. Samuel Taylor Coleridge, *Biographia Literaria: or, Biographical Sketches of my Literary Life and Opinions,* ed. J. Shawcross (Oxford, 1907), I, Chapt. XIII, p. 202.

5. Miller, *The New England Mind: The Seventeenth Century,* p. 360.

6. Donald E. Stanford, ed., "The Earliest Poems of Edward Taylor," *American Literature,* XXXII (May, 1960), 147-48.

7. William Butler Yeats, "The Symbolism of Poetry," *Ideas of Good and Evil* (London, 1903), p. 242.

8. Compare stanza 9 of "Contemplations" with Taylor's 1.22:
> But shall the bird sing forth thy praise, and shall
> The little bee present her thankful hum?
> But I who see thy shining glory fall
> Before mine eyes, stand blockish, dull, and dumb?

9. Richard Baxter, *Poetical Fragments: Heart-Imployment with God and It Self.* 3d ed. (London, 1699), sigs. A$_4$r and A$_3$r.

10. Thomas H. Johnson, "Colonial Voice Reheard in Verse," *Saturday Review,* XLIII (August 6, 1960), p. 12.

Chapter Four

1. Stanford, "The Earliest Poems of Edward Taylor," p. 137.

2. W. E. Lunt, *History of England* (New York, 1950), pp. 448-50.

3. Stanford, "The Earliest Poems of Edward Taylor," pp. 138-43.

4. Stanford, "An Edition of the Complete Poetical Works," p. 522.

5. Harold S. Jantz, *The First Century of New England Verse* (Worcester, 1944), p. 34.

6. *Ibid.,* p. 28 ff.

7. Kenneth B. Murdock, *Hankerchiefs from Paul* (Cambridge, Mass., 1927), p. 25.

8. *Ibid.,* p. lxxi.

9. "Diary," p. 16.

10. An excellent study of the Puritan elegy is Robert Henson's "Sorry After a Godly Manner" (unpublished dissertation, UCLA, 1957).

Chapter Five

1. Malcolm Mackenzie Ross, *Poetry and Dogma* (New Brunswick, New Jersey, 1954), pp. 152, 182, *et passim.*

2. See above, p. 63.

3. Philip Pain, *Daily Meditations,* ed. Leon Howard (San Marino, California, 1936).

4. In Stanford, *Poems,* p. xiii.

5. *Ibid.,* p. xxi.

6. Levy, p. 89.

7. In Stanford, *Poems,* p. xxiii.

8. Austin Warren, "Edward Taylor's Poetry: Colonial Baroque," *Kenyon Rev.,* III (Summer, 1941), 366. This essay appears in revised form in Professor Warren's *Rage for Order: Essays in Criticism* (Ann Arbor, 1948).

9. I am indebted for these observations to William R. Manierre's excellent analysis: "The Puritan Minister as Poet: A Note on Reading Edward Taylor."

10. George Puttenham, *The Art of English Poesie* (1589), ed. Edward Arber, *English Reprints*, VII (London, 1869), p. 211.

11. Samuel Johnson, "Life of Cowley," *Lives of the English Poets*, I (London, 1925), p. 39.

12. John Weemes, *The Christian Synagogue*, 4th ed., corrected and amended (London, 1633), pp. 285-87.

13. Cited in Martz, *The Poetry of Meditation*, p. 257.

14. Joseph Hall, "The Art of Divine Meditation," *The Works of the Right Reverend Joseph Hall, D. D. Bishop of Exeter and Afterwards of Norwich*, ed. Philip Wynter, rev. ed. (Oxford, 1863), VI, 50.

15. Baxter, *Saints Everlasting Rest*, p. 678.

16. As in his poem titled, "Upon a Spider Catching a Fly." Certainly a nature poem in one sense, Taylor is less interested in the insects than in the moral they allegorize: "Strive not above what strength hath got."

17. See above, pp. 90-107.

18. Underhill, pp. 141-46.

19. Inge, pp. 220-21.

20. Rosemary Freeman, *English Emblem Books* (London, 1948), pp. 238-39.

21. *Ibid.*, p. 116.

22. Francis Quarles, *Emblemes*, V, iii, ll. 25-30, in Alexander B. Grosart, ed., *The Complete Works in Prose and Verse* (Edinburgh, 1881), III, 91.

23. Freeman, p. 117.

24. *Ibid.*, pp. 173-203.

25. *Ibid.*, pp. 47-52.

26. *Ibid.*, facing p. 33.

27. Quarles, *Emblemes*, III, xi, in *Works*, p. 75.

28. Cf. Martz's analysis of Meditation 1.29, in Stanford, *Poems*, pp. xxxii-xxxiv, and of the typological poems, Meditations 2.1-30.

29. Warren, *Rage for Order*, p. 17.

30. Stanford's discussion, based on Rosamund Tuve's excellent discussion of typological symbolism, provides another way of accounting for the illogicalities of such poetic imagery, "Complete Edition," pp. clxxiii-clxxxi.

31. Martz, in Stanford, *Poems*, p. xiii.

32. Thomas H. Johnson, *The Poetical Works of Edward Taylor* (New York, 1939), p. 23.

33. Thomas H. Johnson, "Edward Taylor: a Puritan 'Sacred

Poet,'" *New England Quarterly*, X (June, 1937), 290-322, discusses the dating.

34. This stanza is particularly reminiscent of George Herbert's *The Temple*, but only two of its variations were employed by that master of versification: Taylor's familiar *ababcc* stanza matches Herbert's "The Church Porch," "The Agony," and others; Herbert's "The Temper (1)" corresponds to Taylor's *abab*, 5443 of "An Extasy of Joy let in by this Reply return'd in Admiration."

35. Nathalia Wright, "The Morality Tradition in the Poetry of Edward Taylor," *AL*, XVIII (March, 1946), 14-15.

36. Note that Wright—following the judgment of Thomas H. Johnson, Taylor's first editor—includes the "Prologue" as the first poem of *God's Determinations;* Stanford removes the "Prologue" from this position and places it before the *Meditations.* The position of the poem in Taylor's manuscript seems to warrant Stanford's change.

37. The first half of the second "Christographia" sermon devotes itself to establish this tenet.

38. The connection is strengthened if, following Johnson, we include Taylor's "Prologue" in *God's Determinations;* in which case it would function like Loyola's "preparatory prayer."

39. W. C. Brown, "Edward Taylor: American 'Metaphysical,'" *AL*, XVI (November, 1944), 186-97. Emma L. Shepherd, "The Metaphysical Conceit in the Poetry of Edward Taylor (1644?-1729)" (unpublished dissertation, University of North Carolina, 1960).

40. Helen Gardner, ed., *The Divine Poems* (Oxford: The Clarendon Press, 1952), p. xxxv.

41. *Ibid.*, p. xxxvii.

42. In Stanford, *Poems*, pp. xv-xviii.

43. Ross, *Poetry and Dogma*, pp. 6-7.

44. Stanford, "Complete Edition," p. clxiv ff.

45. John Malcolm Wallace, "Thomas Traherne and the Structure of Meditation," *ELH*, XXV (June, 1958), 70-89.

46. Austin Warren, "George Herbert," *Rage for Order*, p. 35.

47. Robert Bridges, ed., *Poems of Gerard Manley Hopkins*, 2nd ed. (New York, 1930), p. 31.

Selected Bibliography

PRIMARY SOURCES

The major poems from Taylor's manuscript "Poetical Works" (Yale University Library) may be read in two editions. Donald E. Stanford, *The Poems of Edward Taylor* (Yale, 1960), contains the following works: "The Ebb and Flow," "An Elegy upon the Death of that Holy and Reverend Man of God, Mr. Samuel Hooker," "A Fig for Thee Oh! Death," "A Funeral Poem upon the Death of my ever Endeared and Tender Wife Mrs. Elizabeth Taylor," "God's Determinations Touching His Elect: and the Elect's Combat in their Conversion, and Coming up to God in Christ together with the Comfortable Effects thereof," "Huswifery" (two versions), "Preparatory Meditations before My Approach to the Lord's Supper, Chiefly upon the Doctrine Preached upon the Day of Administration," "Upon a Spider Catching a Fly," "Upon a Wasp Child with Cold," "Upon the Sweeping Flood Aug: 13, 14, 1683," "Upon Wedlock, and Death of Children," and "When Let by Rain." Stanford describes in detail all other editions and major manuscripts, except the manuscript in the Prince Collection, Boston Public Library (*Poems,* pp. 499-521).

Thomas H. Johnson supplements Stanford by editing the following poems from the "Poetical Works" in "The Topical Verses of Edward Taylor," *Publications of the Col. Soc. of Mass.,* XXXIV (1943), 513-54: Acrostic love poem to Elizabeth Fitch, "An Elegy upon the Death of . . . Francis Willoughby," "An Elegy upon the Death of . . . Mr. Charles Chauncy," "An Elegy upon the Death of . . . Mr. John Allen," "An Elegy upon the Death of . . . Mr. Sims," "An Elegy upon the Death of . . . Mrs. Mehetable Woodbridge," "A Funeral Tear Dropt upon the Coffin of . . . Dr. Increase Mather," "My Last Declamation in the College Hall, May 5, 1671, Where Four Declaim'd in the Praise of Four Languages and Five upon the Five Senses," and "Verses Made upon Pope Joan."

Donald E. Stanford prints the following poems from the Taylor manuscript book at the Redwood Library and Athenaeum in "The Earliest Poems of Edward Taylor," *American Literature,* XXXII (May, 1960), 136-51: "Another Answer [to a Popish Pamphlet]," "A Dialogue between the Writer and a Maypole

Dresser," "The Lay-man's Lamentation," "A Letter Sent to His Brother Joseph Taylor and His Wife After a Visit," and "This in a Letter I sent to My Schoolfellow, W. M."

Taylor's Diary is printed in "Diary of Edward Taylor," *Proceedings of the Mass. Hist. Soc.*, XVIII (1880-1881), 4-18.

All the other major works are still in manuscript, as follows:

"Christographia, or a Discourse Touching Christ's Person, Natures, the Personal Union of the Natures, Qualifications, and Operations Opened, Confirmed, and Practically Improved in Several Sermons Delivered upon Certain Sacrament Days unto the Church and People of God in Westfield" (Yale University Library). Fourteen sermons, 1701-1703. These are soon to be published by the Yale University Press.

"Commonplace Book" (Massachusetts Historical Society). Letters, notes, and extracts.

"Eight Sermons on the Lord's Supper, 1693/4" (Prince Collection, Boston Public Library).

"Harmony of the Gospels" (Redwood Library and Athenaeum).

"A Metrical History of Christianity" (Redwood Library and Athenaeum). Brief extracts appear in Stanford's edition of the *Poems.*

"A Particular Church Is God's House, 1679" (Prince Collection, Boston Public Library).

"The Public Records of the Church at Westfield" (Westfield Athenaeum). Taylor's profession of faith, spiritual relation the account of the church organization, and a copy of "A Particular Church is God's House."

"Two Sermons on Church Discipline" (Prince Collection, Boston Public Library).

"Notes on Stoddardean Controversy" (Prince Collection, Boston Public Library).

SECONDARY SOURCES

BLACK, MINDELE. "Edward Taylor: Heaven's Sugar Cake," *New England Quarterly*, XXIX (June, 1956), 159-81. A mature evaluation of Taylor's Calvinistic modification of his Catholic devotional tradition.

BLAKE, HOWARD. "Seventeenth Century Yankee," *Poetry*, XXXVI (June, 1940), 165-69. A brief, pithy, critical review, relating Taylor's verse to Quarles's.

BROWN, W. C. "Edward Taylor: American 'Metaphysical,'" *American Literature*, XVI (November, 1944), 186-97. Establishes

Taylor's relationship with Donne, Herbert, and the English "metaphysical" poets.

GRABO, NORMAN S. "Catholic Tradition, Puritan Literature, and Edward Taylor," *Papers of the Michigan Academy of Science, Arts, and Letters,* XLV (1960), 395-402. Studies the meditative practice of the Mathers and Samuel Willard to show its acceptance by orthodox New Englanders.

————. "Edward Taylor on the Lord's Supper," *Boston Public Library Quarterly,* XII (January, 1960), 22-36. A detailed summary of Taylor's "Particular Church" and his sermon battle with Stoddardeanism.

————. "Edward Taylor's *Christographia* Sermons: A Study of Their Relationship to His *Sacramental Meditations,* with an Edition of the Sermons." Ph.D. dissertation (University of California at Los Angeles, 1958). An analysis of the sacrament-day sermons and their contribution to Taylor's *Meditations.*

JOHNSON, THOMAS H. "Edward Taylor: a Puritan 'Sacred Poet,'" *New England Quarterly,* X (June, 1937), 290-322. A biographical and critical description of Taylor's manuscript "Poetical Works"; attempts to date several undated poems; prints several poems and excerpts.

————. *The Poetical Works of Edward Taylor* (New York: Rockland Editions, 1939; Princeton University Press, 1943). A selected edition with a general introduction and glossary; contains *God's Determinations,* thirty-one *Meditations,* five miscellaneous poems, and a very useful list of Taylor's library.

————. "The Topical Verses of Edward Taylor," *Publications of the Colonial Society of Massachusetts,* XXXIV (1943), 513-54. Critical comments, notes, and the text of elegies, declamations, etc., from "Poetical Works."

LIND, SIDNEY E. "Edward Taylor: A Revaluation," *New England Quarterly,* (December, 1948), 518-30. A negative appraisal that finds Taylor doomed to mediocrity "by reason of his station in life."

LOCKWOOD, JOHN HOYT. *Westfield and its Historic Influences,* 2 vols. Springfield, Mass., 1922. Vol. I is the most complete record of the area in which Taylor lived and worked; excellent background.

MARTZ, LOUIS L. "Foreword," *The Poems of Edward Taylor.* ed. Donald E. Stanford (New Haven: Yale University Press, 1960), pp. xiii-xxxvii. A splendid appraisal of Taylor's poetry, especially of the *Meditations.*

PEARCE, ROY HARVEY. "Edward Taylor: The Poet as Puritan," *New England Quarterly*, XXIII (March, 1950), 31-46. Attributes Taylor's mediocrity as a poet to his New England Puritanism.

SHEPHERD, EMMA L. "The Metaphysical Conceit in the Poetry of Edward Taylor (1644?-1729)." Ph.D. dissertation (University of North Carolina, 1960). A thorough review of Taylor scholarship and a sane and subtle examination of Taylor as a conceitist; I did not see it in time to incorporate it in this work.

STANFORD, DONALD E. "An Edition of the Complete Poetical Works of Edward Taylor." Ph.D. dissertation (Stanford University, 1953). This edits Taylor's "Poetical Works" and is the basis for the Yale *Poems*. Texts are unreliable, but the 189-page introduction is the longest and most thorough treatment of Taylor's theology and poetry. Although some aspects may be questioned, this is yet a basic study of Taylor.

————. "The Earliest Poems of Edward Taylor," *American Literature*, XXXII (May, 1960), 136-51. The only published text of the Taylor poems in the Redwood Library and Athenaeum manuscript.

————. "Edward Taylor and the Lord's Supper," *American Literature*, XXVII (May, 1955), 172-78. A short review of Taylor's anti-Stoddardeanism from *Meditations* 102-11, second series.

————. *The Poems of Edward Taylor* (New Haven: Yale University Press, 1960). The standard edition of Taylor, this is yet selective. Prints all 217 *Meditations, God's Determinations,* eleven miscellaneous poems, and brief excerpts from the "Metrical History of Christianity." It also provides the only accurate biography and an excellent bibliography of Taylor manuscripts and editions.

WARREN, AUSTIN. "Edward Taylor's Poetry: Colonial Baroque," *Kenyon Review*, III (Summer, 1941), 355-71. Also in *Rage for Order: Essays in Criticism* (Ann Arbor: The University of Michigan Press, 1948), pp. 1-18. A most significant, sensitive, and suggestive critical appraisal of Taylor's poetic qualities.

WEATHERS, WILLIE T. "Edward Taylor and the Cambridge Platonists," *American Literature*, XXVI (March, 1954), 1-31. Often misinformed about Taylor, this attempt to demonstrate Taylor's fall from orthodoxy through his Platonic views is suggestive and interesting.

————. "Edward Taylor; Hellenistic Puritan," *American Litera-ture,* XVIII (March, 1946), 18-26. Suggests Taylor's reliance upon the non-English classical poetry found in his library.

WRIGHT, NATHALIA. "The Morality Tradition in the Poetry of Ed-ward Taylor," *American Literature,* XVIII (March, 1946), 1-18. A very excellent study of *God's Determinations* as a morality play.

Index